Praise for the n

Look for Sharon Sala's next novel in The Jigsaw Files,
available soon from MIRA.

SHARON SALA

BLIND FAITH

mira

mira™

Recycling programs
for this product may
not exist in your area.

ISBN-13: 978-0-7783-1022-8

Blind Faith

Copyright © 2020 by Sharon Sala

This edition published by arrangement with Harlequin Books S.A.

For questions and comments about the quality of this book, please contact us
at CustomerService@Harlequin.com.

Mira
22 Adelaide St. West, 40th Floor
Toronto, Ontario M5H 4E3, Canada
www.Harlequin.com

Printed in U.S.A.

When there's nothing to hold on to but your faith in someone else's word. When the promise they made to you will either be the difference between your life, or your death. That's when you are put to the test. That's when you are asked to believe in something you cannot see.

I dedicate this book to the truth keepers.
To the promise keepers.

And to the people in my life who never let me down.

There aren't many of you, but you know who you are.

BLIND
FAITH

One

The morning sun was hot on Tony Dawson's head, but his anger was hotter. This camping trip in Big Bend National Park was nothing but a setup—a betrayal—and by two people he had considered friends.

The drunken argument the three high school boys had last night had carried over into morning hangovers. They packed up camp in silence, and were nearing the junction that would take them back down to the Chisos Mountain Lodge, where their overnight hike had begun.

Tony had nothing to say to either of them, which obviously wasn't what they'd expected, and as they neared the junction, both Randall Wells and Justin Young lengthened their strides to catch up to him.

"What are you going to do when you get back?" Randall asked.

Tony just kept walking.

Randall pushed him. "Hey! I'm talking to you!"

"Keep your damn hands off me. Not interested. Don't want to hear the sound of your lying voice. You said enough last night," Tony said.

"Are you going to keep seeing Trish? After all you found out?" Randall asked.

Tony fired back. "I had girlfriends back in California. I would assume they moved on when I left, because I did. So what if you dated Trish before I even knew her?"

"What about what Justin said?" Randall asked.

Tony stopped, then turned to face the both of them.

"You want the truth? I don't believe Justin. Why would I? You two lied about wanting to be my friends. You lied about this camping trip. It was a setup. You're both losers. Why would I believe two sore losers over my own instincts?"

Tony saw the rage spreading over Randall's face, but he wasn't expecting Randall to come at him.

Randall leaped toward him, swinging. Tony stepped to the side to dodge the blow, and when he did, the ground gave way beneath his feet. All of a sudden he was falling backward off the mountain, arms outstretched like Jesus on the cross, knowing he was going to die.

Two days later: Dallas, Texas

A Dallas traffic cop clocked the silver Mercedes at ninety-five miles per hour, and was just about to take off after it when his radar gun went dark, and then the car shot through a nonexistent opening in the crazy morning traffic, before disappearing before his eyes.

"That did not just happen," he muttered, but just in case, he radioed ahead for the next cop down the line to be on the lookout.

Wyrick wasn't concerned with the cop's confusion. She was already off the freeway and taking backstreets to get to the office. She knew the cop had clocked her, but she had her own little system for blocking traffic radar, and she was in a bigger hurry than normal because she overslept—a rare occurrence that happened now and then when she dreamed.

Last night had been one nightmare after another… from her mother disappearing at the merry-go-round when Wyrick was five, then being kidnapped and taken to the people at Universal Theorem who had created her, to the years at UT and what she referred to as her life in mental bondage.

From there, the dreams morphed to the man UT had picked out for her to marry…the man she thought loved her…until she got cancer.

Dreaming of the treatments and the chemo, then waking up sick in the night and thinking the dream was real, then falling back to sleep into the same web of disease and deceit.

Reliving the shock and disgust on her fiancé's face when he saw her rail-thin and bald, coldly breaking off the engagement by telling her he didn't want to watch her die.

The look of frustration on Cyrus Parks's face, and his matter-of-fact dismissal of her illness, explaining it away as a flaw in her system, and chalking her up as another failed experiment. She woke up bathed in sweat as Cyrus was walking out the door of her hospital room.

She threw back the covers in anger.

When she was at her weakest and sickest, they threw her away like food gone bad, and it was rage that kicked in her own will to live.

She stomped into the kitchen to get a cold Pepsi, wanting the bad taste of that memory gone, and drank it in the middle of the kitchen, remembering how she'd healed herself in a way she didn't even fully understand. Accepting as she finally calmed down that once in a great while she was doomed to relive the death and downfall of Jade Wyrick, and the resurrection of the woman she was now.

And because she finally went back to bed after the Pepsi, she overslept. Now she just needed to get to the office before Charlie Dodge, or she'd never hear the end of it.

Finally, the office building came into view, and she sped through the last half mile without once tapping the brakes, skidded into her own parking place and breathed a sigh of relief that Charlie's parking spot was still empty.

"That's what I'm talking about," she muttered, as she grabbed her things and got out on the run.

Within minutes of opening the office, she had coffee on, with the box of sweet rolls she'd picked up this morning plated beneath the glass dome in the coffee bar, and had both of their computers up and running.

She was going through the morning email when Charlie walked in, but she refused to look up. She knew what she looked like. She'd spent precious time this morning making sure she looked fierce, because she felt so damn wounded from the dreams.

"Bear claws under glass," she muttered. "Teenager missing in the Chisos Mountains in Big Bend. Are you interested?"

Charlie was used to Wyrick's outrageous fashion sense, and refused to be shocked by the black starbursts she'd painted around her eyes, the blood drop she'd painted at the corner of her mouth, the red leather catsuit or the black knee-high boots she was wearing. But he *was* interested in the sugar crunch of bear claws and kids who went missing.

"Yes, to both," he said, as he sauntered past. "Send me the stats on the missing kid, and get the parents in here for details."

"They're due here at 10:30."

He paused, then turned around, his eyes narrowing.

"Why do you even ask me what I want?"

"You're the boss," Wyrick said.

"I know that. I just didn't know you did," he mumbled, and stopped at the coffee bar.

He filled a cup with coffee, put a bear claw on a napkin and strode into his office. By the time he had his jacket hanging in the closet, his Stetson on the hat tree and a third bite of bear claw in his belly, he was ready to cope with the day, and pulled up the email about the missing teenager.

Tony Dawson—seventeen years old.

Disappeared in Chisos Mountains of Big Bend National Park while backpacking with Randall Wells and Justin Young, two friends from school.

Boys wake to find Tony gone. Think he walked back down alone due to an argument from the night before. But when they packed up and walked down, Tony Dawson's truck was still in the parking lot at the Chisos Mountain Lodge and he was nowhere to be found.

Two-day air and foot search yielded no clues.

Charlie was still reading when he heard the door open in the outer office and then heard a man's voice, followed by Wyrick's responses.

"I need to talk to Charlie Dodge!"

"Your name?"

"Darrell Boyington."

"Have a seat, Mr. Boyington."

Boyington smoothed a hand over his hair, absently patting it in place, and then sat.

Wyrick picked up the phone and buzzed Charlie's office.

"I heard him," Charlie said. "Does he have an appointment?"

"No, sir."

"The Dawsons are due here anytime, and I'm not

going to keep them waiting for a walk-in. Schedule an appointment for him if he wants."

"Yes, sir," Wyrick said, then hung up. "I'm sorry, Mr. Boyington. Mr. Dodge has clients arriving at any moment. Would you like to schedule an appointment?"

Boyington stood.

"No. I need to talk to him now! It's urgent!"

"I'm sorry, sir, but—"

"Look, lady…"

Charlie had heard enough. He strode out of his office.

"Hey! Arguing with my office manager doesn't get you any closer to me," Charlie said. "I have a prior appointment. The end."

Boyington started walking toward him.

"Look, Charlie. My name is Darrell Boyington. I own—"

"You don't own me or my time, Mr. Boyington. Make an appointment or find another investigator, and don't make me say it again."

Wyrick walked to the door and opened it.

Darrell's eyes widened. "What do you think you're—?"

"Hastening your exit?" Wyrick said, and pointed to the hallway.

"Freak. Get out of my way," Boyington muttered, slamming the door shut behind him.

Charlie frowned. "I'm sorry he said that."

Wyrick shrugged. "I suppose I asked for it today."

"Why?"

"Women hide behind makeup," she muttered, then went back to her desk.

"What are you doing?" he asked.

"Running a search on Darrell Boyington. It pays to know your enemies."

"Fill me in when you find out," Charlie said, and went back into his office to finish reading up on the missing teen.

A few minutes later, Wyrick stepped into his office.

"Boyington owns a chain of sports bars. I have no idea why he was here."

Charlie shrugged. "Probably wanted somebody tailed. That stuff is not on my radar."

Wyrick already knew that.

A few minutes later, the door to the outer office opened again, but this time it was the Dawson family, and it was a testament to their panic that they had absolutely no reaction to Wyrick's appearance when she ushered them into his office.

"Mr. and Mrs. Dawson, this is Charlie Dodge."

Charlie stood. "Good morning," he said, and seated Mrs. Dawson, while her husband took the chair beside her.

"Would either of you care for coffee?" Wyrick asked.

They shook their heads.

Charlie glanced at Wyrick.

"Would you please join us?"

She went back to get her iPad to take notes, and as soon as she was seated, Charlie began.

"Mr. and Mrs. Dawson, I've read the highlights from the email you sent. Is there anything else you want to add?"

"We're Baxter and Macie, please," Baxter Dawson said, but it was Macie who kept talking.

"We moved here from California this past summer. Tony is our only child. I didn't want him to go on that trip because it was so far away and in such rough terrain," she said, and then started crying. "But they had this long break from school because of teacher evaluations or something, and then the weekend to boot, and I gave in. They left Dallas last Thursday before daybreak. They hiked and camped Thursday night. Tony went missing Friday morning. Today is Monday, and I don't know where my son is. I don't know if he's even alive. I can't bear it. It's the not knowing that's the worst."

Baxter reached for her hand and picked up the story. "When the park rangers first began searching, we were confident that he'd be found. After the boys mentioned the argument the night before, and Tony being gone when they woke up, it seemed plausible."

"When the argument occurred, were they drinking?" Charlie asked.

Baxter sighed. "The boys said they'd had a couple of beers apiece, but there's no way to know because when they were first questioned, they'd told the park ranger that they had discarded their trash back at the lodge when they hiked back down. Then they said they had expected Tony's truck to be gone. But when it was still in the parking lot and he was nowhere on-site, they realized he could still be up in the mountains. Maybe lost. That's when they went straight to the authorities. Then the authorities notified us about the search. We were at the lodge the whole time, waiting for word."

"Why did they stop the search at only two days?" Charlie asked.

"I don't know, but when we were asked if there was trouble at home, like they thought he would just decide to disappear like this on his own, we knew the heart had gone out of the search."

"I'm the one who wanted to hire a private investigator," Macie said. "I asked around about people to hire, and it appears your reputation for finding missing children is well-known here. And if there is any chance of finding Tony, they said you could do it."

Charlie took a breath. This was going to be hard for them to hear, but it had to be said.

"Are you accepting of the fact that I might not find him alive?"

Baxter paled, but it was Macie whose chin went up.

"Yes. I've faced that possibility, but we have to know. I want my baby back, one way or the other. I gave him life, and if he's already in God's arms again, I want to be the one to lay him to rest."

Baxter moaned. "Jesus, Macie."

"Understood," Charlie said. "I will need the addresses of his two hiking partners. I also have one more question. Was Tony an experienced backpacker, and does he have any survival skills?"

"He grew up in Bakersfield, California, and was used to hiking in the surrounding areas," Baxter said. "I used to go with him until he got older. Then he went with friends. But this trip was a long way from Dallas, and the overnight stay was a new experience."

"I also have a question about the boys being surprised the truck was still in the parking lot. Did they think he would have driven off and left them on their own that far away from home?" Wyrick asked.

"Oh… Tony drove down by himself," Baxter said.

Charlie frowned. "Wait…what? Three boys are going backpacking together…this far away from home…and they don't all go down together?"

"See? I'm not the only one who thinks that decision was strange. They had a car. Tony had the truck, so he took all the equipment, but his truck had a front and a back seat. There would have been plenty of room for all three of them," Macie said.

Charlie's frown deepened. This story wasn't making sense.

"I'll definitely do everything I can to help, and I will stay in constant touch, because I know this is a hard time for the both of you."

"Thank you," Macie said. "We're grateful."

"What kind of a retainer do we need? Whatever it is, we'll pay," Baxter said.

"Wyrick will deal with that before you leave, and get contact info from the both of you so we can stay in touch. She's also my ace in the hole when it comes to research."

Wyrick stood. "If you two will follow me, I'll get your info and a receipt for the retainer."

Charlie shook their hands, then watched Wyrick usher them out with quiet grace. She was a walking dichotomy. A freaking warrior of a woman hiding her reality behind a bizarre appearance, daring someone to cross her, before they decided to do it on their own.

A short while later, he heard them leave, and the moment they were gone, Wyrick was back in his office.

"I sent the names and addresses of the two boys to your phone, but they're both in school right now. It will be evening before they're available to question. Do you want to wait?" she asked.

"No. My gut says there is a lot wrong with this story and they've made their statements. How long would it take to get your chopper ready?"

"I already notified Benny to get it ready. It'll take a couple of hours to get you there. If you need more info, all you have to do is call. I can research from home or at work."

"Then I'm going home to pack. Text me with a timeline. I'll meet you at the hangar," Charlie said, and put his jacket back on and grabbed his Stetson.

"Don't forget to pack your sat phone," Wyrick said.

"Yes, ma'am," he drawled, and left her standing.

She took a moment to admire his wide shoulders and sexy butt, then looked away. Too much of a good thing was never wise.

* * *

Trish Caldwell couldn't sleep, and trying to eat made her sick. The knot in her stomach was almost as big as the ache in her heart. Having Tony go missing like this was the worst thing that had ever happened in her seventeen years of living, and she didn't know how to handle it.

Her mother kept telling her it was all in God's hands, but that felt like giving up. It felt like she'd already written him off as dead, and it was just a matter of finding his body.

But Tony Dawson was so sweet, and handsome, and funny. She wouldn't let herself believe that he was gone.

She'd refused to go back to school today, unwilling to face well-meaning friends, and cried herself sick. The only people who seemed to understand how she felt were Randall and Justin. They were just as upset as she was, and were organizing a prayer vigil tonight at the high school football field.

As Tony's girlfriend, everyone expected her to be there, but the thought of it was overwhelming. Everyone would be looking at her to see if she was crying enough, or if she was hysterical, and then they'd all talk about how hard she was taking it.

They thought he was dead, too. She didn't want to hear it. Not even an insinuation of it, and yet she knew she would hear that and so much more. She was scared. Scared that their beliefs would become her truth.

When Randall called, offering to take her to the vigil, she agreed. At least she wouldn't be there on her own, and he and Justin could run interference for her. She was still holding the phone and staring out her bedroom window at the park across the street, remembering that was where she and Tony had shared their first kiss, when there was a knock at her door. Then her mom appeared in the doorway.

"Hey, honey, who was that on the phone? Was it news about Tony?"

Trish shook her head. "No, just Randall offering to take me to the prayer vigil at the field house tonight."

"Are you going?" Beth Caldwell asked.

Trish's eyes welled. "I have to, Mom. If I don't, people will think I've already given up on him."

Beth sat down beside her and reached for her hand.

"Do you want me to go with you? I will."

"Yes, would you?"

"Of course," Beth said. "I'll always have your back."

Trish laid her head on her mother's shoulder. "I'm scared, Mama. The more time passes…"

"I know. And I can only imagine what Baxter and Macie are thinking, so let's stay positive until life gives us a reason not to, okay?"

Trish nodded. "Help me find something to wear. It's supposed to be colder tonight."

And with that, mother and daughter got up to pick

out something to wear for the weather, and the occasion, unaware that Baxter and Macie Dawson had enlisted more help to find their son.

Charlie was packed and standing in the kitchen of his apartment eating a salami-and-dill-pickle sandwich. The sandwich made him think of Annie. She loved salami, but the kind with the black peppercorns. And she liked mustard and onions on her sandwich, not pickles.

God, he missed her…her and her onion breath, and the laugh when she kissed him afterward. It was getting harder and harder to remember her from before, for what the early-onset Alzheimer's she now suffered from had done to her…to them.

He finished off the sandwich and the glass of sweet tea, and then put the glass in the sink and the napkin that had served as a plate in the trash, and wondered what the hell was holding Wyrick up.

No sooner had he thought it than his phone signaled a text. It was her.

Chopper is ready now. I'm en route. Pack your iPad and a power pack. I uploaded info to it that you're going to want, but you're not going to have wifi there, so read on the way.

He sighed, then went back to his office, picked up the iPad and dug a couple of power packs out of a drawer and put them in his bag, along with his regular cell phone, then gathered up his things and headed out the door.

Dallas was experiencing its first cold spell, which wasn't that unusual for October, but Big Bend National Park was at the southern end of the state of Texas, bordering Mexico. It had a far different weather pattern than the northern part of the state.

He wondered if the weather was going to impact his search, then knew it would all hinge on how far up they'd hiked before Tony Dawson went missing. The nights would be cold. The weather during the day would vary with regard to warmth. But he'd find all that out when he got there, and right now, his biggest issue was traffic to get to the airport.

It was at its usual breakneck pace, and Charlie was already thinking about the upcoming trip and the job ahead. He didn't have any preconceived notions about what he'd find, but he'd been doing this for a long time, and his instincts were telling him there was more to those boys' story than what they'd admitted. What didn't make sense was why they'd keep anything a secret when their friend was missing. Getting so drunk they didn't remember much was possible, but why keep it a secret when a friend's life was at stake?

Wyrick changed clothes in the office before heading to the hangar where she kept her chopper. Benny had it fueled up and ready, and now all she had to do was get there. But when she left the building and headed for her Mercedes, she caught a glimpse of

Darrell Boyington sitting in a black Lexus at the back of the parking lot.

What the hell is he trying to prove?

But getting Charlie to the Chisos Mountain Lodge was uppermost in her thoughts, and she forgot about Boyington as she jumped in the Mercedes and sped out of the parking lot.

She was on the freeway before she happened to glance up in the rearview mirror and see a black Lexus about thirty yards behind her.

Boyington?

It had been a while since she'd been tailed by people hired by Universal Theorem, but she could spot a tail within seconds. She was accustomed to UT's interests in her whereabouts, but knowing it was someone Charlie turned away was a little creepy, and yet there he was. She didn't have time to deal with him, and she didn't want to lead him all the way to the location of her hangar. The less people knew about her personal business, the better.

Thinking she would lose him in the traffic, she accelerated, but so did he. When the little warning system went off on her phone, alerting her of a speed trap up ahead, she grinned.

Boyington was going down.

She accelerated even more, and when she did, Boyington surged forward, moving through traffic behind her like a bloodhound on a hot trail. She was doing ninety, and he was gaining, when she activated the cloaking device on her Mercedes and shot past the cop and his radar gun, leaving Boyington to the cop and her home free.

About a quarter of a mile later, she deactivated the cloaking, took the next westbound exit and headed for the airport.

Charlie was there and waiting by the chopper when she sped through the gate and then parked her car in the hangar and grabbed her bag.

"Everything okay?" Charlie asked.

"It's fine," she said. "I changed clothes at the office. Traffic was weird. That's all."

He nodded. "Dallas traffic is always weird."

"Mount up," Wyrick said, and began her preflight checkup while Charlie climbed in.

He had already stowed his gear behind his seat, so he buckled in and waited for her to finish outside, then waited again as she went through a flight check inside, as well.

They put on headphones as she powered up. The rotors started spinning as every instrument on the dash lit up like the console on a Starfighter. And in another universe, Jade Wyrick would have been the Jedi manning it.

Wyrick glanced at her flight partner. He was grim-faced and staring out the windshield in front of him, and she knew he was already thinking about the case.

When the rotors reached full power, she lifted off—going up and then making a half circle before taking a heading of south by southwest to Big Bend National Park.

As soon as she had time to think about something besides flying, she mentioned Boyington again.

"Just so you know, Boyington was waiting in the parking lot and tailed me part of the way here. I lost him on the freeway."

"What the hell?" Charlie said.

She could feel him staring at her.

"Did you feel threatened?" he asked.

She shrugged, keeping her gaze on her business. "I don't know what I felt, but I wasn't afraid, if that's what you meant. However, it was creepy, and whatever he wants, I don't think we need to be working with him."

"Agreed," Charlie said. "Let me know if he shows up again."

She nodded. "No worries. The missing kid is far more important than whatever is on some frustrated man's agenda. Did you see the map of the trail they took that I uploaded to your iPad?"

"Not yet."

"You can read it now."

He gave her a thumbs-up and powered it up.

"I also preregistered you for the hike they took. The permit is on your phone. You'll have to show up with your ID, but they know you're coming, and they know the family has hired you to aid in the search for their son."

Charlie glanced at her then, marveling at her attention to detail.

"Remind me to give you that raise," he said.

She snorted.

He grinned.

They both knew she could buy a whole country and have money left over. That constantly promised raise was a running joke between them.

After that, the two-hour-plus flight was mostly silent until they were five minutes out from their destination.

"Coming up on the lodge. I have permission to land nearby to unload you."

"Let me know you make it back," Charlie said.

"I will. You check in with me tonight when you can. I'm going to go back and do some more research on all three boys. Maybe I'll have something more."

Minutes later, she set down.

"Good hunting," she said, right before Charlie took off his headset.

"Safe flight," he said, and then grabbed his gear and started toward the lodge.

He turned to watch as she lifted off and waited until she was out of sight before going in. A park ranger was inside the door talking to a couple of hikers who'd just come down from one of the trails. They were asking about the searchers they'd seen, and if the missing hiker had been found. Charlie stopped, curious as to what the ranger would have to say.

"No, he's still missing," the ranger said.

"That's tough," one of the hikers said. "We saw a group of people down in one of the canyons yesterday. We wondered if they were searchers, but we didn't see any today. Have they called off the search?"

"I think they've moved farther up the canyon. I don't know where they're at now," the ranger said. "Thanks for checking in to let us know you're back. Are you leaving now?"

"Yes, sir," they said. "We're going to load up and head back to Austin. It was an amazing trip."

"Hope to see you again," the ranger said, and then the hikers left the office.

"Excuse me," Charlie said. "My name is Charlie Dodge. I'm a private investigator out of Dallas. I've been hired by the Dawson family to look for their son, Tony, and just wanted you to know I'll be on the trail searching for him, too."

The ranger shook Charlie's hand. "Ranger Arnie Collins."

"If I find anything, who do I contact?" Charlie asked.

"Cell service is bad here. You'll likely need a two-way radio or—"

"I have a sat phone," Charlie said.

"Then call the office," the ranger said. "They'll know how to get the information to the right people. Do you know the trail they took?"

"Yes. Did they discover anything during the search, or pinpoint a specific location of any kind?"

"No, and I was part of one of the search teams, so I would have known."

"Okay. Thanks for the info."

A short while later, Charlie left with a map of the trails and started on the same hike the boys had chosen. Even though he would keep an eye out all the way there, his first goal was to reach the same area where they'd made camp, and he was going to have to hustle, because his day was already half over.

Two

Wyrick had a good tailwind all the way back to Dallas, cutting almost fifteen minutes of flight time off the trip. Benny was waiting when she landed.

"Welcome back," Benny said. "You made good time."

Wyrick nodded. "Check her over and keep her serviced and ready. I'll have to make a trip back to pick him up, too."

"Will do," Benny said, and as soon as Wyrick drove her Mercedes out of the hangar, he towed the chopper back inside and went to work.

She drove straight back to the office, changed into the clothes she'd left home in and stowed the jeans and work clothes. She'd washed the makeup from her face when she left, and she needed something more to hide behind than the red leather and black boots, so she added red eye shadow and black lipstick and called it good.

After making a fresh pot of coffee, she took a bear

claw to her desk to make up for having no breakfast or lunch and went to work. The phone rang periodically. She took messages and answered questions while going through new email and paying bills.

It was late afternoon before she had time to dig into the social media aspects of the three boys. Since she wasn't one of their "friends," she was going to have to hack to research, but saved the hacking for home, where the security on her personal computers was impenetrable.

By the time she left the office, she was starving. She picked up Chinese on her way home, while keeping an eye out for Boyington and his black Lexus, but it was a no-show, which was a relief.

She got home, stripped and showered, then dressed in old sweats and a T-shirt. She took her food to the living room, turned on the TV and finally ate her first meal of the day.

Having Merlin for a landlord and living in the basement of his mansion was the safest she'd felt in years. Having Charlie Dodge for a boss wasn't safe for her emotional well-being, but she'd already figured out her life wasn't worth shit without him in it, so there was that.

Darrell Boyington was standing on the balcony of his penthouse, looking out across a city of lights. Dallas was the ninth most populous city in the US—almost four hundred square miles of city, with nearly a million and a half people within that area. Everything was big in Texas, including the state itself, and Darrell had earned his way to the penthouse in a most unique manner.

His sports bars were a cover for the hit man he was. And the only jobs he took were ones with a target that challenged him. It was easy to just walk up and shoot someone, but in this day and age of cameras everywhere, doing it completely unseen, unnoticed, and getting away with it was impossible.

So he came at his work from a different angle. He not only located his target beforehand, but he found a way to meet them face-to-face, making sure his face was familiar enough that they dismissed him, and then he followed them for days, sometimes longer, until he found the opening…the weakness…the place that allowed him to slip in and out unnoticed. It was, after all, about the hunt.

And today, he had walked into Dodge Security and Investigations with only one thing in mind. He'd introduced himself to his next target. He'd made a pest of himself enough so that the next time Jade Wyrick saw him, that was how she would remember him, and she would see him again. He would make certain of that. She might be pissed off at him, but she would never see him as a physical threat—not until it was too late.

Randall Wells arrived just after six thirty to pick Trish up for the prayer vigil. He knocked on the door, then stepped back and waited, but it was Trish's mother who answered.

"Good evening, Randall. We're almost ready," she said, and then called out to Trish. "Randall is here."

"Coming," Trish called.

She said "we're"—as in, she's going, too?

Randall was still trying to wrap his head around the fact that Trish's mother was going with them when Trish came down the stairs in jeans and a white hoodie. She looked different. Older. Sadder. It made Randall uncomfortable. He hoped she didn't spend the night crying.

"I hope you don't mind that I'm going with you," Beth said. "Trish wanted me to."

"Of course not, Mrs. Caldwell," Randall said, and hurried ahead to open both the front and back doors of his car.

Trish got in front, her mother in the back, and they headed to the field house.

"Mr. and Mrs. Dawson are coming," Randall said.

"Yes, I know," Trish said. "They called me."

"Right," Randall said, and that was the extent of his conversation until they reached the school.

He circled the parking lot beside the football field until he found an empty space and parked. A huge crowd was already gathering, and more were arriving by the minute.

"Justin and I thought you would want to say something tonight," Randall said.

Trish panicked. "No. I'm not making a speech. I'm not putting myself on display. I'm here. And I'll stand beside his parents if they want, but this is about them and Tony."

"Right...totally understood," he said.

Trish and her mother got out together, then waited for Randall to walk them through the crowd.

Justin saw them coming and ran to meet them.

"Hey, Trish. Hey, Mrs. Caldwell."

Beth smiled. "It's good of you and Randall to organize this," she said.

Justin shrugged. "It's the least we could do."

There were volunteers in school colors at the gates handing out prayer candles.

"We're praying for you," one girl said, as she handed Trish a candle.

"I'm not lost. Pray for Tony," Trish said, then walked away with the candle in her hand and an ache in her chest.

They made it through the crowd all the way up to the makeshift stage before they spotted Baxter and Macie near the steps.

When they saw Beth and Trish approaching, Macie went to meet them and gave Trish a hug.

"I know this wasn't easy for you, honey, but we're really glad you're here," she said.

Trish's eyes welled, and all she could do was nod.

Her mother spoke for them. "We wouldn't have this any other way. We love your Tony, too."

A few moments later, the school principal took the stage and the ceremony began. People jostled her from behind, and when they did, her mother moved closer, putting her arm around her and pulling her close.

Trish was blinking back tears again when Tony's parents took the stage to thank everyone for coming, and then Randall and Justin were recognized for organizing the vigil, and through it all, Trish was growing numb.

This is a dream. It has to be a dream. I'm going to wake up and it will be morning, and Tony will have sent me two texts while I was asleep, telling me how he couldn't sleep for thinking of me.

But the air was getting colder, and there was a mist starting to fall as the pastor moved to the microphone and started praying, and the silence that descended upon the crowd was eerie.

The mist got heavier, and candles began going out, leaving the whole crowd in momentary darkness, which only added to the eeriness of the night. Then someone thought to use the flashlight on their phone, which prompted others to do the same. Within moments, they were holding their phones up over their heads. Someone began singing "Amazing Grace," and the crowd was awash in light.

Trish took a deep, shuddering breath, then closed her eyes.

Please, please, God, don't let Tony be dead.

Long after everyone had finally gone home, the solemnity of the ceremony had stayed with them. The mist had turned into rain, and Trish was lying in her bed, listening to it hammering on their roof, and praying that wherever Tony was, he had shelter, too.

Randall was in his room on the phone with Justin. His parents were in bed watching television. He could hear late-night TV host Stephen Colbert's voice coming from their room.

"How do you think the prayer vigil went?" Randall asked.

"Good," Justin said. "What did you think?"

"Yeah, it was good," Randall said.

Justin sighed, hesitated and then asked in a quiet, shaky voice, "Where do you think Tony is?"

"I don't know," Randall said. "I expected the searchers to find him the first day."

"Yeah, me, too," Justin said. "I can't figure this out. I just can't figure this out."

"Same," Randall said.

Justin's belly hurt, but he stayed quiet. There was nothing else to be said.

Randall kept talking, because the silence was painful.

"I heard Mr. and Mrs. Dawson telling Trish's mom that they'd hired a private investigator to go look for him," he said.

Justin frowned. "What can one man do that two days of air and ground searchers couldn't?"

"I don't know. I just heard them say he was famous for finding lost kids," Randall said.

"Well, I hope he does find him. This needs to be over," Justin said.

"Right. The sooner the better," Randall said.

"Yeah," Justin said, and disconnected.

Macie had cried herself to sleep in Baxter's arms, but he couldn't sleep. His thoughts were filled with what-ifs and worst-case scenarios, and every time he closed his eyes, he imagined Tony's broken body unprotected, exposed to the elements and the wildlife. It was a parent's worst nightmare come to life, and he felt like Charlie Dodge was their last best chance.

Back in the Chisos, Charlie had hiked almost three hours before he walked up on an old man sitting on the side of the trail. The old man's eyes were closed, his legs crossed in a meditative position as he rocked back and forth, muttering the same chant over and over beneath his breath. His long hair was braided and hanging over his shoulders, his skin was so brown it looked like leather, and the multitude of wrinkles on his face were creased with sweat and dust.

Charlie had no intention of disturbing him, and was about to step off the path to give him space when the man suddenly opened his eyes.

"Do you hear the ghost?" he asked.

Charlie stopped. "Uh, no, sir. Do you hear ghosts?"

The old man tilted his head back and squinted.

"You're a big one, aren't you?"

"Yes, I guess I am," Charlie said.

He nodded. "Are you camping over tonight?"

"Yes," Charlie said.

The old man closed his eyes again. "Maybe you'll hear the ghost. I heard him, but I couldn't find him."

Charlie started to walk on when it dawned on him what the old man was saying. He stopped and went back.

"Why did you think it was a ghost?"

"Because it woke me from my sleep, moaning, then screaming down the canyon like a banshee."

"Are you sure it wasn't someone crying for help?" Charlie asked.

"Nobody was talking. Just a scream. I know a banshee when I hear one. I'm praying it away."

"Where did you hear it?" Charlie asked.

"Up there," the old man said, pointing in the direction Charlie was heading. "Bloodcurdling. Spine-chilling, I tell you. I've been hiking up here for years and I've never heard anything like that."

"You know there's a teenager somewhere up there who's gone missing, don't you?"

The old man nodded. "I saw the searchers. They told me. I told them about the ghost, but they didn't listen."

"I hear you," Charlie said. "I'll watch out for the ghost." Then he walked away.

He hiked all the way to the site on the trail where the boys had made camp. It was dusk and getting dark fast by the time he stowed his food in the bear box and put up his tent.

He built a fire and made coffee, but settled for jerky and protein bars instead of cooking. Once his belly was full and the coffee had warmed him up from the inside, he got out his iPad, but there was no reception, so he went for the sat phone to check in with Wyrick.

Wyrick had been working for almost three hours, going through the boys' social media accounts, when she discovered a very interesting link between the missing boy and Randall Wells. Now she just needed Charlie to call in. It might not help him find Tony Dawson, but it could explain the holes in the other boys' story.

It was just after 10:00 p.m. and she was sitting cross-legged in bed with a bowl of popcorn in her lap and a cold Pepsi on the table beside her, watching a country-music awards show. Even though she didn't know much about country music, living in Dallas, it seemed like the appropriate thing to do.

A singer named Blake Shelton was onstage, and Wyrick was thinking to herself that Shelton was as tall as Charlie when her phone rang. She hit Mute and answered abruptly.

"Hello."

"Hey, it's me," Charlie said.

"Are you okay?" Wyrick asked.

Charlie sighed. "Yes, Mother. I'm getting ready to go inside my little tent and tuck myself into my little sleeping bag."

"Shut up," Wyrick said. "I have news."

Charlie grinned. He'd gotten under her skin, which was rare. Score one for him.

"So, talk to me," he said.

"Remember Baxter and Macie saying they haven't lived here but a few months?"

"Yeah, so?"

"So, over a year ago, before they ever moved here, guess who Randall Wells was dating?"

"I don't do guessing games," Charlie said.

"Trish Caldwell!" Wyrick said.

"Wait...what? The same girlfriend Tony has now?" Charlie asked.

"Yes. I found pictures of Randall and Trish together on Snapchat and Instagram. They were a couple for about six months, and then evidently they parted ways. Trish went back from being 'in a relationship' to single, and so did Randall."

"How long ago was this?" Charlie asked.

"Their breakup was at least four months before the Dawsons moved to Dallas, so Trish was a free agent for at least six months before she hooked up with Tony. Now she and Tony are a couple."

"No one mentioned this," Charlie said. "I wonder if Tony knew."

"If you want, I can find out tomorrow," Wyrick said.

"I want," Charlie said. "Interview Trish first. Find out if Tony knew that. Then when you talk to Randall and Justin, find out when they started hanging out with Tony. See if it was before he hooked up with Trish or after they began dating, and then let me know."

"I'll call parents and set up interview times first thing tomorrow," Wyrick said.

"Thanks," Charlie said. "I'll be on the trail. No iPad signal, so you'll have to call the sat phone."

"I know. Now go tuck yourself in your itty-bitty tent and try not to get into trouble."

She disconnected before Charlie could respond, but she heard him chuckle, and that was enough to sleep on.

* * *

A coyote howled from a nearby ridge, and another one answered way down in a canyon. A cougar was on the way back to its lair, dragging the carcass of her kill to her cubs—a great horned owl her only witness as it soared silently above her, going in the other direction.

A half mile away, a steady trickle of water was seeping out from the walls of a deep, narrow cave, falling near Tony Dawson's motionless body and into his outstretched hand.

His face and clothes were caked with dirt and dried blood. The visible skin on his fever-racked body was cut, scratched and purple with bruises.

In his delirium, his mother was sitting beside him and crying. Sometimes it was his father's voice telling him to hang on, but the pain was constant. His body was on fire, and when he was conscious, he wondered why it took so long to die.

Charlie's sleep was fitful. He kept dreaming about Annie. Then the dreams would change to a kid crying for help, but he couldn't find him. Once he woke up to an animal snuffling around the outside of his tent, but stayed quiet until it moved away.

He was up, dressed and having an MRE for breakfast with his camp coffee when a porcupine waddled into camp. Charlie eyed it carefully, and then took another bite of meat ravioli from the pouch as the critter sidled off into the underbrush.

He broke camp and was back on the South Rim

Trail by sunup. There was a junction up ahead where two trails merged, one of which was Boot Canyon Trail, which would take him down a narrow canyon trail into forest, and he was leaning toward taking that one at the junction. As it got lighter, he used his binoculars constantly, stopping periodically to scan the vista.

And all the while he was looking, he was wondering what magic Wyrick was going to pull out of her hat today. They needed a break of some kind to point him in the right direction.

Wyrick made the calls to set up the interviews just after 7:00 a.m. She apologized for the early time, then explained what she needed.

Trish's mother, Beth, was immediately on board.

"Yes, ma'am. Trish will be more than willing to help you in any way she can. She's in the shower right now. What time do you plan to come here?"

"I'm beginning with her, so eight o'clock."

Beth glanced at the clock. That was forty-five minutes away.

"She's staying home from school, so we'll be waiting," she said.

"Thank you," Wyrick said. "I'll see you soon."

The next call she made was to Nita Wells, Randall's mother. She was immediately on the defensive, and complaining about the timing of the call.

"You should have called sooner. My son is getting ready to leave for school, and he's already talked to the police," Nita said.

"So, he's going to be late for school today, and it doesn't matter what Randall told the police. Charlie Dodge is not the police. He was hired specifically by Tony Dawson's parents. Are you unwilling to help them find him?"

"No, no, of course not," Nita Wells said.

"I have your address. I'll be there a little after 9:00 a.m.," Wyrick said, then hung up and made her last call to Justin's mother, Andrea Young. She answered in a sleepy voice.

"Hello?"

"Mrs. Young, my name is Wyrick. I work for the private investigator the Dawson family hired to look for Tony."

"Oh, uh, yes, what can I do for you?" Andrea said.

"Charlie Dodge is already on-site searching, and I need to talk to Justin this morning."

"I don't know what else we can tell you, and he's getting ready for school."

"I'm sorry, but he's going to have to be late for school, and you can't tell me anything, Mrs. Young. I need to talk to Justin because he was there."

"He told the police every—"

"Charlie Dodge is not the police. Are you refusing to help?" Wyrick asked.

"No, of course not. When do you want me to—?"

"I have your address. I'll be there before ten."

"But Justin has a test and—"

"With all due respect, Tony Dawson is our priority. No one knows where he is. If he needs medical attention. If he has no shelter from the elements. Just make sure your son is there when I arrive."

"Fine. But we'll be right there with you when you talk to him," she said.

"I fully expect you to be," Wyrick said, leaving her to think about that for a while.

She guessed teenage boys with things to hide would be hard to break, so this morning she dressed to intimidate.

They'd smirk about her bald head and flat chest and she knew it, so she chose a low-cut black leather vest that revealed more than enough of the red-and-black dragon tattoo, a black bolero jacket, red leather pants and knee-high black boots. Then she slashed black shadow across her lids, bringing the shape to wicked winged points at the corners of her temples. If they weren't scared before, they were going to be when she got through with them.

She gathered up an extra phone to video the interviews and her iPad with the notes she already had on it, then left her apartment.

Her landlord, Merlin, was outside in the driveway picking up the morning paper as she circled the mansion and headed for the main gate. Wyrick smiled. Merlin was old-school. He refused to read newspapers online. She waved at him as she passed.

When he smiled and waved back, she thought he looked pale, and when she glanced up in the rearview mirror, he appeared to be walking stooped over.

It made her wonder how old Merlin was. In her mind, he was timeless and ageless—like the Merlin of fantasy. She made a mental note to check in on him tonight, and headed for the Caldwell residence.

Since all four of the kids went to the same school, they lived within easy driving distance of each other, and talking to Trish Caldwell was first on today's agenda.

The Caldwell residence was a nice but unassuming home. Wyrick already knew Beth Caldwell was a widow, and she was also a teacher in an elementary school in the same district where her daughter went to high school, which meant they were off for the same holidays and school breaks. A handy setup for a single parent.

Wyrick pulled up in the drive and parked. She grabbed her bag and slung it over her shoulder, then went up the steps and rang the doorbell. When it opened, she started talking before Beth Caldwell had time to react to her appearance.

"Mrs. Caldwell, I'm Wyrick, Charlie Dodge's office manager. We spoke on the phone."

Beth blinked and then smiled. "Come in. I called and told school I'd be delayed a bit. We're in the kitchen having waffles. Would you join us?"

"I'll have coffee with you," Wyrick said, and followed her through the house and into the kitchen, where Beth introduced her.

"Trish, this is Wyrick, the lady I told you about."

Trish looked suitably impressed by Wyrick's appearance.

"Fierce! I love it," Trish said.

Wyrick had hard questions to ask and didn't want

to establish any kind of friendly rapport, but she appreciated the positive response.

"Thank you," she said, and sat down as Beth put a cup of hot coffee in front of her.

"How can we help?" Beth asked.

Wyrick took a sip of the coffee, then set it to the side, taking out the phone she was going to record on and a mini tripod.

"Normally, my boss is the one doing all of the interviews for his cases, but timing is critical here, and so he took off to the site where Tony went missing, and I'm videoing everything for him," Wyrick said.

Trish's eyes welled. "I look terrible. I didn't sleep much last night. I just can't quit thinking about Tony."

"No one is going to see this but the boss. Just go ahead and finish your breakfast. The questions are easy." Then she started the video.

Trish nodded and took another bite, chewing as she waited for Wyrick's first question.

"So, how long have you and Tony been dating?" Wyrick asked.

"Three months and a couple of days," Trish said.

Wyrick nodded and made a note in her iPad.

"Where did you meet?"

"At school," Trish said.

"Are you an official couple, or—?"

"Yes, we're official," Trish said.

Wyrick nodded, waiting while Trish took a few more bites, because she suspected when she moved into the next sets of questions the girl was going to lose her appetite.

She glanced at Beth. The worry on her face was evident, as was the love she had for her daughter. Wyrick could feel it.

"Trish, how long have Tony, Randall and Justin been friends?" Wyrick asked.

Trish blinked. "I'm not sure, but I didn't meet Tony until just before school began this fall."

"Did Tony know you used to date Randall Wells?" Wyrick asked.

Trish paled. "I don't know."

Beth frowned. "Honey…you didn't tell him?"

Trish looked nervous. "At first I didn't think it mattered. We'd just met, and I didn't know who his friends were. We'd been dating barely a month when Mom and I saw them all together at the mall. It was awkward and weird."

"Did Randall and Justin seem surprised that you and Tony were a couple?" Wyrick asked.

Trish thought a moment and then frowned. "No. No, they didn't. Randall was cool, and so was Justin. I mean…it had been months and months since Randall and I had dated. He'd even had a girlfriend or two since."

"After you and Randall broke up, did you date other boys before Tony?" Wyrick asked.

Trish shook her head. "No."

"Who broke up, you or Randall?" Wyrick asked.

"I guess I did," Trish said.

Beth interrupted. "What are you suggesting?"

"I'm not suggesting anything, but the boys stated they all had a fight the night Tony went missing. And that they'd been drinking. So, if Tony had no idea he was dating Randall's former girlfriend, things could have been said that caused the argument. And that could have been the reason Tony left."

Trish dropped her fork and started crying.

"Oh my God. It's my fault! It's all my fault. I should have told him, but by the time we got close, I didn't want to lose him…and now maybe I've lost him for good."

Beth jumped up and went to her daughter.

"No, no, don't think like that. We still have to have faith he'll be found alive, honey. And you didn't cheat on him. You are all young and will date lots of people as you grow up. You were single. Tony was single. You were both fine."

"I should have told him," Trish said.

Beth sighed. "Yes, probably so, but you can't change any of this now. And you're not responsible for what happened to three boys who got drunk on a camping trip, understand?"

"Your mother is right," Wyrick said. "A woman has the right to date who she wants, and granted, it might have been an uncomfortable conversation, but it shouldn't have made a difference. I'm sorry to upset you, but we always need the whole truth when we're trying to solve a case."

"It's okay," Trish said, wiping her eyes. "I just pray you find Tony alive. I love him, and if he's too mad at me to want to be with me anymore, then that will have to be okay, because all I want is for him to be safe."

Beth glanced at Wyrick. "If your boss has news, will you keep us updated?"

"Yes," Wyrick said. "Thank you for the coffee and the information. It's been helpful."

Beth walked her to the door. "If those boys are hiding something, they aren't going to tell."

"But I'll know it if they're lying, so there's that," Wyrick said, and left without explaining herself.

Three

Charlie had been hiking down Boot Canyon Trail for the better part of two hours when he paused to use his binoculars again. He swept the horizon, then aimed them down and started a slow search of the area below him.

As he did, something flashed in the sunlight below, catching his attention. He looked down, but saw nothing that would explain the flash. He looked again and again through the binoculars without ever relocating the flash, but he couldn't ignore it. So he began looking for a landmark to mark the area where he'd seen the flash, and picked a pinyon tree that had been struck by lightning. Using it as a marker, he found what looked like a natural path on the slope and started down. The incline was steep and rocky, but there was just enough growth of pinyon and juniper to hang on to as he began to descend. The going was slow, but safety demanded it.

It took over thirty minutes to get down the slope

to the dead pinyon tree, and then he began searching the area for something shiny. It could have been anything that would have caused that flash, from an empty glass bottle, to a piece of metal. But he had to find it to be sure it wasn't some kind of signal from someone in need, so he began poking around in the underbrush and looking among the crevices.

Another fifteen minutes passed before he saw what looked like a canvas strap on the ground beneath some brush, and as he reached down and pulled it, he quickly realized it was attached to a hiker's backpack.

His heart skipped a beat as he knelt down to check it out. It was obvious that animals had been at it. He could see drag marks where they'd pulled it out from beneath a rock. A portion of one side had been torn open, and the wrappers from the protein bars that had been in it were scattered beneath the pack and caught in the underbrush.

Charlie turned it around, and when he did, he saw a metal dog tag clipped to a zipper pull…the kind of identification a soldier would wear. That was what had caused the flash of light. Sunlight caught on that shiny piece of metal. He turned it over and saw the name, Grant Dawson. It was from WWII. The timeline would have made him a great-uncle or a great-grandfather to Tony.

"Dammit," Charlie muttered, and began digging inside the pack. He found Tony's wallet and ID.

He stood there a moment and then looked up the slope he'd just descended. If Tony had fallen down from above, then why had his backpack been beneath the rock? It would have been on the ground or on top of the rock. And if he'd fallen, then where was Tony? He would not have left this behind.

All of Charlie's warning signals were going off as he began circling the area, looking for signs of blood or drag marks that would indicate animals had dragged a body away. But he found nothing that would lead him to believe Tony was ever here.

"What the hell is going on?" Charlie muttered, and then reached for his phone.

He called the ranger station first to notify them of what he'd found, then gave them the GPS coordinates and said he was leaving it for them to recover.

"But that area was thoroughly searched," the woman said.

"I don't doubt that," Charlie said. "I think it had been hidden before, because there are visible drag marks where it had been pulled out from beneath some rocks. I think animals are responsible for moving it back into view, because it was torn into and food wrappers are all around it."

"Okay. We'll get someone out to retrieve it, and good work, Mr. Dodge. Are there any signs of the boy?" she asked.

"No, ma'am, and there are no signs to indicate he fell from above. There's no blood or signs of a body being dragged off by predators. I don't think he was here, but I can't explain the hidden backpack. I'm going to continue searching down here in the canyon."

"I'll make note of that for the rangers," she said.

"Oh, one other thing," Charlie said. "Yesterday I met an old man on the trail. He was meditating, and when he saw me, he asked me if I'd heard the ghost. He said he hikes the trails up here a lot, so I walked off and left him meditating. Is he okay? I mean, is he competent to be out on his own?"

"That sounds like Leroy. Really dark skin, long white hair and a face full of wrinkles?"

"Yes, ma'am. Was it okay to leave him on the trail like that?"

"I don't know anything about a ghost, but he's a savvy hiker, and while he's a bit eccentric, he's sharp as a tack. Don't worry about him."

"Okay, then," Charlie said. "If I find anything else, I'll let you know." Then he hung up and called Wyrick, hoping she would have worked her magic and learned something that would help him find the kid.

Wyrick's appearance at the Wells home resulted in a cool reception.

Nita Wells answered the door, looked somewhat horrified, then almost shut it in Wyrick's face.

"I'm Wyrick. You are expecting me."

"Oh! Well, I wasn't expecting all this," Nita said.

Wyrick stared the woman down without comment, forcing her to break the silence.

"We're in the living room," Nita said. "Follow me."

Wyrick entered with her head up, her stride long

and purposeful. The look on the teenage boy's face was both fascinated and shocked.

"Do we need a lawyer?" Nita asked.

Wyrick turned, fixing her with a cool, studied stare. "I don't know. Do you?"

Nita blushed.

Randall frowned. "Mom. Chill."

"This is Wyrick," Nita said.

Wyrick sat down without an invitation, choosing the sofa so she could use the end table to set up the video.

"You're recording this?" Randall asked.

"For my boss," Wyrick said. "He's already in the mountains searching, so he sent me."

Randall nodded, but he couldn't quit staring at the dragon tattoo where her breasts should have been. It was obvious there was much more to the dragon than what the eye could see, and that fascinated him.

"I'm ready," Wyrick said, and hit Start on the video. "Okay, Randall, whose idea was it to go camping in the Chisos?"

Nita leaned forward. "I think it was—"

"I asked Randall, so I want Randall's answer," Wyrick said.

Nita flushed. She didn't like this wild woman, and she resented any implication that her son might be at fault.

"Me and my friend Justin went last year. We made friends with Tony after he moved here, and when he mentioned he used to backpack and hike back in California, we invited him to go with us," Randall said.

"Why didn't all three of you drive down together?" Wyrick asked.

Randall shifted in his seat. "Tony had a truck. He offered to bring all the gear, and so we drove down in our car. He followed us."

"Not a very fun trip for Tony…driving all that way for hours and hours alone," Wyrick said.

Randall shrugged.

"Did you meet Tony before he started dating Trish Caldwell or afterward?" Wyrick asked.

Nita gasped. "What does that have to—?"

Randall flushed. "I don't remember. Besides, what does that have to do with—?"

Wyrick went straight to the point. "Trish never told Tony that she had once dated you. Is that what your fight was about?"

Nita gasped. "She didn't? I mean…are you sure she—?"

Wyrick kept looking at Randall. "Trish said she never told him. So when we find him, is he going to tell us that's what the fight was about, or would you rather come clean and tell me now?"

Randall was wild-eyed and looking from his mother to Wyrick and back again.

"Randall?" Nita said.

"We drank some beers," Randall said.

"Too many, I assume," Wyrick said. "Three drunk teenagers on a mountain, and two with a secret the other doesn't know. Who told?"

Randall looked down at the floor. "He kept talking about his girl this and his girl that, and I blurted out…'I know all about her, because she was my girl first, before you ever moved here.' Then Justin laughed and said she'd been with a lot of guys before Tony."

Nita groaned. "Randall, that's not true. Trish is a good girl and you know it."

Randall shrugged. "I didn't say it. Justin did."

"So what happened after that?" Wyrick asked.

"We had a little scuffle. Traded a few punches, and then we all got in our tents and passed out. When we woke up the next morning, he was gone."

Nita was pale and shaking. "Did you tell the police this?"

He shook his head.

She got out her phone and started texting.

"What are you doing?" Randall asked.

"Texting your father to come home."

Randall covered his face.

"Was he just missing, or had he packed up and left?" Wyrick asked.

Randall shrugged. "All of his stuff was gone. That's why we assumed he just walked back down. We didn't expect his truck to still be in the parking lot when we got there."

"Just to be clear. You didn't look for him at all?" Wyrick asked.

Randall shook his head. "No, ma'am. We did not."

Wyrick stood abruptly, shifting her focus to Nita.

"I'm going to ask the both of you not to call the Young family. I'm going over there right now. And if you care anything about Tony Dawson's life and getting to the truth, you will do as I ask."

Nita was shaken, but her whole attitude toward Wyrick had changed.

"You have my word. Randall and I will be sitting right here together, waiting for his father to get home."

"I'll see myself out," Wyrick said, then stopped the video, packed up her things and walked out.

As she was driving away, she was already thinking about Justin Young. Would he be as open, or would he try to lie his way out?

She already knew there was more to the story than what he had admitted. Because, while Randall was telling her they didn't search for him, she'd seen all three of them arguing, and it had been daylight, and they'd all been wearing backpacks. She didn't know what that meant, but only two of them came off that mountain. Tony Dawson was still there, but did they leave him in trouble, or did he go off on his own?

She pulled up to the Young residence about fifteen minutes later, and as she got out, she saw someone briefly look out the window and then move away.

"Yes, I'm here," Wyrick muttered, glad this was the last interview. She wasn't a people person and had generated more conversation during these interviews than she did in a week. She knocked, and moments later, the door swung inward.

"Mrs. Young, I'm Wyrick."

"I guessed," Andrea Young said. "Come in. Justin

is in the living room, and just so you know, you're causing my husband to miss work this morning."

"No, ma'am, I am not. Your son misplaced a friend. He's the reason this is happening."

Andrea's nose went up in a disapproving sniff. "Follow me," she said. As soon as they entered the living room, father and son stood. "Peter, Justin, this is Wyrick."

Peter Young shook her hand. "Ms. Wyrick. I've heard great things about Charlie Dodge. We're happy to do anything we need to help find Tony."

"Thank you," Wyrick said, and then looked at Justin. Like Randall, he appeared startled and fascinated by her. "I'm recording all of this for my boss. As soon as I get set up, we'll begin. There are only a few questions, so it shouldn't take long."

"Did you already talk to Randall?" Justin asked.

"Yes, I did," Wyrick said. "Take a seat, please, so I can set the camera up."

"Oh, yes, sure," Justin said, and sat beside his father.

As soon as Wyrick was ready, she got straight to the point.

"Did you and Randall make friends with Tony Dawson before you found out he was dating Trish Caldwell or afterward?"

Justin's mouth dropped.

Andrea gasped. "What are you getting at?"

Peter frowned. "Wait...what's happening?"

Wyrick shrugged. "Trish Caldwell never told Tony that she'd dated Randall before he moved here.

It shouldn't have mattered, but teenage boys being teenage boys, it probably did. So, was that what the argument was about? And how drunk were you before the fight started?"

Justin looked from one parent to the other, suddenly wishing they weren't in the room.

Andrea stared. "Justin wasn't drunk…right, son?"

Peter frowned. He knew boys better than that, because he'd been one.

"Justin, the truth," Peter said.

Justin sighed. "We were drunk."

"And what started the argument you said you had with Tony?" Wyrick asked.

Justin glanced at Wyrick, then looked away. "Randall did. He was jealous of Tony."

"But why?" Andrea asked. "Randall and Trish Caldwell broke up months before Tony Dawson moved here."

Justin glanced at his mom and then answered. "Trish is the one who broke it off. I think Randall held a grudge about that."

"Even though he's dated other girls since?" Wyrick asked.

Justin frowned. "How did you know that?"

"I know stuff. All kinds of stuff," Wyrick said.

Justin shrugged. "Tony kept talking about his girl, and Randall got sick of it. He told Tony that Trish was his girl first, before Tony ever moved here."

Wyrick leaned forward. "And you added to Tony's shock by telling him that a lot of boys had dated Trish Caldwell. You insinuated she slept around."

Peter groaned and looked at his son in disbelief. "You didn't."

Justin shrugged. "Well, dammit, Dad. I was drunk, okay?"

"That's how girls' reputations are ruined," Wyrick said. "A lie. Just one lie and everybody runs with it."

"I'm sorry," Justin said. "I'll make it up to her."

"Right now, no one knows you said it but Randall and Tony, so don't say it again, and the lie doesn't grow."

Justin frowned. "How did you find out, then?"

"Randall told me," Wyrick said.

Justin glared at her. "I don't believe you. Randall wouldn't rat on me."

"He didn't 'rat' on you. He told me the truth. And I know something else you're not telling. All three of you were together the next morning. You were on the trail and you were all wearing your backpacks. And you were arguing," Wyrick said.

Peter stood. "How do you know that?" he asked.

"Ask Justin if it's true," Wyrick said.

Justin was ashen and trembling. "You can't know that. No one was there. No one saw us."

"Actually, you just admitted that was true by the way you denied it," Wyrick said. "I also know you're scared shitless about something else. Something worse. What did you two do to Tony Dawson?"

"We didn't do anything. We didn't touch him!" Justin shrieked, and got up and ran out of the room.

Andrea jumped up and followed him, leaving Peter alone and in shock.

"I don't know what to say…what to think," he mumbled.

"If he confesses anything more, I would appreciate a phone call. If Tony Dawson is still alive, his life might depend on someone willing to tell the truth."

Wyrick handed him a card from Dodge Security and Investigations, and then picked up her video equipment and left on her own. She was back in the Mercedes and on her way to the office when her cell rang. When she saw it was Charlie, she put it on speaker.

"What?"

"I found his backpack. It appeared to have been hidden, which is why searchers would have missed it before, but I think animals are responsible for the fact that it had been dragged out into the open enough for me to find it. They'd torn into the backpack for the protein bars. Tony's ID was inside, but there's no sign of his body anywhere. No blood. No drag marks that would indicate animals got to him."

"I have news, too. Randall admitted they were all three drunk. Tony kept bragging about his girl, and Randall fired back and said she was his girl first. Then Justin added a little fire by claiming Trish slept around with lots of boys, which isn't true, but Randall didn't deny it. What they told Tony must have gutted him."

"Well, shit," Charlie said.

"That's not all," Wyrick said. "When I was talking to Randall, I saw all three of them with their backpacks, but it was morning, and they were on the trail together, and they were arguing. So either they fought before that night, or Tony was there the next morning, and they lied about not knowing what happened to him."

Charlie was silent a moment, but he was thinking about Wyrick's uncanny ability to know what people were thinking when they were being questioned.

"You saw that…like when we interviewed that convict in Phoenix, and you saw the truth of where Fourth Dimension was, and what was happening to those little girls?"

"Yes, like that. I saw the boys together and it was morning."

"What would happen if you were holding something that belonged to Tony? Do you think you could key in on him?" Charlie asked.

"I don't know. I've never tried to do that," Wyrick said.

"Call his parents. Tell them you're coming by and that you need a personal item that belongs to Tony. Something he wears or uses all the time. See what happens and call me. I've got a gut feeling they might have hidden his body like they hid his gear, and I want to be wrong."

"Yes, okay, and if it works, I'll call you."

"In the meantime, I'll continue the search," Charlie said.

Wyrick disconnected, then pulled up the Dawsons' home phone and called.

Macie Dawson answered. "Hello?"

"Mrs. Dawson, this is Wyrick."

There was a gasp, and then Macie's voice began to shake.

"Oh my God, do you have news?"

"No, not yet," Wyrick said. "But I have a favor to ask. I need something personal of Tony's. Something he uses or wears all the time. I'll get it back to you."

"Yes, of course. I'm home. I'll have it ready for you."

"I'll be there in about fifteen minutes," Wyrick said, then put the address in her GPS system and headed to the Dawson home.

She kept trying to focus on Tony, but she couldn't establish a mental or emotional connection. She didn't feel good about any of this now. Finding out that his hiking gear had been hidden wasn't a good sign. And the fact that there were no physical signs of him around the gear was disheartening.

What had they done to him, and what had they done with his body?

Four

Macie Dawson went to Tony's room, then paused in the doorway. What would she choose to give to Wyrick? Then she saw his baseball caps. He wore a cap all the time, and his Dallas Cowboys cap was one of his favorites.

She took it off the bedpost, then carried it downstairs, put it in a paper bag and waited. When she saw Wyrick pull up into their drive a little over fifteen minutes later, then get out at a jog, it made Macie nervous, like something was imminent, that there was news they weren't telling her. But if they'd found him, they wouldn't be wanting this baseball cap.

When Wyrick rang the bell, Macie was there. She opened the door and thrust the paper sack toward her.

"Will this do?"

Wyrick looked inside. "Does he wear this a lot?"

"All the time," Macie said.

"I'll get it back to you. I promise," Wyrick said,

and sped off, anxious to get back to the office, where it was quiet. She needed to be able to focus.

"Godspeed," Macie said, but Wyrick was already gone. She stepped back into the house and closed the door.

Another thirty minutes passed before Wyrick made it back to the office. She parked in her space and was heading for the building when Darrell Boyington jumped out of a car and stepped between her and the building.

"Wait! Wait! I just want to talk," he said. "I'm sorry I was rude. I'm sorry I called you a freak. I need help."

"You didn't listen before, but I want you to listen to me now. You're lying to me, but I don't have time to figure out why."

Boyington blinked.

"What do you mean, you don't have time to figure it out?" he muttered.

Wyrick ignored him and kept walking straight toward him, but Boyington didn't like being thwarted, and stood his ground.

When he wouldn't move, Wyrick poked a finger into the hollow between his collar bones, pressing so hard it made him wince.

"This is the second time you have staked me out after being asked to leave the office. Am I going to have to file stalking charges against you?"

Boyington backed off. Cops were the last thing he needed. "No, no, I just need help and—"

"Find someone else, because if I see you anywhere around here again…or if you try and chase me down on the freeway again, I will tell Charlie Dodge. And trust me, you do NOT want that to happen. There are dozens of other investigators in Dallas. Go hire one of them. Now get your ass in that car and get the hell out of this parking lot, or I'm calling the police."

"Sorry," Boyington said. "I'm leaving. No cops. No cops."

And the moment he said that, Wyrick's heart skipped a beat. He knew Cyrus Parks. She didn't know how, but she saw Cyrus's face superimposed over Boyington's and knew that was who he was thinking about. Holy hell! Was he working for Parks? Was she in danger again? So, now was the time to put a stop to it before it went any further.

"While you're at it, call Cyrus Parks and tell him you quit, because I'll destroy the both of you if I see your face again."

The shock on Boyington's face was real.

"How did you—?"

Wyrick took another step toward him. "Get away from me. Now!"

The thought ran through his head to just break her neck now, but he already knew there were video cameras everywhere. And naming the man who'd hired him had been shocking. How the fuck had she known that?

He turned around and headed for his car, and was

running by the time he got inside. He started it up and peeled out of the parking lot without looking back.

Wyrick was worried all over again. Just when she thought Parks had backed off for good. Maybe he found out she'd been part of taking down Fourth Dimension. Or maybe he just hated being thwarted enough to want her dead. Either way, her sense of safety was gone. She hurried into the building, then up to the office.

Once she was inside, she locked the door behind her, then began turning on lights. She started coffee brewing, then took the sack into Charlie's office and sat down. The moment her fingers touched the cap, she could see Tony Dawson's face, so she closed her eyes and followed the vision.

Charlie marked the coordinates of the backpack on his GPS and then paused, trying to decide whether to go back up onto the trail to continue his search or shift to this lower location. He felt like a crime had been committed, but he still hadn't decided if it was premeditated or a crime of chance.

As he looked around at the heavier forested area, he thought he could hear water, and remembered the map showing the location of a creek down in this canyon. If Tony was hurt, it stood to reason he would seek a water source, so he began walking toward the sound.

The canyon he was in now was rife with juniper, oak, cottonwood and ash, all of which afforded shelter to a diverse assortment of wildlife. Birdcalls and the occasional chatter from a squirrel above him were evident, and more than once, he came across deer tracks. The farther he went down into the canyon, the more animal signs he found.

When he found the creek, the cougar and bear tracks gave him pause. If Tony Dawson was no longer alive, the chances of finding him in pieces was real. And even though he'd seen enough of that when he was still serving as an Army Ranger, the possibility put a knot in his belly, so he kept walking, looking for signs of human footprints, too.

The sun was moving too fast across the sky for Charlie's peace of mind. If he didn't get a break soon, he would be spending his second night under the stars, and for Tony Dawson, it would be night five.

When a rattlesnake slithered out from the scrub, moving across the rocky path without concern that Charlie was even there, he froze, waiting motionless for it to pass.

When it finally disappeared into the brush on the other side of the path, he moved on until he got to an open space on the trail and caught a glimpse of something moving off to his right. Once again, he stopped, watching as a doe and a half-grown fawn moved through the trees and then, like the snake, moved out of sight.

By his estimation, he was about a quarter of a mile from where he'd found the backpack. Logic would lead anyone to believe that a hiker would never leave that behind, and certainly wouldn't hide it. But what if he had been the one to hide it? What if he'd meant to come back for it and something happened to him?

Charlie paused again, looking around at the area, then up through the trees, trying to get a glimpse of the trail above where he was standing.

"Where the hell are you, kid? Where did you go?" Then he pulled out his phone and called Wyrick.

The cap Wyrick had been holding was on the floor between her feet. She was sitting with her head down, gripping the arms of the chair so tightly that the ends of her fingers had turned white, but she was no longer in Charlie's office.

It was dark and narrow here. And cold.

Water. She could hear water dripping.

Something was back there—growling—no, no, not a growl. A moan. It was a moan.

Sweat broke out across her forehead as a wash of heat swept through her, but she was focused on the moan. It connected to pain—pain she could feel now.

God, oh God! The pain!

She was about to move deeper into the darkness when her phone rang. The sound yanked her out of the vision so fast she fell forward out of the chair onto her hands and knees.

Her phone kept ringing, and she couldn't focus on where she was, and then she saw the dark red pattern of the area rug in Charlie's office and groaned.

"Shit," she muttered, and scrambled to her feet to

get to the phone she'd left on her desk. "I'm here!" she said, and then heard Charlie chuckle.

"Where else would you be?"

"Never mind," she said. "He's alive."

Charlie froze. "What? Where?"

"Inside something…something long and narrow. It's cold. I heard a trickle of water. I heard what sounded like a moan. The pain…the pain is bad. I don't know where it is, but I think he's in a cave. I can't explain what any of that means. I don't know if that was a vision from the present or if it was something from the past. You might find him, and he's not alive anymore…understand?"

"Yes. And thank you," Charlie said.

Wyrick sighed. "You're the one who thought of it. Now go do your thing, Charlie Dodge. Figure it out. Find the kid before it's too late."

"Jesus, Wyrick! I'm down in this canyon without a freaking clue as to where to go next. Do you see a landmark, or something specific that would tell me where to even start looking?"

She ran back into his office and picked up the cap. Again, the room disappeared and this time she was standing in a small clearing, looking toward a wall of rock and scrub brush.

"Get off the path," she said. "I think you need to move into the trees toward the cliffs. Whatever you need next is in plain sight, and that's all I know."

"Heading that way now," Charlie said. "If you get anything else, let me know." He left the trail.

The going was slow now, moving through trees,

scrub brush and uneven, rocky ground. His focus was on looking for something that didn't belong… maybe something man-made…something that Tony Dawson might have dropped. Wyrick said plain sight, and he trusted what she said.

The trail he'd left was about thirty yards behind him now, but he could no longer see it. It would be easy to get lost in here, especially if someone was sick and disoriented.

And then he came upon what looked like a garden of rocks and large boulders. At some time in the past, a part of the mountain had broken off and fallen down here, scattering the rocks about until they looked like they'd come up from the earth like seeds of mountains-to-be.

The canyon wall was on the other side of the rock fall, and as he started making his way through it, he saw something strange near the bottom of the wall and headed toward it. Within seconds, he realized it was a hiker's boot and started running.

The boot was wedged in a crevice between three large rocks. There was dried blood all over the boot, and on the rocks, as well, and then a whole lot of coyote tracks around the area. The tracks had obliterated any signs that might tell him more.

"Son of a bitch," Charlie muttered.

He looked up. The trail was right above him. If Tony fell from there, Charlie didn't think he would've survived it. But where was the body? Coyotes could have dragged it away, but it would have been in pieces. There was no way they would have neatly removed the foot that had been in that shoe. At the least, he would be seeing pieces of clothing. None of this was making sense.

But Wyrick said it felt like he was in a cave, and she'd heard him moan. Right now, it didn't matter how the kid got hurt. He just wanted to find him alive, and Wyrick hadn't been wrong yet, so he was going to look for caves. Judging from the blood on and around the boot, mobility had to have been compromised. He couldn't have gone far. He glanced back at the boot one last time, then took a deep breath and started yelling.

"Hello! Hello! Tony! Tony Dawson! Where are you?"

And then he kept yelling as he fanned out from the boot, looking for signs that someone had either walked or crawled away from that bloody boot, looking for anything that could be an opening to a cave.

Tony was sitting on a pier, looking out across the ocean at the sunset. He felt a pull toward the fading light, as if he was supposed to follow it. But he hesitated, and then all of a sudden, he was no longer alone.

A man had joined him. He looked at Tony and grinned.

"Hi, kid."

The man looked familiar, but Tony was certain he'd never met him.

"Hi."

"So, what's going on?" the man said.

Tony shrugged. "I'm waiting."

"Oh yeah? Who are you waiting for?"

"I'm not sure," Tony said, then looked at him closer. "Do I know you?"

"Not really, but I know you, and your dad and granddad."

Tony looked back at the setting sun. The sky was turning vivid shades of yellow, and red, and orange. He took a deep breath and then slowly exhaled.

The man put his arm around Tony.

"You can do this, kid. It's your choice, but if you want to stay, you're tough enough to do it."

"Thanks," Tony said.

"Hey, no problem, kid. It's what I do for the people I love," the man said, and then he put something in Tony's hand and closed his fingers around it.

Tony stared back at the sun. It was almost gone, and the pull to follow it was easing. He'd chosen to stay.

"Thanks, mister," Tony said, and then realized he was alone.

He opened his fingers. There was a military dog tag in the palm of his hand with the name Grant Dawson on it.

And then all of a sudden the pier was gone, the sun had set and there was nothing in his hand. He was in darkness, and in a kind of pain he didn't know a human could endure.

He opened his mouth to call for help, but the only thing that came out was a moan.

Then he stilled, struggling to stay conscious, because he could hear someone calling his name, but what if it was them, coming back to finish him off?

He didn't want them to know where he was. Then he heard the voice again…a man's voice… Was it a real person, or was it a dream?

Someone was shouting—shouting his name. He needed help or he was going to die. He wanted to answer, but he was too weak to shout.

He heard the voice again…and in his mind, he remembered the man at the pier. He'd chosen to stay. Now he had to choose to live.

With every ounce of strength he had left, he rolled over onto his back. The scream that came up his throat was born of pain—fired by the guts it had taken to move all his broken bones. But the pain was too great, and he slipped into unconsciousness again.

Charlie was moving at a jog, trying to cover as much ground as he could and still search. Twice he saw what he thought was an opening to a cave, only to discover it was nothing more than a deep crevice below an outcrop of rock.

And each time the spurt of adrenaline he'd felt downshifted to a growing feeling of defeat. Time was running out for Tony Dawson. He could feel it, and in desperation, he paused, cupped his hands to his mouth and started shouting over and over at the top of his voice.

"Tony! Tony Dawson! Where are you?"

When he first heard the scream, he thought, *Old Leroy's banshee*, and spun around and started running through the brush and trees toward the direction of the sound, still shouting all the way to the canyon wall.

Scrub brush grew in clumps against the wall, and even more had grown up between the dead branches of a fallen tree. He began searching for an opening behind it, and then looked down the wall to his right and saw a gap in the rock and ran.

The opening was long and low, barely five feet high. He shed his backpack, grabbed the LED lantern he'd brought with him and turned it on, then crawled inside.

He swept the area before him to make sure he wasn't crawling in on snakes, but when the light fell on the partial skeleton of a deer, he wondered if he'd stumbled into a cougar's lair instead.

Had he mistaken a cougar's scream for a human one? He knew from his childhood that the scream of a cougar was often mistaken for that of a woman. Hesitant, he lifted the lantern as high as he could, trying to get a look at how deep this tunnel went, and that was when he saw the boy.

"Oh God, oh God," Charlie muttered, and started crawling.

The first thing he felt for was a pulse. It was there!

Then he moved the light down to the boy's legs. One foot was bare and purple with bruises, swollen to twice its size. The broken bones at the ankle were unmistakable. He knew the boy had somehow crawled in here, but he didn't know if he'd fallen from the trail above first, and was too afraid of internal injuries to pull him out.

He put a hand on Tony's head. He had a fever

and it was high, and the boy's lips were cracked and bleeding from dehydration. He pulled out a handkerchief, dipped it in the little pool of water beside the body, then squeezed a few drops between his lips.

Tony moaned.

"Hang on, Tony… Hang on, kid. I'm getting you out of here," Charlie said, then left the lantern by the boy and crawled out.

The moment he was outside, he called the park office.

"Chisos Mountain Lodge," the clerk said.

"This is Charlie Dodge. I just found your missing hiker."

"Oh my God! Hang on a moment. Ranger Collins is out in the parking lot. Let me get him."

Charlie heard her drop the phone and run. A couple of minutes later, Collins picked up.

"This is Arnie."

"Hey, Arnie. It's Charlie Dodge. I found Tony Dawson. He's alive, but in bad shape. I can give you a GPS location, but you're going to have to airlift him out from somewhere nearby, because he's not going to tolerate being carried."

"Give me the coordinates," Arnie said, and wrote down what Charlie gave him. "How the hell did you find him?"

"I went down Boot Canyon Trail. Then after I found the backpack, I stayed in the canyon to search further. I found a boot wedged between some rocks, guessed it was his, and I found him nearby in a cave."

"A cave? No wonder we didn't find him. Good job, Charlie. Good job."

"Have you picked up his backpack yet?" Charlie asked.

"Yes. That's what I was doing out in the parking lot. A couple of rangers retrieved it and brought it in."

"Hang on to it for me. It was a reflection of sunlight on that metal dog tag on the zipper that I saw. It set me on the right track to find him. His parents are going to want it back."

"Will do," Arnie said. "Is he still in the cave?"

"Yes. I was afraid to move him. I don't know if he fell from the trail above or if he got hurt another way, but his ankle is badly broken, and maybe his leg above it, too. His fever is in the danger zone, and he's unconscious."

"Got it," Arnie said. "Just hang on. I'll get help to you."

"Tell them to call out for me when they get here, because I'm going back into the cave to stay with the kid. He's been in there on his own long enough."

"Will do," Arnie said, and hung up.

Charlie heard him disconnect and then called Wyrick. He guessed she was sitting beside the phone because she picked up while it was first ringing.

"Hello? Charlie?"

"I found him. He's in bad shape, but he's alive. Take down this number. It's for the office at the Chisos Mountain Lodge," he said, and then read it off.

Wyrick breathed a slow sigh of relief that he'd been found and wrote the number down.

"Got it," she said.

"Call Baxter and Macie Dawson. Tell them he's

alive and we're waiting to be airlifted out. That will take some time. They'll have a million questions. I found him unconscious, so I don't have answers for anything. Give them the number I just gave you. They can coordinate everything else from there, via the rangers on-site. And tell them not to tell anyone else he's been found yet."

"Why? What about calling Trish Caldwell?"

"Not even her. Not yet," Charlie said. "For sure don't tell Randall's or Justin's families. I know Tony Dawson did not hide his own backpack. There's still more to this story than we know."

"Understood," Wyrick said. "As soon as I get the calls made, I'll head your way to pick you up."

"I'm a long way from the lodge, and I don't know how long it will take for help to get here."

"Well, hell, that means I'm going to miss my hair appointment because of you," she drawled.

Charlie grinned. "Okay, fine. Suit yourself."

"I always do," Wyrick said. "I'll be at the lodge waiting...whenever you show up."

She hung up on him. Before he could say *thank you* or *kiss my ass*.

"Damn woman," he muttered, then got a bottle of water from his backpack and crawled back inside the cave.

Macie Dawson was in the kitchen making coffee. Baxter was at the table eating a piece of the coconut cream pie she'd made that morning.

"This sure is good pie, honey," he said.

"It's Tony's favorite," Macie said, and then burst into tears.

Baxter jumped up and wrapped his arms around her.

"I know. Don't give up hope," he said.

Macie leaned into him. "At this point, hope is all we have."

Baxter felt the same way, and was at a loss for words to ease what felt like growing grief. And then his phone rang. He went back to the table to get it.

"It's from Dodge's office," he said, and put it on speaker as he answered. "Hello, this is Baxter."

"This is Wyrick. Charlie found your son. He's alive."

"Oh my God! This is wonderful!" Baxter said. "Charlie Dodge is a miracle man."

Macie ran to the phone. "Is he hurt?"

"Yes, ma'am, he's hurt, but Charlie is with him, waiting for an airlift. He doesn't know anything, because Tony was unconscious when he found him, so questions will have to wait."

"Is he hurt bad?" Baxter asked.

"All Charlie said was that he was in bad shape. I don't know exactly what that entails. But I have a phone number for you. It's for the office at the lodge. Charlie said you will be able to stay in touch with the rangers from there and find out where they're taking him."

Macie's tears were gone. She had hope *and* purpose again. Her boy was alive, and whatever that meant, it was enough.

Then Wyrick delivered the last of the message. "Charlie also said for you not to tell anyone Tony has been found. He will explain the reasons why later, but I think he's still suspicious of the circumstances in which he went missing."

"What circumstances?" Baxter asked.

"Randall and Justin's story doesn't jibe with some things we've learned. Charlie will explain everything to you once Tony is taken care of."

"Yes, all right. I'm not going to question a damn thing Charlie Dodge asks of me," Baxter said. "He found our boy. That's enough. Thank you. Thanks to the both of you. More than you can know."

"Feel free to call me if you run into problems," Wyrick said. "I'm good at finding solutions."

"Thank you," Macie said.

Wyrick disconnected, then called Benny to get the chopper ready, gathered up her things, along with the sack with Tony's cap, locked up the office and headed home to change.

Five

As hard as it was to see him in this condition, Charlie knew documenting it mattered, so he used his iPad to take pictures of Tony and the visible injuries, as well as pictures of the inside of the cave, using the LED lantern for a light source.

As soon as he'd finished, he sat down beside the boy, poured some water on his handkerchief and dabbed the boy's lips again as he began to talk.

"You are one tough kid, Tony Dawson. About as tough as the man who wore that dog tag you have on your backpack. I found that, by the way. I found your boot, too. I don't know what happened to you, but when you get better, you can tell us how this went down."

Tony moaned.

Charlie laid a hand on his arm. "My name is Charlie, and I'm going to stay here with you. We're waiting for a medical team. You're gonna be okay. Just don't let go."

The boy's lips were moving now, but no sounds were coming out. Tony was so feverish that even if Charlie could have heard him, he wouldn't have trusted anything said in delirium. What mattered was that the boy knew he was no longer alone.

"Your mom and dad know you're alive. We called them. You're going to be home with them before you know it. Stay with me."

"Mama…"

Charlie poured more water on the handkerchief, then patted it on Tony's lips again. It wasn't going to heal anything, but it was all he could do in the way of comfort.

"I had a fever like this once," Charlie said. "And a dislocated shoulder, and I was lost as hell, too. This woman I know found me. And she's the reason I found you, too. Maybe you'll meet her one day, and when you do, she'll change your opinion of women forever…but in a good way, okay?"

Tony shifted slightly, and as he did, pain shot through him so fast that, even in his unconscious state, he screamed.

Charlie winced. "I'm sorry, kid. I'm so sorry."

And for a few seconds, he was back in Afghanistan, sitting watch beside one of his men who'd just lost a leg because of an IED.

Silence followed the shriek. A long silence. The kid in Afghanistan had died. This silence was a stark reminder of that day, and he reached out to check Tony's pulse again, then breathed a sigh of relief. This kid was still breathing.

He glanced at his watch. They'd been waiting for over an hour now, and each moment Charlie measured the time by the continuing intake and exhalation of the kid's breath. When he finally heard voices outside the cave, and then someone calling his name, he yelled out.

"In here! In here!" Then he rolled over onto his hands and knees and began crawling toward the opening.

Within seconds, men were crawling in, and pushing a backboard and their EMT bags.

"Charlie Dodge?"

"Yes. The boy is back here."

"I'm Larry. We heard him scream."

"Yeah. I don't know whether it's from the delirium, or if he's in so much pain that being unconscious isn't enough to block it," Charlie said, then grabbed his lantern and held it up for the medics, giving them light to assess and stabilize the boy for transport.

"How far will we have to carry him to get to Medi-Flight?" Charlie asked.

"Not far, and it's already en route. By the time we get him ready, they should have landed," one of them said.

Charlie watched in silence as they cut away Tony's pants, revealing the rest of his injuries, some of which were obvious—like another broken bone below his knee that had pierced his skin.

When they cut away his jacket and shirt and began examining the upper portion of his body, they found ribs that appeared to be broken, but they had been broken from the back, rather than from an impact to his chest, and there was an odd bruising pattern on his back that was worse than the one on his face.

"Look at the shapes of those bruises," Charlie said. "I found his hiker's pack back on the trail. It had an internal metal frame that would fit those marks."

"So he fell from the trail?" Larry asked.

"Still not sure what happened to him," Charlie said. "I found his backpack in one location, and then found him and his missing boot here."

"Well, wherever he fell, he did not walk here! His injuries are too severe, but if he did fall from the trail, I'd guess that backpack likely saved his life by absorbing a lot of the impact."

"I can't explain the backpack, but his injuries occurred in this area. His other boot is wedged between some rocks about a hundred yards away. Somehow he got his foot out of it and crawled in here," Charlie said.

The medic shook his head and kept working to get an IV established and his broken leg immobilized, until they finally had him covered up and strapped in on the backboard.

"Okay. Let's get him out of here," Larry said, and they began moving the backboard toward the opening.

Charlie pushed as they pulled, and finally they were out of the dark and in sunlight again.

Charlie shouldered his backpack and then picked up

one end of the backboard, while the medics took the other sides, and started walking toward the pickup site.

"I hear a chopper," Charlie said.

"Medi-Flight. Right on time."

"Where will they take him?" Charlie asked.

"First stop will be Big Bend Regional Hospital in Alpine. It's a small hospital. Twenty-five beds—general surgery—but it's his best bet right now. If they have to move him to a bigger place for more extensive surgery, they'll stabilize him there first," Larry said.

Charlie sighed. He'd done what he'd come to do, which was find him. Now all he could do was trust that the people Tony needed next would be there for him, so he tightened his grip and kept moving. They walked out of the forest area into rocks and sand to the waiting chopper.

The moment they appeared, medical personnel spilled out of the chopper and came running. Within minutes, they had the boy loaded up, and then the chopper lifted off.

Charlie watched until it disappeared.

"Walk with us," Larry said. "We drove a Jeep partway up. We'll get you back to the lodge."

"I'll gladly take the ride, but I need to stop and get some pictures of the kid's boot that's stuck in those rocks, and then I'll take it back with me."

"Take pictures of a boot?" Larry asked.

"You'll know what I mean when you see it," Charlie said, and led the way to the bloody boot still wedged between the rocks.

The medics looked up at the height of the trail above and then back down at the boot.

"Holy shit. If he fell all that way, no wonder the boot is wedged in so tight. I'm surprised he was conscious enough to even move."

"He had to. See all those coyote tracks? He would be easy prey trapped like this," Charlie said. "But I wonder how many times he tried and passed out from the pain before he got himself free."

Charlie pulled out the iPad again, and this time, he began taking pictures of the boot from every angle and then pictures of the trail above. It took two men pulling as hard as they could to get the boot free.

Charlie put the boot and the iPad in his pack, then followed the medics as they returned to where they'd left the Jeep.

The men talked among themselves as they walked, but Charlie had tuned them out. He was already thinking about getting home. Finding that kid so near death made him think of how quickly a life could end, and his Annie was failing. He didn't know how much time he had left with her. He knew he was going to lose her, but he felt an urgency to be with her. He didn't want to be left with regrets.

When they walked up on the Jeep, Charlie was glad to see the ride. He tossed his pack in with their medic bags and got in the back seat, still thinking about the kid. God, he hoped they could put him back together again. Even though delivering justice was not part of his job, he needed to know this kid got it.

They were almost back at the lodge when Larry

got a call. All they heard was his side of the conversation, but it didn't sound good, and then Larry hung up.

"So, they assessed the boy's injuries in Alpine, did what they could, and he's already en route to the Medical Center Hospital in Odessa," the medic said.

"What's his condition?" Charlie asked.

Larry grimaced. "Critical. But he was stable enough to transport, and that's good. The paramedics on board are top-notch. The doctors at Alpine made the call to get him to a trauma center."

Charlie checked the time again. Wyrick should already be at the lodge waiting on him. He was going to take a chance she was there and call. If she didn't answer, then he'd know she was still in the air.

Wyrick was in the store at the lodge buying pop and candy for the flight back.

"Is this all you need?" the clerk asked, as Wyrick slid two bottles of Pepsi and a handful of Snickers bars on the counter.

She nodded and pulled out a credit card, inserting it in the reader.

"Y'all want a sack for that?" the clerk asked.

"No, I'll put them in my bag," she said, and bagged up all but one Snickers as she walked out.

She sat down on the bench out front, peeled back the wrapper and took a bite, rolling her eyes in delight from the taste of nuts, chocolate and caramel. Her phone rang while she was still chewing, and when she saw it was Charlie, she swallowed fast.

"Yes?"

"Are you here?"

"Yes. What do you need?"

"Call Baxter and Macie again. Tell them they're taking Tony on to Medical Center Hospital in Odessa."

"What's his status?" Wyrick asked.

"Critical. Did you tell them not to tell anyone?"

"Yes. I'll call now."

"I'll be there soon. Caught a ride back with the medics, but I'm going to have to change before we fly back."

"Change? Why?"

"You'll understand when you see me," he said.

"Copy that," Wyrick said. "Anything else?"

"No," Charlie said, and then blinked when the line went dead in his ear. She'd hung up on him again, but he was too damn tired to care.

Wyrick knew hanging up on him like that ticked him off. It was why she did it. She took another bite of the candy bar and then wiped her fingers on her jeans before she made the next call.

Baxter and Macie were already on the road, tight-lipped and silent. The last time they had taken this route, their son was lost, and they didn't know if he was alive or dead. This trip, the only difference was that Tony was no longer lost. They'd been on the road a little over two hours when they got Wyrick's call.

"You get it, honey," Baxter said, and Macie answered.

"Hello, this is Macie."

"Macie, this is Wyrick. Are you on the way?"

"Yes. We've been on the road about two hours."

"I have an update. The hospital at Alpine sent him on to the Medical Center Hospital in Odessa. They'll be better able to care for his needs."

"Oh! That's closer. We'll get to him sooner. Do you have an update on his condition?" she asked.

"Charlie said he was designated as critical."

Macie moaned.

"He's alive, Macie. Focus on that," Wyrick said.

"Yes, you're right. Thank you for the update."

"Of course," Wyrick said. "Travel safe."

After that, she dropped her phone back in the bag, took out a Pepsi to wash down the last of her candy bar and then headed to the lodge. If Charlie was so dirty that he felt the need to change, he was going to need more than a change of clothes.

An hour passed and Wyrick was just hanging around the lodge admiring the scenery when she saw a Jeep pull into the parking lot. She stood, watching as Charlie got out. He was filthy, as promised. Crawling around inside a cave would do that. He looked tired, and had a two-day growth of whiskers, and still looked like he could kick ass if the need arose. She sighed.

Dude, dirt and all, you are one sexy man.

The fact that she even thought that pissed her off. She did not want to feel anything for another man as long as she lived, and yet Charlie Dodge got under her skin without even trying. Thankfully, he didn't know it, and she intended it to stay that way. She went to meet him as he walked toward the lodge.

* * *

The feeling Charlie had when he saw Wyrick walking toward him always settled whatever chaos he was feeling, which didn't make a lot of sense, since she was also responsible for the aggravation in his life, as well.

Maybe it was because she was steadfast. She had never once let him down in anything he'd asked of her. Maybe it was because she didn't live with the guile most women had. With Wyrick, there was no subterfuge. She was exactly who she appeared to be. A one-of-a-kind warrior woman with an oversize sense of responsibility.

Today, she was the calm in his storm.

And then they were face-to-face.

"You stink," she said.

His eyes narrowed. "It's good to see you, too."

She ignored the sarcasm. "I reserved a room for you inside the lodge long enough to shower and change. They were quite accommodating for the hero of the day."

Charlie sighed. "Your prior comment on my aroma is forgiven. That's freaking awesome."

She shrugged. "I thought you might want to swing by Odessa on the way home to check on Tony Dawson…and I didn't want to smell you all the way home, either, so there's that."

Charlie laughed.

The sound moved through her like a bolt of lightning, leaving goose bumps on her skin as she led the way into the lodge.

The manager met them at the front desk to greet Charlie personally.

"Here's your key, Mr. Dodge, and on behalf of all of us, we are grateful you found the lost boy."

Charlie took the key, then glanced at Wyrick.

"I had help. Invaluable help."

Wyrick ignored the praise. "I'll be waiting here in the lobby."

Charlie nodded. "I won't be long."

As soon as he left, Wyrick headed to the restaurant to pick up the food she'd ordered for him, too.

He returned about a half an hour later in clean clothes, with his hair still wet, and still sporting his two-day growth of black whiskers, giving his appearance a slightly dangerous edge.

Wyrick glanced at him once.

"You smell better," she said.

"No, I smell good, woman…damn good, compliments of the pine-scented soap in the shower. Almost as good as you smell," he said.

She held up the bag in her hand. "You smell your roast beef hoagie," she said, and led the way out of the lodge and across the area to the chopper.

Charlie dumped his backpack inside.

"Oh wait! The kid's backpack. It's at the ranger station."

He took off running, and a few moments later, he came out carrying it and put it inside the chopper, then climbed in.

Wyrick gave him the sack with his food, handed him a cold Pepsi from the cooler behind their seats and then did a follow-up check before takeoff, even though she'd done one after landing.

By the time she got in, Charlie's sandwich was gone. She pulled out two more Snickers bars and gave him one, and then got one more cold Pepsi for herself and began preparing for takeoff. By the time they were in the air, Charlie was licking the last of the chocolate from his fingers.

"We're still good for Odessa?" Charlie asked.

"Yes."

He leaned back in the seat and closed his eyes.

She glanced at him once, thinking his eyelashes were as black as his whiskers, and then peeled back the wrapper from her other candy bar and headed north.

Tony Dawson was on the beach at La Jolla. He knew the water would be cold, but he loved the feel of the hot sand between his toes and the scent of salt water in the air.

Two gulls were fighting over a scrap of bread beside a trash can near a pier, and a pair of seals were sunning on the rocks just offshore.

The sun was in his eyes, and he was wishing he'd brought his sunglasses when he heard someone calling his name. He turned to look, and then everything exploded in a flash of light.

He was no longer at the beach. He was on a ledge, then falling backward and looking up at his friends who were watching him fall. After that, everything began happening in slow motion—looking up at the near-perfect blue of the sky, seeing a hawk dip toward the earth, knowing he would never see his parents again, accepting that these were the last things he would ever see.

Then a miracle was happening. He couldn't see it, but he could feel it, arms encircling him, holding him, like they were bracing him for impact, and then everything went black.

He knew nothing about the race to save his life, or that he'd even been found.

A trauma team was waiting when the Medi-Flight helicopter landed at the hospital in Odessa. They'd already been briefed about his injuries, and the X-rays they'd taken at the hospital in Alpine were already there and waiting. After four long days, Tony Dawson was finally where he needed to be.

Six

Charlie woke up as Wyrick was radioing for permission to land at the Midland-Odessa airport. He shifted his headphones back into place and looked down. The last time he'd flown over the Permian Basin, the landscape had been rife with pump jacks. But the oil boom had come and gone, and oil prices per barrel were half of what they used to be. There were still pump jacks, but they weren't all working, and nowhere near the quantity that they'd been before.

This made him think of Annie. Lots of things weren't like they'd been before, including them. He was no longer part of a couple. He was alone. Married. Still in love. But alone.

And then the chopper was landing, and Wyrick was all business, shutting it down.

"I rented a car to get us to the hospital. Get what you want out of the chopper. I'm going to lock it."

"I plugged my cell phone into a power pack back

at the lodge. Let me get it," he said, and dug it out of his backpack.

Wyrick didn't comment. She understood it was his connection to Annie now. As soon as he dropped it in his pocket, he dug a boot out of his backpack and put it into Tony Dawson's backpack.

"Here's the cap Macie gave me that helped me see Tony," Wyrick said.

Charlie took the sack, shouldered the backpack and waited as Wyrick locked up the chopper. Then they headed toward the terminal to pick up their rental, a late-model SUV.

"I'm driving. You navigate," Charlie said, as they got in the white Ford Explorer.

Wyrick was already in the midst of locating the hospital, and slipped into the passenger seat while Charlie got in behind the wheel.

The airport was midway between Midland and Odessa, and, compared to Dallas, the traffic was minimal, and the drive was short. It was nearing sundown when they arrived at the hospital.

"God, I hope there's good news," Charlie said.

"His parents won't be here yet," Wyrick said.

Charlie patted his pocket to make sure he had his phone. "One of the downsides of Texas. It's a long way to anywhere here," he said, and got out.

Wyrick was right beside him all the way into the lobby, then up to the front desk.

"We're here for Tony Dawson," he said. "Medi-Flight brought him in a couple of hours ago."

The lady checked her computer for a room number.

"He's in surgery."

"Where's the waiting area?" Wyrick asked.

The lady gave them directions, and they headed for the elevator, then up to the surgical floor to the nurse's desk.

"We're here for Tony Dawson," Charlie said.

The nurse looked up, first at Wyrick, then at him.

"Are you family?"

"No, ma'am. The family hired us to find him. They're en route from Dallas, and likely won't be here for another couple of hours."

"I can't give you any—"

Charlie interrupted. "I can give you some. The kid was missing for four days in the Chisos Mountains. His family hired me to find him, and I did… in a cave. He was in bad shape when I found him, and I didn't think he'd make it here alive. So the fact that he's in surgery is good news to me. We'll just be in the waiting room. Do you need the phone number of his parents?"

She pulled up Tony's records. "No, we have it, but thank you for offering. The surgical team will give periodic updates. I'll let them know he has people here. The waiting room is that way," she said, pointing toward the elevator they'd just exited.

They went back down the hall and into the waiting area and sat down—Wyrick chose a chair in the corner, Charlie in a chair by the window, directly across the room from her.

The physical distance between them was telling.

It was only when they were working that their connection went live.

Wyrick pulled out her phone.

Charlie shoved a hand through his hair and then rubbed the back of his neck. Between sleeping on the ground last night and crawling around in a cave this afternoon, he had a stiff neck. He was too damn tall for small tents and low ceilings.

And so they sat while the sun went down, and night came to West Texas.

About two hours into their wait, Baxter and Macie Dawson walked into the waiting room. When they saw Charlie and Wyrick, Macie burst into tears and hugged him.

"We'll never be able to thank you enough," she said.

"Thank Wyrick, too," Charlie said. "If it hadn't been for her, I would still be looking."

"I thought you were in Dallas all this time," Macie said.

"I was," Wyrick said.

Macie frowned. "Then how—?"

"She flew herself down. Now that we have the waiting room to ourselves, we need to talk. Come sit down, both of you," Charlie said.

"They said he's still in surgery," Baxter said. "Thank you so much for being here."

"Yes, I did the job you asked me to do, but there are things you need to know about this case before I leave. I don't know how it's going to play out, but there's a whole lot about Randall and Justin's story that doesn't match up to what I found."

Macie gasped. "What do you mean?"

"It all started with Wyrick's research. I thought the whole story Randall and Justin told didn't sound right. So I had Wyrick do some research after I left, which included interviewing Tony's girlfriend, Trish, and both Randall and Justin. I'm going to let her tell you what she found out and what they told her."

"I'll be brief," Wyrick said. "What none of you knew, including Tony, is that Trish Caldwell dated Randall before you all ever moved to Dallas. They broke up months before your arrival, but that old history was there, and she never told Tony."

Macie gasped. The implications were immediate.

"Also, all three of the boys were drunk that first night, and both boys admitted it. Randall said Tony kept talking about Trish and how great she was, and Randall popped off and told him she'd been his girl first, and then Justin added fuel to the fire by lying, insinuating that Trish slept around. They had a fight. And supposedly, they all finally went to bed and passed out."

Baxter groaned.

Wyrick kept talking. "Neither boy has admitted it, but Randall and Justin made friends with Tony because he was dating Trish. Justin said Trish was the one who dumped Randall, and that Randall was jealous of Tony and Trish. It's looking like the hiking trip was some kind of a setup, but I don't think what happened was intentional."

Macie was pale and shaking, and Baxter's face was flushed in anger.

"Why did you want Tony's cap?" Macie asked.

Wyrick wouldn't look at Charlie, but she never hesitated.

"To see if I could tune in to where he was."

Macie's eyes widened. "You mean…like a psychic? Are you a psychic?"

Wyrick shrugged. "I am many things, Mrs. Dawson. I can't take credit for any of it. It's just how I am."

Charlie picked up the story.

"When she was interviewing Randall, despite the answers he was giving her, she saw a different truth. She saw them on a trail, and they were arguing. It was daylight, not night, like they claimed."

"Oh my God," Baxter said. "And if it wasn't for you two, their lies would have stood as truth."

"Not for long," Charlie said. "I found Tony's backpack first," he said, and set it beside them. "And that's Tony's cap we borrowed, in the sack. The backpack had been hidden in the crevice beneath a rock. Animals had dragged it out, likely after the searchers had passed that area, and it was the reflection of sunlight on the metal dog tag that revealed it to me."

"Oh wow. Granddad's dog tag from World War II," Baxter said.

Charlie nodded. "That's what put me on the right track. I left the hiking trail above and took one that led down into the canyon and found the pack. I radioed the rangers of the location and then kept searching. But there was no sign that Tony had ever been anywhere near the pack. No footprints. No body. No blood. No nothing. All I could think was either he hid it for some reason and was going to come back for it and didn't, or someone did something to him and hid it to delay his being found."

Macie moaned. "This is a nightmare. My poor boy…what he must have been going through…what he must have been thinking."

"I think I would still be looking if it hadn't been for Wyrick. Once she got hold of the cap, she keyed in on Tony and told me she thought he was in a cave of some kind… She knew it was dark and long, like a low tunnel, and it was. She said she thought he was still alive, and he was. And she told me to get off the trail and which direction to go into the woods, and I did, and that's when I found the boot. That put me on the right trail to finding him."

"Found what boot?" Baxter asked.

"I found one of Tony's hiking boots wedged in between some rocks. I brought it with me, but it was wedged so tightly that it took two men to pull it out. I think he fell from the trail above. With all the injuries he had, and the length of the fall, I don't know why he's still alive. I have no explanation for how he got his foot free from that boot, because he broke his leg and ankle. I don't know how he got across a rock field into that cave, but I assume he crawled, because that's where I found him. After I found the boot, I began calling his name, and he finally answered with one scream. But it was enough. I found him in the cave, and the rest you know. He's going to have to fill in the blanks, but those boys lied. I don't know whether his fall was an accident or intentional, but they knew what happened to him. I think they just expected the searchers to find a body, and that would be that. Only he lived through the fall. And if he hadn't gotten free, he would have died from exposure or animals, and that would have sealed their story."

"What do we do?" Baxter asked. "Wait for Tony to get better so he can tell the police or—?"

"No. I have a plan," Charlie said. "When we get back to Dallas, I'll take it from there and keep you updated. You two just worry about your son, and when you get back, I'll return the backpack and his boot."

"And his cap," Wyrick added.

"Yes, and his cap," Charlie said.

A short while later, a doctor walked into the waiting room.

"The Dawson family?" he asked.

"Yes," Baxter said, as he and Macie jumped up.

Charlie and Wyrick stood with them, waiting.

"I'm Dr. Mack. He made it through surgery better than I expected. He had some internal injuries and has a concussion. We removed his spleen, repaired some muscle tears and set two broken ribs. He has pins and screws in his leg and ankle and two broken fingers on his right hand. We're concerned about infection and pneumonia. He was without medical treatment too long, but we're pumping him full of antibiotics. He's in a drug-induced coma to let his body work on nothing but healing, and he'll be in ICU for the time being."

"What about his leg? Can you save it?" Baxter asked.

"We're going to do everything we know how to make that happen, but he's fighting some serious infection right now. It's too soon to make any kind of predictions," Dr. Mack said.

"When can we see him?" Macie asked.

"They'll move him into ICU. There is a waiting room there. The nurse's desk will tell you how to get there. After that, the visiting times are posted. Our ICU is one of the best. We'll take good care of him here."

"Thank you," Baxter said. "Thank you for saving our son's life."

Dr. Mack shook his head. "A whole lot of people are responsible for that. Try to get some rest. I'll check in on him off and on all night, and they'll call me if the need arises."

Baxter and Macie began gathering up their things.

"We're going to be leaving now," Charlie said. "Keep us updated on Tony's progress, will you?"

"Yes, of course," Macie said.

They parted ways in the hall, and Wyrick led the way back to the elevator. Charlie was silent all the way back to the car.

"Do we need to get rooms?" he asked.

"Not unless you're afraid of the dark," Wyrick said.

He snorted. "You're scarier than the dark. But if you're up to flying home tonight, I'm game."

Wyrick rolled her eyes. "Big baby," she muttered. "Do you think you can find your way back to the airport without me?"

He sighed. She had him there. "Not in a timely fashion."

"That's what I thought," she said, and proceeded to direct him through the streets of Odessa and back onto the highway leading to the Midland-Odessa airport.

They returned the rental and then headed back to where she'd left the chopper, ran through her usual preflight check while the chopper was being refueled, and then they got in and ran through her preflight check inside, as well, before starting it up.

He'd never flown in a chopper at night, but there was always a first time for everything. But when she fired up the chopper, what he hadn't expected was to be able to clearly see beyond the lights of the terminal. The entire windshield had the same capability as the night-vision goggles they'd used in the war.

"Holy shit, Wyrick! The whole windshield is night-vision."

She shrugged. "I just took existing technology and gave it a tweak. It's a prototype of something I developed a couple of years back, and yes, I hold the patent on it, too."

As soon as they reached full throttle, she radioed the tower and lifted off.

The flight back took almost two hours, and when

she homed in on the landing strip at the private airport where she kept her chopper, she saw the lights at the helipad and set down.

She was shutting it down when Benny came walking out of the hangar.

"Hey, there's Benny," Charlie said.

Wyrick looked up in surprise and then got out. "I didn't intend for you to wait for me."

He shrugged. "You don't let people take care of you," he said.

"Guilty," Wyrick said. "But thank you."

"Go home, boss. I will tow the bird in and lock up," he said.

Charlie shouldered his backpack, then paused.

"Don't open the office for business in the morning. Just be there. I'm going to get both boys and their parents in there together to give them the news."

"They're going to wonder why they have to come to your office."

Charlie shrugged. "Let them stew about it. The unknown keeps everyone on edge."

"Once they find out Tony is alive, they're going to think he told us everything, aren't they?" Wyrick said.

Charlie nodded. "And we're going to see two friends turn on each other to shift the blame. They'll tell on themselves without ever knowing Tony is still unconscious. But I want some Feds with us when it happens."

"I'll be there," Wyrick said.

Charlie left first, but she wasn't far behind. She

followed his car on the freeway until his exit came up. Once he was off the freeway, she turned on her stealth mode and floored it.

By the time she finally pulled up to her landlord's estate, entered the code to get herself onto the grounds and then drove around back to her apartment, she was so tired, she was punchy.

She managed to get herself inside, and the security on, before staggering down the hall to her bedroom.

She kicked off her boots, took off her jacket and went belly down on top of the bed and passed out.

The next thing she knew, it was morning.

She stripped, then went to the kitchen to start coffee, before heading to the shower. Two fine upstanding young men were going to bust their public personas to hell and back this morning when Charlie told them the friend they left for dead was in a hospital in Odessa.

Alert and *fierce* were the words for today.

Charlie's sleep was dream-filled, and when he woke, the first thing he did was call to check on Annie.

"Morning Light Memory Care. This is Pinkie."

"This is Charlie Dodge. I'm calling to get an update on Annie."

"Good morning, Charlie. Just a moment and I'll ring the nurse's office."

Charlie rubbed at the back of his neck as he

waited. Still stiff, but a hot shower would take out the kinks.

"Mr. Dodge, this is Nurse Egan. I'm new to Morning Light. I don't believe we've met. How can I help you?"

"Annie Dodge is my wife. She's in Room 204. I'm well aware of the deterioration of her condition, but I wanted an update."

"Of course," Nurse Egan said. "Actually, Dr. Dunleavy is still here making rounds. Would you care to hold and speak to him personally?"

"Yes, please," Charlie said. He put his phone on speaker and headed for the kitchen to make coffee.

He filled the reservoir, popped in a coffee pod, put his mug beneath the spigot and was watching the thick, dark brew filling his cup when the call was answered.

"Good morning, Charlie."

"Morning, Dr. Dunleavy. Glad I caught you. I want an Annie update. Have there been any changes since we spoke last?"

Dunleavy hesitated. "Let me check my notes… Let's see. The last cognizance tests we ran were about two weeks ago, right?"

"Yes. That's when you called me and told me she was losing abilities faster than before. I was there four days ago, but she was asleep. I didn't stay long. I've been out of town on a case and just got back and wanted to check in."

"Right, right. So, the notations here indicate that feeding her is becoming more difficult."

"What can you do to offset that? Different kinds of foods? Or just drinking supplements?"

"I'm sorry, Charlie, but we're getting to the point where any nutrition she receives may be through an IV."

Charlie groaned. "But why?"

"It's actually a facet of the disease's progression. Forgetting tastes. Forgetting to chew. Forgetting to be hungry. Forgetting how to swallow. That's pretty much the issue we're dealing with now. She doesn't remember how to use a straw, and doesn't remember how to swallow liquids, either."

The helplessness Charlie felt at that moment was unlike anything he'd ever felt before.

"What are you saying?" he asked.

"I just wrote up orders for hospice to be called in. This doesn't mean she's in her last hours. But the kind of care for what's left of her life is best left to them."

"Will I have to move her?" Charlie asked.

"No. They come here."

Charlie looked down at his feet. He'd spent two days and taken thousands of steps looking for a lost boy, and found him.

Yet, even if he began right now and started running, there was nowhere to go and nowhere to look for the Annie he was losing. She was already gone, and it was breaking his heart.

"Okay, and thank you. I have some loose ends to tie up this morning on the case I just finished, but I'll be in this afternoon to see her."

"Don't worry, Charlie. We're taking good care of your girl. She's not in pain or suffering. That part of this disease is always harder on the family. Call me anytime. I'm forever grateful for what you did for my family, and anything I can do for yours, I do gladly."

Charlie disconnected, then carried his coffee back to the bathroom, sipping it between his shower and a much-needed shave.

By the time he was finished, it was just after 8:00 a.m., a decent enough time to call in a couple of favors from the Texas branch of the Federal Bureau of Investigation.

Special Agent Hank Raines owed Dodge Investigations big-time for finding and identifying all those missing children who were being held at the Fourth Dimension, and they owed Wyrick for finding them a way into the compound without alerting them that they were there.

Hank Raines was on his way to work when his cell phone rang, and when he saw who it was from, he grimaced. He and Charlie Dodge hadn't parted on the best of terms, but that was all Hank's fault, so whatever it was Charlie wanted, it must be important.

"Hello."

"Agent Raines, this is Charlie Dodge."

"Good morning, Charlie. What's going on?"

"I have a favor to ask," Charlie said, and then began to explain the story from the beginning.

"Holy shit! That's some bad stuff," Hank said. "But you said the kid you found is still unconscious."

"Yes, but I'm not telling them that. And the crimes… on whatever level they fall under…happened in a national park, which means it falls under the auspices of the federal government."

"Under the Investigative Branch of the National Park Service," Hank said.

"Yes, but you're still a Fed. And I'm assuming if someone confesses to a crime committed on federal property, you have the authority to arrest them."

Hank chuckled. "You would assume correctly. But they'd have to confess."

"Oh…they're going to, because Wyrick will be with me. She scared the shit out of them enough on the first interview she had with them that they gave more info up to her than they did the park rangers when they reported Tony Dawson missing."

Hank remembered all too well how Wyrick had reacted when he'd tried to confiscate one of her "inventions."

"Okay, I'll buy that, and yeah, sure. I'll get my partner and meet you at your office later. What time?"

"Eleven o'clock. I've got to get the parents to bring their boys into my office, which means they'll have to get them out of school."

"See you then," Hank said.

Charlie disconnected, then went to the kitchen to make breakfast. Toasted frozen waffles and more coffee would have to suffice. No time to make eggs.

He called the Wells family first while his waffles were in the toaster, and Randall's mother answered.

"Hello, this is Nita."

"Mrs. Wells, this is Charlie Dodge, of Dodge Investigations."

"Oh! Yes! Mr. Dodge! Do you have news?"

"I have information you and your family need to hear. Will you please bring your son to my office this morning at 11:00 a.m.?"

"What? Wait! Why can't you just tell me now?"

"Because I'm only going to tell it once, and I want both families here."

"Well, Randall is in school and—"

"Check him out, Mrs. Wells, and bring him to this address," he said, and then gave her the address to his office.

There was a long moment of silence as the tone of her voice shifted.

"Do we need a lawyer?"

"I don't know. Do you?" Charlie asked.

Nita froze. It was the same response Wyrick had given her.

"I'll call my husband. We'll be there at eleven, but I just want you to know I do not appreciate all this secrecy."

"This isn't about appreciating anything, ma'am. It never has been," Charlie said, and disconnected. Then he made the same call to the Young family, but it was Peter Young who answered.

"This is Peter."

"Mr. Young, this is Charlie Dodge, of Dodge Investigations."

Peter's heart dropped. He already knew Justin hadn't told the whole truth, and he still wasn't talking. But he hadn't expected a call from the investigator.

"Do you have news?" Peter asked.

"I have information. I've already spoken to the Wells family, and now I'm asking the same thing of you as I asked of them. I need you to bring Justin to my office this morning." He gave him the address and then added, "Be there at eleven."

Peter's heart skipped. "What's happening?"

"All will be explained then."

"We're all going to be there together?" Peter asked.

"Yes, sir," Charlie said. There was a long moment of silence, and then he heard the man sigh.

"Yes, okay. We'll be there," Peter said.

"Thank you," Charlie said, and disconnected.

He heard the toaster pop up the waffles and grabbed a plate. *One thing at a time, Charlie. One thing at a time.* After he'd eaten, he sent Wyrick a text about the eleven o'clock appointment, but that was all. She would find out Raines was coming when he showed up.

Randall Wells was in shock when his parents showed up at school and checked him out, and when he found out where they were going, he seemed anxious. The closer they got to the address, the more nervous he became.

"Why do we have to go talk to that man?" he asked.

Harve Wells glanced at his wife, who was unusually silent.

"I don't know, but if it helps them find Tony, we're doing it," he said.

"Yeah, of course," Randall said.

"I suspect none of this would be happening if you'd been honest with the rangers when this all began," Nita said.

At that point, Randall shut up. His mother had been riding him ever since that Wyrick woman's visit, and he'd be glad when all of this was over.

It was ten minutes to eleven when they arrived and parked.

Randall looked around as they got out, recognized the same Mercedes he'd seen Wyrick driving and frowned, then reminded himself she worked for Dodge. Of course she would be there.

The family was silent in the elevator, and walked down the hall to Dodge Investigations without talking.

Wyrick glanced up as they walked in.

"Be seated," she said, and then went back to what she was doing.

The trio did as she directed, and realized they were the first ones there. All three of them looked at each other, then took out their respective cell phones and stared at the screens instead.

Peter and Andrea Young all but dragged Justin to the car.

"I don't want to go," he kept saying.

Finally, Peter grabbed him by the arm and yanked him around to face him.

"This isn't about what you want. It's about Tony," Peter said.

Justin paled, ducked his head and got in the back seat without further comment.

"Do you think we should have asked our lawyer to be there?" Andrea asked, as they backed out of the driveway.

Peter frowned. "Which signals we have something to hide." He glanced up at his son in the rearview mirror as he put the car in Drive and accelerated. "Justin, *do* you have something to hide?"

"God, Dad! I'm sick of talking about this. Give it a rest."

"How do you think Baxter and Macie are feeling?" Peter asked. "They're probably sick, too. Heartsick. I have to say, I am very disappointed with the attitude you've taken. A friend you were with went missing, and all of a sudden you can't be bothered."

Andrea frowned. "Peter, for goodness' sake. You act like Justin is guilty of something. He's a kid. He doesn't know how to process this grief, that's all."

"I don't see tears," Peter said. "I haven't seen tears once. Just a lot of yelling about wanting to be left alone."

Andrea glared. "You just don't understand him. You never understood him. You're always at work. I'm the one who's there for him. I'm the one who knows him."

Peter sighed. "Way to go, Andrea. It's always about you, only this time, it's not. And supposition won't make any of this easier. Let's just wait and see what this is about, before you decide someone is hurting your baby…who, by the way, will be eighteen in two months."

"Dang, Dad," Justin said.

"I'm not talking to you," Peter said.

Justin slumped back down in the seat and the rest of their trip was made in stone-cold silence.

"There's the Wellses' car," Andrea said, as Peter pulled into an empty spot and parked.

"Good. Randall is already here," Justin said, already perking up.

They walked single file into the building, and rode the elevator up without looking at each other, walking into the office the same way.

Wyrick looked up again.

"Take a seat," she said.

Andrea glared at the woman, resplendent in shiny purple leather pants and a gold satin vest revealing far too much of that appalling tattoo. She obviously did not own a decent blouse.

And then she realized Wyrick was staring back at her, waiting for her to do as she was told.

Andrea sat down on the other side of the room between her husband and her son, and looked at Nita and rolled her eyes, as if to say, *What are we doing here?*

Moments later, Charlie Dodge walked in, accompanied by two men in dark suits.

Wyrick blinked. *Special Agent Raines and company.*

She stood.

Charlie gave her a steady look.

"If you'll please bring the families into my office, and your notes, as well, we will proceed."

Wyrick nodded.

"Morning, ma'am," Agent Raines said.

"Good morning," Wyrick said, and then looked at both families. "Follow me."

Seven

Wyrick had seating for Charlie and the families, but she hadn't set up chairs for the agents. When she started to get two more, Raines stopped her.

"Thank you, but we'll stand, ma'am."

She nodded, then took a seat near Charlie's desk, facing the families.

Both agents were at the door.

The families were looking worried now.

"What's going on?" Harve Wells asked.

Charlie put his elbows on the desk and leaned forward.

"I called you all here to give you the news. Tony Dawson is alive, so if anyone wants to change their story, now's the time to do it before shit hits the fan."

The boys looked at each other, and then Justin stood. His voice was shaking when he started to talk.

"I told Randall the whole camping trip was a bad idea, but he thought it would teach Tony a lesson. We didn't mean to hurt him. It was an accident."

Randall started shouting. "You went along with everything. You even lied about Trish to make it worse. You made Tony believe he was dating some whore!"

Both sets of parents were in shock, but it was Wyrick who shut it all down. She stood abruptly.

"Sit down, both of you. Stop shouting. We already know you saw him fall. We know he was alive when you went off and left him. You lied to the park rangers. You could have told them immediately where your friend was, but you didn't."

Peter Young stared at his son in horror. "Justin! What the hell made you do something so vile to a friend?"

"He wasn't a friend. Not a real one," Justin said.

Charlie was angry, and Wyrick knew it, even though he had yet to raise his voice.

"So, because he wasn't your real friend, it was okay to leave his body for the animals? Is that what you're saying?" he asked.

Justin looked away.

Wyrick pointed at Randall. "So, you're the one who wanted him dead?"

"Not dead. Just to put him in his place," Randall muttered.

"You left him for dead," Charlie said.

"We thought he already was," Randall said. "But we didn't touch him. He fell off the trail on his own."

Justin pointed. "No, he fell when he ducked to dodge your fist."

Randall came out of his chair in a rage, but before

he could get to Justin, both agents grabbed him and pinned his hands behind his back.

Harve and Nita Wells were in shock, and Andrea Young was bawling. Her husband, Peter, was the only one aware of the reality of what was happening. His son was going to be arrested, and the charges were serious.

"If you thought he was dead, why didn't you just go back and tell the rangers that he fell?" Charlie asked.

"He fell into those rocks and jammed his boot in so tight we couldn't get it out. We tried to get him free. We took off his backpack and were trying to pull him free, but his boot was stuck. We finally got his foot out of the boot, but he screamed so loud and so long when we did it and then passed out. We thought he was dead," Justin said, and started sobbing. "We thought we'd killed him. I panicked. I grabbed my pack and we started running. I didn't realize until a few minutes later that I had his pack, and not mine. Randall said we had to hurry, that we couldn't be found anywhere near the body or they'd blame us, so I dropped his backpack and ran back to get mine."

"Why did you hide the pack?" Charlie asked.

Randall shrugged. "Justin was stupid for leaving it. I just shoved it out of the way to—"

"I found the damn thing, so don't lie to me," Charlie said. "If it hadn't been for animals dragging it out, it might never have been found. You didn't shove it anywhere. You hid it."

Randall glared.

Justin was still crying. "I didn't mean for all this to happen. When I went back to get my pack, Tony was just lying there. I thought he was dead. I thought the rangers would find him that day. I just didn't want to get in trouble."

"Oh my God," Peter muttered. "I have no words. I'm horrified, and saddened beyond words that my son was a part of all this."

"I'm sorry, Dad," Justin said. "I'm so sorry."

"Some friend you turned out to be," Randall said. "You ratted me out. I didn't touch him! I didn't touch him!"

"They're all yours, Agent Raines."

Harve Wells gasped. "Agent?"

"Special Agent Raines with the FBI," Hank said, and then addressed both boys as they put them in handcuffs. "You lied to the park rangers, who are federal employees, who work on federal land. You caused the accident, then left a friend to die. You pretended you did not know where he was. If he had died, you would both be facing murder charges."

Andrea Young screamed and fell back in her chair in a faint.

"I'm calling my lawyer," Harve Wells said.

Agent Raines shrugged. "Be sure to let him know that your son will face charges in federal court, and if he does time, he will do it in federal prison. My partner and I are arresting these boys and will be escorting them to jail. Charges will be determined and filed accordingly."

Both boys were in shock. Even Randall's bravado was gone. He kept looking at his parents, waiting for them to rescue him, but they were silent.

When the agents began reading the boys their rights and leading them out of the office, Justin sobbed.

Both sets of parents followed, with both fathers on their phones calling lawyers.

Once the office was quiet again, Wyrick spoke. "They still don't know Tony Dawson has not recovered consciousness."

Charlie nodded. "And that is its own kind of justice."

"Trish Caldwell?" Wyrick asked.

"Now you can tell her Tony's alive. I'm going to Morning Light."

Wyrick's gut knotted. Annie must be failing, and Charlie wasn't talking about it.

"I'll call her, then catch up on email and billing. Are you available for another case?"

"I'll let you know," he said, then left the office.

Wyrick sighed, then stopped at the coffee bar to get a cheese Danish and a cold Pepsi, taking them to her desk.

She ate about half the Danish, then pulled up Trish Caldwell's phone number and made the call.

Trish was in her room, sitting by the window in her favorite chair, staring off into space. The house was quiet. Her mother was at work, and she was supposed to be doing homework, but she couldn't focus.

She'd said so many prayers to God, and made so many deals with Him over what she'd do and what she'd give up if He'd only let Tony live, that she didn't remember what she'd offered up last.

When her phone suddenly rang, she jumped. Then when she saw who was calling, she was almost afraid to answer. But the need to know…good or bad…was stronger than her fear.

"Hello?"

"Trish, this is Wyrick. Charlie found Tony alive."

Trish cried out, then slid out of the chair onto the floor, sobbing.

"Trish! I need you to listen to me," Wyrick said.

"Yes, yes, I'm listening," she said. "Is he okay?"

"No. He's far from okay. His injuries are severe. He's in ICU in Medical Center Hospital in Odessa, Texas."

"Odessa?"

"He was airlifted there. Broken bones. Infection. Concussion, and the list goes on, but the surgeon was hopeful. What you need to know is that Randall and Justin were complicit in the injuries. They caused him to fall. They thought he was dead and left him where he fell."

"Oh my God! Why? Why?"

"It's not pretty," Wyrick said, "but you have to know the whole truth. Randall and Justin planned the trip to 'teach him a lesson,' they said. Randall did it out of jealousy, and Justin went along with it."

"I should have told him. It's my fault. I should have told him," Trish said.

"They blindsided him with the news. Randall bragged you were his girl first, and Justin lied and alluded to the fact that you slept around."

"Oh my God! He will hate me forever," Trish wailed.

"His parents are at the hospital. You can keep up with the updates on his healing from them. After that, the rest of it is up to the two of you."

"Where was he?" Trish said. "Why couldn't they find him?"

"He still hasn't regained consciousness, so we don't know all the details, but we know for sure what Randall and Justin admitted. And Charlie found Tony in a cave. He probably crawled in there as protection from predators and the elements."

Trish was sobbing again. "I don't care if he hates me for the rest of his life. I'm grateful he's alive."

"Do you know how to contact his parents?"

"Yes, I have their number," Trish said.

"So, the rest of this is up to you."

"What happens to Randall and Justin?" she asked.

"They were arrested this morning by the FBI. I don't know what they'll be charged with, but they're both in big trouble."

"Thank you for letting me know," Trish said.

"Of course. And don't give up on the relationship. Give it time. If it's meant to be, it will happen," Wyrick said, and then rolled her eyes after she hung up. "What the hell, Wyrick? You are such an expert in the romance department that you're giving out advice?"

She took a drink of her Pepsi and then finished off the Danish before she went back to sorting through the emails from prospective clients.

Charlie's gut was in a knot all the way back to Morning Light.

Please give me one more Christmas with her.

But the prayer was silent desperation. And why did it matter? She hadn't known him or anyone else for months. His Annie was already gone. All that was left was the shell of her—a taunting reminder of the beautiful, vital woman she'd been.

Charlie had always been good at seeing past people's public facades, but love had made him blind to what was becoming painfully obvious. All he could do for Annie now was make sure she was safe and comfortable, and be grateful she was ever in his life.

By the time he parked and got out, he'd shifted into quiet mode.

Pinkie, the receptionist, was on the phone when he walked into the lobby at Morning Light. He paused to sign in, then walked to the inner door for her to buzz him in. She was still talking when he heard the click, and he turned the knob to let himself in.

The faint scent of old bodies and the residents' diapers was almost masked by the aroma of antiseptic cleaners and some kind of artificial spray—maybe lavender. Whatever it was, it was cloying.

An old man came shuffling up the hall and passed him without acknowledging he was even there. He heard a nurse from somewhere behind him talking to the old man.

"There you are, Jerry. It's time for bingo. Do you want to play bingo?"

"Bingo?" the old man said, and let her lead him into another hallway.

Charlie walked past the common room, remembering the puzzles he used to work there with Annie. Working jigsaw puzzles had been her favorite pastime.

An orderly he knew came out of a resident's room.

"Hey, Charlie. Still looking for lost people?" he asked.

Charlie nodded.

"Well, you came to the right place," the orderly said, and laughed, like he'd made a great joke.

The comment pissed Charlie off and he didn't respond. It wasn't fucking funny.

The door to Annie's room was open. He knocked once and walked in. A woman was standing beside Annie's bed, adjusting an IV.

"Hello," Charlie said.

The woman turned around and smiled. "Hello, I'm Doris, Annie's hospice nurse."

"I'm Charlie. Annie is my wife," he said, and walked to the foot of her bed. Her eyes were partly closed, but they were moving beneath the lids, and her fingers were twitching.

"Is she asleep?" he asked.

"Not in the sense you mean," Doris said.

Charlie swallowed past the lump in his throat. "Is she unconscious?"

"Again, not in the sense you mean," she said. "The brain is a repository for a lifetime of memories. We don't believe they're really remembering incidents. It's more like a reflexive action you get when someone hits that funny bone on your knee that makes it jerk. In the rare instances when an Alzheimer patient's brain fires, they might see a random image, or a memory of a time long ago, which triggers a momentary physical action."

"Jesus," Charlie said, and pulled up a chair beside her bed, taking her hand. "Hello, sweetheart. It's me, Charlie."

Annie didn't react to his voice or his touch.

"How do you feed her now?" he asked.

Doris paused, then pulled up the other chair and sat down with Charlie.

"She has a living will," Doris said. "It came with the paperwork when she was admitted."

Charlie frowned. "Yes, I remember her filling that out on the day we got her diagnosis."

"Did you ever read it?" Doris asked.

Charlie shook his head. "No. She took it back to the next doctor's visit and asked him to put it in her medical file."

"She agreed to taking fluids intravenously, but not nutrition. In other words, that is a refusal to allow a feeding port to be inserted. She will no longer receive sustenance since she can't chew or swallow."

The words felt like a physical blow to the chest. He couldn't take a breath without bursting into tears.

Annie had chosen this, and he'd never known.

He felt Doris's hand on his arm, but he couldn't take his eyes off Annie's face. She'd done the brave thing. The thing he would never have been able to do *to* her. The thing he would never have been able to do *for* her.

"I'm going to step outside for a few minutes to give you some time alone." She pointed to the buzzer near Annie's bed. "Just ring the bell if you need me."

Charlie heard her footsteps as she walked away, then the click of the door as she closed it behind her. Now was his chance to say whatever he wanted to say to Annie, and he couldn't, because he'd said it all a thousand times before. There was nothing left to tell his sweet Annie but goodbye, and he wasn't ready to let her go.

Baxter and Macie were camped out in the ICU waiting room, living from one visiting hour to the next. They had a blanket apiece and a pillow apiece, and had taken a room at a nearby motel to go bathe and change, and took turns leaving the hospital to do that. Tony wasn't conscious, but according to the nurses, his vital signs were stronger. They wouldn't ask for more.

It was midafternoon when Macie got a text from Trish. She read it, sighed, then handed her phone to Baxter.

I just found out Tony is alive. I asked God for that and nothing more, so it was the answer to my prayers. I should have told him I used to date Randall, but I didn't even know they were friends until Tony and I had been dating for over a month. And then I didn't know how. I was stupid. It nearly got him killed. It doesn't matter if Tony hates me for the rest of his life. Or if you two blame me for all of this. It doesn't matter. I am just so grateful to God that whatever sadness comes to me is nothing more than I deserve. Forgive me.

"Well, hell," Baxter said, and wiped his eyes.

Macie leaned her head against his shoulder. "I know. Young love isn't wise. It's wild and wonderful and scary. The choices those two boys made have nothing to do with her. They're the ones who tried to hurt our son. She just wanted to love him."

"We don't know how Tony will feel about her," Baxter said.

Macie was silent a few moments, and then she reached for her husband's hand.

"Is Tony going to wake up and be our Tony again?" she asked.

Baxter shrugged. "He can be any Tony he chooses. I just want him to wake up, but that's not going to happen until they decide he's strong enough to be conscious."

The whole afternoon at the office was quiet. Wyrick knew when Charlie didn't return or call that something was going on with Annie. Her heart hurt for him—for the whole situation—but stoic and tough were what got her through each day, and today was no different. When it was time to lock up, she gathered up her things, pausing in the doorway to look back.

The security lights gave the suite of rooms a pale, eerie glow. It was so quiet and peaceful up here. Almost as quiet and peaceful as her basement apartment at Merlin's estate. Every day, she had to run the Dallas gauntlet to get from one place to the other, but this was the most satisfied she'd been since childhood.

She didn't belong to Charlie Dodge. But she belonged with him—helping him do what he did, bringing closure to other people, even though there was no way to fix what was wrong in their own lives.

She sighed, then pulled the door shut and headed for the elevator. A couple of other businesses on their floor were still open. She could hear the soft murmur of voices as she walked, and as she got in the elevator, she was thinking of what she was going to have for dinner tonight on her way down.

The security lights were coming on in the parking lot. She always parked beneath the one closest to the door, but she still paused and looked around, making sure all was well. After her last dustup with Boyington, she was antsy all over again.

Once she was inside the Mercedes, she started it up, then paused to order a pizza to go. It was a fast pickup on her way home, and the question of what was for dinner would be solved.

After that, she gunned the engine, leaving remnants of tire tread on the parking lot as she shot out onto the street.

Speed was her escape. Chocolate was her drug. Pepsi was her habit. Considering the makeup of her DNA, it could have been worse.

Randall Wells and Justin Young were no longer friends. Getting caught in their lies had changed that, and the lawyers their parents hired for them had turned them into adversaries, posing the questions as to which one of them had the edge and the information to bargain with, which was Justin, and which one of them bore the greatest guilt and had the most to lose, which was Randall.

One was the instigator.

One had abetted in the act.

They would be arraigned tomorrow.

They were in juvenile detention, facing federal charges, and waiting to see if they would be charged as juveniles or adults.

Their lives were no longer their own, and Tony Dawson's was still a question mark.

Trish Caldwell was having dinner with her mother, catching her up on what Wyrick had told her, both of them rejoicing that Tony had been found alive, when Trish's cell phone signaled a text. Normally, they ignored calls at their dinner hour together, but there was too much in limbo to ignore.

"You better answer that," Beth said.

Trish nodded, then jumped up from the table to get her phone from the counter. When she saw who it was from, she was almost afraid to read it as she opened the text.

Please don't feel guilty about other people's actions. You did not hurt Tony. You loved him. That is never a crime. We just wanted you to know we don't harbor any hard feelings toward you at all. Tony is still in ICU. They are keeping him sedated on purpose so he can heal. Feel free to reach out for updates whenever you wish.
Macie and Baxter.

"Oh, Mom," Trish said, and handed Beth the phone so she could read it, as well.

Beth read it and then hugged her. "There you are... See? Even his parents don't blame you."

Trish sighed. "You're right. That's a huge relief."

"And maybe Tony will feel the same," Beth said.

Trish shook her head. "All that matters is that Tony heals. I won't ask for more."

"Okay, but I'm going to ask something of you," Beth said.

Trish frowned. "Okay...what is it?"

"Go back to school tomorrow. Be the one who lets everyone know Tony is alive."

"Oh, I'm sure they already know," Trish said.

"Who would have told? The Dawsons are in Odessa. The Wells family? The Young family? I don't think so.

You are going to school tomorrow and you're going to tell everyone the truth."

"You mean, tell them it happened because of me?"

"You know that old saying about the truth setting you free? Tony is the new kid and all of you are seniors. Randall and Justin grew up with everyone. You don't want anyone assuming even a part of this mess was Tony's fault. Even if you and Tony are no longer together, at least he'll be completely vindicated."

Trish's eyes widened. "I never thought of that. And you're right. I need to make sure everyone knows he was an unsuspecting victim in all of it."

"That's my girl," Beth said.

"Yes! I'll go to school tomorrow. I'll make sure the truth is known."

Eight

Wyrick was eating pizza and watching a movie when she remembered she had been planning on checking on Merlin. She glanced at the clock. It was almost 9:00 p.m., probably too late now, but she muted the sound to see if she could hear his footsteps in the house above her, and heard nothing.

The old mansion was so huge that he could easily be in another part of it and she would never know, or he could have already gone to bed. At any rate, it was too late for visiting, so she finished watching the movie and put up the pizza that was left over, which would likely be tomorrow's breakfast.

After cleaning up the kitchen, she carried the garbage out to the bin, and glanced up at the house as she walked back. She couldn't see lights on anywhere in the house other than the dim glow of night-lights. She was glad she hadn't tried to call him after all.

A siren screamed its way through the neighborhood, setting a couple of dogs to barking. Wyrick shivered and hurried back inside.

Later, as she was getting into bed, she thought of Charlie. He'd never texted her back about his availability to start another job, so tomorrow she'd have to play it by ear.

Charlie stayed with Annie all afternoon, watching Doris, the hospice nurse, and the employees of Morning Light coming and going in her room, quietly witnessing the team of people it took to provide her with the level of care she was now needing.

It was heartbreaking to see her like this, but he was grateful for their presence.

Finally, it was Doris who told him to go home.

"You need to rest. You need to eat."

"I'm afraid to leave," Charlie said.

"I understand, but she's not at that point, yet. I promise. Her heart rate is strong and steady."

"You can tell that?" Charlie asked.

"Fourteen years at this job, and yes, I can tell," Doris said. "If there is any sudden or drastic change, you will be notified immediately. I promise."

Charlie glanced back at Annie, then at Doris. "I can be here in a little under twenty minutes."

"I'll remember," Doris said.

Charlie stroked the side of Annie's face, then leaned down and whispered in her ear.

"Your name is Annie, and a man named Charlie loves you."

Walking out of her room felt like he was running away, but she didn't need him. Her journey from here on would be taken alone. And now that he was out, he couldn't wait to get out of the building. He got to the exit and hit the buzzer. As soon as he heard the lock click, he opened the door.

All he'd done was walk through a doorway, but it was like stepping into another dimension. The lobby was the transition point between the real world outside and the lost world within.

Pinkie was gone, and a young man was on night duty.

"Have a nice night, sir," he said.

"Thanks," Charlie said, and walked outside.

His Jeep was one of only two in visitors parking.

Part of him was afraid to leave, and the other part of him wanted to get in the car and drive away so fast that he outran the nightmare behind him. Instead, he drove straight home, and once inside his apartment, he took a deep breath, tossed his things onto the sofa and then headed for the shower.

It wasn't until he was getting into bed that he stopped long enough to check messages.

There was one from Baxter and Macie. Good news. Tony was holding his own.

His eyes blurred with tears.

Annie was holding her own, too, but she was on her way out of a life, and the kid was just getting started. God willing, the kid got the chance to live it.

He checked to see if there were any from Wyrick, but there were none. Then he remembered he was the one who was supposed to let her know if he would be available for another case, so he pulled up her number.

No new clients.

He hit Send, and then put his phone on the charger and turned out the lights.

Wyrick was just getting out of the shower when she heard her phone signal a text. Thinking it might be Charlie, she wrapped a towel around her to catch the drips and went to see who it was from.

To her surprise, it was from Merlin.

I need to talk to you. Do you have time this morning? It won't take long. I unlocked the door at the top of your stairs. Come up if you can.

Wyrick frowned. This was very unlike Merlin. He was not a social person, but she certainly wasn't going to ignore the request. She ran back to dry off, then put on sweats and tennis shoes. The stairs leading from her basement apartment to the kitchen above had two doors. One at the bottom of the stairs. One at the top. She unlocked the one from her side and ran up the stairs. Knocked once and then walked into his kitchen.

Merlin was sitting at the kitchen table with a cup of coffee in his hands, holding it as if to warm his fingers, and a half-eaten sweet roll on a napkin that he'd pushed aside. His long white hair was tied back at the nape of his neck, and he'd shaved off his beard, which exacerbated the thinness of his long face even more, but his smile was one of delight when she walked in.

"Good morning, Jade. Seeing your dear face is a wonderful way to begin my day. Coffee and rolls are on the counter. Please help yourself."

"What's wrong?" she asked.

He shook his head, then pointed. "Coffee first."

She poured herself a cup, added cream because it was there and got an apricot Danish, then sat down.

"You shaved off your beard," she said, and then took a bite of her Danish.

He nodded.

"My hair is next," he said.

She frowned. "Why?"

"Maybe I like your look," he said.

The cryptic comment hit like a fist to the gut. "You're sick, aren't you? What's wrong? How can I help?"

"You can't help, dear. No one can. It's end-stage liver cancer. I don't have long, and there are things I need to confirm before I'm too ill to focus."

She reached for his hand. "Oh, Merlin. I'm so sorry. I know people in the medical field. I might be able to get you into some kind of trial on a new cancer drug."

He shook his head. "No, no, I'm past that. I'm not upset. I've lived a good long life. I won't begrudge this fate."

"Do you need me to move? I mean… I can under-stand not wanting a renter at this point."

"On the contrary. I wanted to tell you that I've named you my sole heir."

Wyrick's vision suddenly blurred. She'd never belonged to anyone, and would never have thought she mattered enough to anyone else for something like this to happen.

"Oh, Merlin! I don't know what to say other than I am so touched."

He smiled and patted her hand. "It doesn't matter to me what you do with this old barn once I'm gone, but I would like to finish out my days here. I've hired around-the-clock nursing for when the time comes, and if it's not too much of an intrusion into your personal life, I would ask that you monitor them for me and pay bills and the like…when I can no longer do that for myself."

"Yes, I will. I would have done that for you anyway. You don't have to give me anything."

"But I have all this…and no family. I don't even have friends anymore…except you."

"I'm not much of a friend," Wyrick said.

"I'm something of a loner, and you know it. You were all the friend I needed," Merlin said. "I like knowing you're under my roof. I like knowing you trusted me enough to stay here."

Wyrick sighed. "You didn't know it, but I had been toying with the idea of finally buying a place of my own, so I will be honored to be able to stay here."

"Sell it if you need and find something nice… something shiny and modern," Merlin said.

Wyrick frowned. "I'm not a shiny and modern

woman. I love this place. It's the only place I've felt safe since I moved to Dallas."

"Excellent," Merlin said, and then his doorbell rang.

"Would you get that? It's Rodney Gordon, my lawyer. There are papers we need to sign."

She jumped up and ran through the house, and then opened the front door.

"Good morning. I'm Rodney Gordon. Art is expecting me."

Wyrick stared. "Art?"

"Arthur Merlin, if you will. You are Jade Wyrick, are you not?"

"Uh, yes. But I've only ever called him Merlin. Please come in. He's in the kitchen," Wyrick said, and then led the way through the house.

"Morning, Art!" Rodney said.

Merlin nodded. "Morning, Rodney. Help yourself to coffee and a Danish."

"I'm good," Rodney said, and sat down. "I understand time is important this morning, so I'll get down to business."

Wyrick sat, watching in disbelief as the lawyer pulled out page after page of legalese she had to sign—everything from giving her access to Merlin's checking account to giving her power of attorney in all aspects of his life, and then making sure Rodney knew his wishes in allowing Wyrick to live in the main house at any time she chose, and make any changes she wanted, even if he had yet to pass.

When it was all said and done, she had an entire file folder of copies, the code to the main security system and keys to the main house. At that point, Merlin waved her away.

"I know you have a job to go to. We'll talk again when you have a little more time."

Wyrick stood. She was being dismissed, but she stopped long enough to throw her arms around Merlin's neck.

"Thank you, dear friend."

"No, thank you, Jade. You're the only person in my life I trust enough to help me out of it."

She left the kitchen in tears and ran back down the stairs to get dressed. She was going to be late for work, and she sent Charlie a quick text.

I'm going to be late. Nothing is wrong.

She started to reach for black pants and a gold vest, then stopped, shoved them aside and chose skinny-leg blue jeans, powder blue cowboy boots with red stitching and a blue denim jacket with three-quarter-length sleeves.

She kept her entire face clean of makeup except for the slash of bloodred lipstick on her mouth, then grabbed her bag with her purse and laptop and headed out the door.

The moment Charlie was awake, he reached for the phone. He saw Wyrick's text and shrugged it off. He was going to be late, too, and called Morning Light, then asked to speak to Doris.

Pinkie put him on hold, and a few moments later, Doris answered.

"Good morning. This is Doris."

"It's me, Charlie. How is Annie this morning?"

"The same, Charlie. Steady pulse and heartbeat."

"Should I be there?"

"She's not failing, if that's what you're asking. But I never make decisions for family."

"Okay. I'll check in later today, then."

"Another nurse from hospice will be with her today. Her name is Rachel. She's a sweetheart. I'll tell her you're planning on stopping by…and don't worry. Everyone here has Annie's contact information."

"Okay," Charlie said, and hung up, then sat on the side of the bed, listening to the silence.

He hadn't slept much last night, and the urge to go back to bed was there, but that wouldn't accomplish anything, and he needed to stay busy, so he headed for the shower to get ready for work.

Darrell Boyington had spent all night thinking about Jade Wyrick. She was scary. She knew about Cyrus Parks, but he wasn't sure she knew he'd come there to kill her.

And then it dawned on him that he might not be the first person Parks had sent on this task. If that was the case, he was already in the hole. His hits had all been on people who were unaware…unsuspecting.

Jade Wyrick had not only seen him coming, but

knew who'd sent him. He needed to contact Parks before committing himself further.

He continued getting ready for work, then went down to breakfast. He'd already called down to the kitchen to order Belgian waffles and bacon this morning and, as always, fresh squeezed orange juice, which he drank before his coffee. It was his routine, and Darrell didn't like to be detoured from his routine. He considered it bad luck.

The food he'd ordered was in chafing dishes on the sideboard, and his juice and coffee were at his place at the table. As soon as he finished his juice, he buttered three waffles, then poured syrup over the stack and cut his first bite. Hot, crispy waffle…warm, salty butter melting in the little brown squares, filled with pure maple syrup. The breakfast of champions.

He ate in silence, reading the newspaper on his phone, and then left his house just before 9:00 a.m., as was his habit. But as soon as he got in the car, he pulled up the number he'd been given and contacted Parks.

Cyrus was in his car on the way to a meeting when a call came in on his secure line. He was already expecting a successful report and answered with an upbeat tone.

"This is Parks."

"Who the hell is that woman?"

"Is this the man I—?"

"Answer my question."

"Why?" Cyrus said.

"She looked at me the other day and, out of the blue, said to tell Cyrus Parks if he didn't leave her the hell alone, she would destroy the both of us. So what is she? Because there is no one on the face of the earth who knows what I look like, or what I do, or that I even know your name."

Cyrus shuddered. "She said my name?"

"Yes, and she's seen my face and knows I'm connected to you, which is not good for me. So I have a choice. Kill you or kill her. Or maybe kill both of you and cut my losses."

It was cold where Cyrus was, but he was sweating. How could he protect himself from a man he didn't know?

"No, no—no need for all that," he said. "I'll send the balance of the money into that account and release you from the contract."

"That'll work, because she's toast, regardless," Boyington said.

"She has powers and skills beyond human comprehension," Cyrus said.

Boyington was furious. "So you set me on a task you knew would fail?"

"I didn't know then, but if she connected us simply by looking at you, then that means her skills are growing exponentially."

"Skills? What kinds of skills?" Boyington asked.

"There is no secret you will be able to keep from her…at least not for long. You won't be able to get close enough to her to take her out. You can't track her. We've tried."

"I asked you before, but you didn't answer me," Boyington said. "What is she?"

"I created a monster I can no longer control," Cyrus said. "Let her be."

Wyrick was preoccupied by the news Merlin had given her this morning, and was walking down the hall in the office building when she heard the phone ringing in their suite.

She ran the last few steps, unlocked the door, then turned on the lights and dumped her stuff on the desk before answering.

"Dodge Security and Investigations."

All she got was a dial tone. They'd hung up, and at this point, she didn't care. Either they'd call back, or they wouldn't. She hung her coat in the closet and turned on her computer before going to make coffee.

She was in a mood about Merlin. Sad for what he was facing, and taken aback at being named his heir. But she knew how much he loved that old mansion, and the level of security he already had in place there was high. It was a gift she would never have seen coming.

She started coffee. Booted up the computers. And put out the fresh doughnuts she'd brought at the coffee bar, then took personal mail and a stack of messages from yesterday and left them on Charlie's desk before pausing to gaze out the bank of windows behind it.

The Dallas skyline was particularly dramatic

today, thanks to a building storm front. Clouds were piling up and darkening, and she could tell by the way people were holding on to their hats and coats that the wind was rising. It made her wish she was down in her basement apartment, and not on the upper level of a high-rise office building, staring down the possibility of a late-season tornado.

Charlie drove straight to the office without conscious thought, then wondered how the hell he'd gotten there as the high-rise suddenly appeared before him.

It wasn't until he turned off the street into the parking lot that he even noticed the building storm. He got out, facing the wind, and then hurried across the parking lot into the building.

Wyrick was still at the windows when she heard the office door open out front. Before she could get turned around, the door slammed shut and Charlie strode into his office, bringing energy and the scent of cold air with him.

"Looking rough out there, isn't it?" he said, as he left his Stetson on the hat rack and hung his jacket up in the closet.

"I hate stormy weather. You have mail and messages from yesterday on your desk," she said, and left the room.

Charlie ignored the brusqueness of her comment as typical Wyrick, then got a coffee and a doughnut and took them to his desk.

He went through the mail, then the messages,

made notes on some of them and tossed the others, but he couldn't focus. He could hear Wyrick's voice in the outer office and knew she was on the phone, so he pulled up his email and began reading through the messages.

There were a couple of local cases he would have considered taking, but none of them were urgent, and none had to do with missing children. As soon as he heard her hang up, he headed to her desk.

She was obviously preoccupied and staring off into space. And there was a look on her face he'd never seen before.

"Hey," he said.

Wyrick flinched and then turned her head.

"Everything okay?" he asked.

"Merlin is dying."

Charlie blinked. He thought (a) Merlin was fictitious, and (b) he was already dead. Then he remembered that was her landlord's name.

"So is Annie," he said.

Wyrick took a deep breath and then put both hands on her desk, almost as if she was holding herself in place.

"'I'm sorry' is a weak and stupid thing to say about something like that, but I am at a loss for anything better."

Charlie heard the tremor in her voice.

"I'm sorry about Merlin," he said.

She nodded.

"Come into my office," he said.

Wyrick followed Charlie to the wet bar, then watched him pour two shots of whiskey.

He shoved one at her and picked up the other.

"What's this for?" she asked, as he lifted his glass in a toast.

"For Annie and Merlin," he said.

"On a wing and a prayer," Wyrick said.

Their glasses clinked, and then they tossed back the shots in one quick gulp.

It was like swallowing fire.

Wyrick's eyes watered.

Charlie took a deep breath.

"I hate this is happening," she said, and then set the glass down on the bar and walked out.

"So do I," Charlie muttered, blinking back tears as he set the glasses in the sink.

Trish Caldwell walked into the principal's office and approached the secretary.

"I need to speak to Mr. Ramey."

"He's getting ready to leave for a meeting across town. Can you—?"

"It's about Tony Dawson," Trish said.

The secretary didn't hesitate further. "Just a moment," she said, and buzzed the office.

"Angie, I told you to hold my—"

"Trish Caldwell is asking to speak with you, sir. She says it's about Tony Dawson."

"Send her in," Ramey said, and then stood. A few moments later, Trish Caldwell came in. "Have a seat."

Trish sat, her hands fisted in her lap. "I need to tell you several things. First… Tony Dawson is alive."

"Oh my Lord! That is wonderful news!" Ramey said.

Trish's stomach was in knots. "You also need to know that Randall Wells and Justin Young have been arrested for lying to the FBI about what happened to Tony, and then leaving him for dead."

Ramey gasped. "What? You're not serious."

"Yes, sir, I am." And then she began to explain the whole story, including her unwitting part in it. By the time she had finished, she was in tears. "He would never have been tricked into the trip if I'd just told him I'd once dated Randall. Yes, I should have told him, but I take no blame for what those two did to him."

"Where is he?" Ramey asked.

"He's in ICU in a hospital in Odessa, Texas. I've already been in touch with his parents. The only thing I can do for Tony now is make sure none of Randall's or Justin's friends try to attribute any blame to him. Tony is an innocent victim in all of this, and it's a miracle he's still alive."

Principal Ramey was silent for a few moments, considering the ramifications of what he should and should not say.

"Okay, Trish. I can announce to the whole school that Tony was found alive, because everyone knew he was missing. I can also state that the other two have been arrested on federal charges for lying to the park rangers, and then abandoning him because they thought he was dead. I won't speak to any other details, and I'm not going to say anything about Tony being ignorant of your past relationship with Randall Wells. In my eyes, that's immaterial to their crime, and should be between you and Tony. What happened to him was because of jealousy. Period."

"Yes, sir," Trish said.

Ramey gave her a handful of tissues.

"Now wipe your eyes and get a note from Angie because you're late to first hour. You can celebrate the good news with your friends today, and we'll all pray for Tony's healing."

"Thank you, Mr. Ramey."

"Of course," he said. "Go ahead to class. I'll make the announcement in a few minutes."

She left his office in haste, stopping long enough to get a note from Angie before hurrying to first hour.

About ten minutes later, they heard the PA system come on and then Principal Ramey's voice.

"Good morning, students. I have news to share with all of you. We have all been in prayer for our fellow student Tony Dawson, and I have the pleasure of telling you that Tony Dawson was found alive. He has undergone surgery for a number of serious injuries, and is in critical condition in ICU in a hospital in Texas. But I have it on good authority that, at this time, he is holding his own. Normally, I would not be sharing this information with you, but the guilty parties have already confessed and it has become a federal case. Also, Tony Dawson deserves the justice and truth of what he suffered. The truth is, Randall Wells and Justin Young have been arrested by the FBI. They are responsible for his injuries, lying to the rangers and leaving him for dead. I ask that you keep Tony and his family in your prayers through this time of healing."

The shock within Trish's class was instantaneous, as it was throughout the building, and then they all looked at her.

"Did you know?" one girl asked.

Trish nodded. "They notified me last night," she said, and then let the talk go on around her. God had answered her prayers for Tony. She wasn't about to ask anything more for herself.

Nine

Darrell Boyington was having a positive workday. The quarterly profits were up almost 12 percent. Holiday shopping always made people celebratory, and lunching at the high-energy level of a sports bar only added to their experience.

And since they were still in November with profits already climbing, he predicted a stellar season. It should have been enough to keep him satisfied, at least for the day, but he couldn't let go of the thought that Jade Wyrick was a threat to all of this.

Not once had he ever regretted his other life. It was the adrenaline rush he needed to cope with the mundane part of being a business owner. There were no broken or lost shipments with his other job. No drop in profits due to a downtick in spending. For him, there was the thrill of the chase, and the slight surge of enjoyment at watching a life go out in a stranger's eyes. It was the closest he would ever be to God, since his soul was already damned to hell for killing. But he needed to find out more about the Wyrick woman before he decided how to remove her. He sat down at his computer and Googled her name, using the state of Texas as his first parameter, and got nearly a hundred hits. He needed to break it down further and localized it within the city of Dallas. He still got more than a dozen hits, but with different middle names. And since he didn't know what that was, he broke it down even more by age and got three within a ten-year span, but none of them were her.

He knew she drove a Mercedes. Those were expensive cars to own, but she was just an office manager. He couldn't find a single debt in her name, and decided she must be independently wealthy. But if this was the case, then why the hell was she working for a PI? The moment he thought that, he laughed at himself for being so blind. People could ask the same thing of him. He knew how he was doing it, but how the hell was Jade Wyrick hiding in plain sight?

He was already ignoring Cyrus Parks's warning that she was dangerous. She was intriguing, which made the hunt that much better. A prey worthy of hunting was what made a hunt worthwhile. But the only thing he knew for sure was where she worked, and that she had some kind of psychic abilities. He was an open-minded man. He believed such things were possible, and it was the only explanation for her being able to connect him to Parks.

What he needed now was to find out where she lived. He had two options. Try to follow her again, which had proved futile before, or track her from a distance, which meant he needed to bug her car.

Unaware that Parks's prior employees had tried that and failed miserably, he opened his safe, picked up a couple of GPS tracking devices in magnetic cases, then put them and a laptop into his briefcase and left his office, pausing at his secretary's desk long enough to tell her where he was going.

"I'm leaving for an early lunch, and will be out the rest of the afternoon scouting locations. You know how to reach me."

"Yes, sir," she said, and then went back to work as he walked out of the office into a blast of cold air and glanced up at the gathering storm clouds.

"Damn," he muttered, and ran for the car.

Charlie was at his desk all morning, but was accomplishing nothing. His heart and thoughts were with Annie. It was just before noon when he finally signed off at the computer and stood. He stretched, then turned to face the bank of windows behind his desk. The thunderstorm was almost on top of them.

He glanced down at the parking lot, and as he did, he saw someone come speeding into the lot, then brake to a sliding halt behind Wyrick's Mercedes.

Charlie frowned, and when he saw the driver get out on the run with something in his hand and drop to his knees behind her car, he turned and ran.

Wyrick looked up as Charlie flew past her desk and then out the door. She didn't know what was wrong, but if Charlie was running, she was following. She ran out into the hall toward the elevator. But as she passed the stairwell and heard the sounds of footsteps going down, she took the stairs, as well, leaping several steps at a time.

She came out onto the main floor just as Charlie hit the exit door with the flat of his hand and ran outside.

Charlie came out of the building just as the man was coming back from the front of Wyrick's car.

Boyington saw him coming and, all too late, remembered Wyrick warning him that he did not want to make an enemy of Charlie Dodge. He had but a few brief seconds to brace himself, before Charlie hit him in a flying leap.

And Wyrick came out just as the two men went down in a tangle of arms and legs—a tackle worthy of the NFL.

At that point, the heavens decided to unleash. A nearby crack of lightning followed by a rumble of thunder was the only warning they were going to get. And then the rain came down.

Boyington was cursing a blue streak, struggling against the weight of the man on top of him, and pummeling Charlie's chest and shoulders while still trying to breathe.

Disgusted, Charlie just pulled back his fist and knocked him out.

"Call the cops," Charlie said, and rolled off Boyington, only to wind up with the rain in his face.

At that point, he stood up to keep from drowning, and then rolled the unconscious man onto his side for the same reason.

Wyrick stared. "That's Darrell Boyington."

Charlie sighed, took the phone out of her hand, made the call, then handed it back. Wyrick was still in shock, and it showed. He'd never seen her with this inability to function.

"What happened?" she asked.

"Check beneath your back bumper and the front of your car," Charlie said.

And just like that, the fire in her eyes relit. "Are you kidding me?"

"No, ma'am. I am too damn wet for jokes."

She shoved the phone back in her pocket and dropped to her knees, then began running her fingers beneath the length of the bumper.

She found the first tracker within seconds, and the rage that shot through her elicited nothing but a scream. She scrambled to her feet and headed for the front fender, found the second one as far inside the wheel well as she could reach and pulled it out. She was drenched, and so angry she was shaking when she walked back.

Charlie had Boyington handcuffed and sitting in a puddle against the bumper of her car.

"You bastard!" she said, and kicked the bottom of his shoe. "Obviously, you did not talk to Cyrus Parks or you wouldn't be here. And you are a dumbass for doing this right under Charlie Dodge's window, so there's that."

Boyington blinked and then looked up through the downpour to the windows above them. This was, without doubt, the stupidest move he'd ever made. It was worse than a beginner mistake, but the stupidity of it was what was going to get him out of it, too.

"You are an intriguing woman. You wanted nothing to do with me. I wasn't ready to give up. I just wanted to know where you lived so I could send flowers…secret admirer and all that," he said.

Charlie stared. First at Boyington and then at Wyrick.

But Wyrick obviously wasn't buying it and kicked the bottom of his other shoe.

"You lie. Cyrus Parks hired you, just like he hired all of the others. And he has just opened the doors on his own level of hell."

The mention of Cyrus Parks sent Charlie into shock. Way more was going on here than she'd told him.

As for Boyington, his head was spinning. *All of the others? Shit, shit, shit. Parks's lies of omission are going to take me down.*

"I don't know what you're talking about. I don't know anyone by that name. I am a business owner. Unlike your boss, I do not tail people for money."

Wyrick squatted down in front of him. "But you tried to buy those services."

"No. I just wanted to meet you," Boyington said.

"You wanted to meet the woman Cyrus sent you to take out, didn't you? Cyrus Parks is way past trying to get me back to Universal Theorem. He just wants me dead, and you're the most recent dumbass he's hired to do that."

Boyington was stunned. This woman had no filters.

"No, of course not!" he mumbled.

"You can tell your story to the cops, because I'm filing stalking charges against you."

"My lawyer will destroy that," Boyington said.

Thunder rumbled again as the rain came down, and then the approaching sirens drowned out the sound.

"In the meantime, you can tell your story to the cops. There will be a record of the speeding ticket you got on the freeway the other day, trying to chase me down. There is a record of you harassing me in this parking lot the other day on the video cameras here, and I have video of you planting these GPS trackers, and Charlie Dodge's eyewitness account of seeing you do it, so we'll see about that," Wyrick said.

Boyington groaned. She was the first woman he'd ever encountered who wasn't afraid of him. She was weird. Seriously, weird—like not afraid of anything. Now he just wanted her dead for free.

Charlie's heart was racing from the shock he'd felt at seeing someone at her car. At the time, he didn't know if it was another tracking device or a bomb, but from what he knew of her enemies, it could have been either. Now finding out this man had approached her more than once was shocking. He'd been so wrapped up in finding Tony Dawson and then what was happening with Annie that she'd kept it all to herself. He'd failed to protect her.

And so he stood a silent witness to her rage. He didn't begin to understand the level of betrayal she'd suffered from Universal Theorem or Cyrus Parks, but he knew it was criminal and inhuman, and that was enough for him.

At that point, the police arrived. Seeing that no one was armed and one man was down and in handcuffs tempered the urgency with which they got out of their patrol cars.

Charlie Dodge and Wyrick were well-known to them, so the usual caution they might have used was set aside as they holstered their guns.

"Mr. Dodge. Ma'am, I'm Officer Ramos. What's going on?"

"It's not what it looks like," Boyington said.

"Yes, actually it is," Charlie said, and proceeded to tell them Boyington's name and what he'd witnessed, and how he'd caught him as he was trying to leave.

"And these are the GPS trackers he put on my car," Wyrick said, and handed them over. "This is not the first instance he has intruded upon my privacy. He followed me from the parking lot once, but I lost him on the freeway, and then he was waiting for me here again, after being told to leave me alone. This is the third instance, and I want to file charges against him for stalking. I have video of him on two separate occasions harassing me here, and video of what he did today."

"If you need further statements, could we do it out of the rain?" Charlie asked.

"I think we're good for now," Ramos said. "We have your names and contact information in the system, and the evidence you have turned over. You will need to come down and make a formal complaint and sign it." Then he pointed at Boyington. "Load him up and read him his rights."

For the first time in years, Darrell Boyington was worried. He'd taken Parks's money on the pretext that he quit the contract. From Wyrick's accusations, if he didn't wind up in jail, he still might wind up dead.

Wyrick and Charlie were soaked to the skin, so hurrying to get out of the rain wasn't worth the effort. They walked back into the office building in silence, then took the elevator back up to the office in the same manner.

The moment they were inside, Charlie stopped her with a look.

"Take what you need from here, and for the next few days, work from home. I don't want you here by yourself with this shit going on, and I can't be here to protect you. There are two women in my life whose well-beings matter to me, and you are one of them. My Annie is the other, and she is dying. The last thing I can do for her is be there. I can't help, but I can stand witness to the person she was until she's gone."

Wyrick ached for his sadness. There were tears on his face hiding within the raindrops. She wouldn't argue, and she couldn't touch him, so she waited in silence as he took a slow, shuddering breath so he could continue.

"I need to know you are safe before I can walk away from this job to be with her. Will you do this for me?"

She met his gaze without flinching.

"Yes."

"Thank you. For now, you *are* Dodge Security and Investigations. I will not be available for another job until I know I can put my full attention to it. If there is anything you can solve by simply researching it from home, then do it. Otherwise, turn it down. If there are decisions to be made, make them. Tell them I am unavailable and nothing more."

"Yes, sir."

Charlie searched her face for fear or uncertainty, and saw nothing but resolve.

"Thank you for always having my back," he said.

"Ditto," Wyrick said. "You have a change of clothes here. Get dry, then go home. Pack what you need to stay with her. If you need anything else, message me. I will always know how to find you."

Charlie sighed. "So you're finally going to admit you're psychic?"

"No. Because after the last time I lost you, I put a tracker app on your phone, remember? If you don't lose your phone, then I'm not going to lose you."

Charlie shook his head. "Remind me to give you that raise."

"Right after you go get changed," she said.

He went through his office, then into the bedroom beyond it to get out of his wet clothes, while Wyrick went to her private bathroom to do the same.

She was changed and packing up her gear when he came out.

She paused and looked up at him, then had to turn away to keep from crying. She kept working until she heard the door shut behind him, and then she dropped down into her chair, put her head down on the desk and sobbed.

A couple of hours later, Charlie arrived at Morning Light with a duffel bag over his shoulder.

"Good afternoon," Pinkie said.

Charlie nodded and signed in, then walked to the door to be let into the residents' quarters. Upon entering, he headed straight for Annie's room.

The other hospice nurse was there, just as Doris told him she would be when he walked in.

"I'm Charlie, Annie's husband," he said.

"I'm glad to meet you, Charlie. My name is Rachel. You can put your bag in her closet. We had a recliner brought in that makes into a bed. You are welcome to stay as long as you wish."

"Thank you," Charlie said, then put the bag in the closet, hung his Stetson and his coat on a hook on the wall and walked to Annie's bedside.

He stood in silence for a few moments, allowing himself to accept the reality of what was happening after denying the truth for so long.

She was thin. So thin. Her skin was so fragile he

was almost afraid to touch her, and so pale that the blue veins beneath it were easily visible. The IV was taped down to her arm, the visible bruising evidence of trying to find a viable vein.

Her long blond hair was matted and tangled. He wanted to brush it, but let go of the thought. Her appearance was less important than her comfort.

He glanced at Rachel, and then pulled up a chair and sat down by her bed.

"Hello, sweetheart. It's me, Charlie. I told you I'd be back," he said, and then he slid his hand beneath her palm, letting her hand rest there lightly.

Rachel put a hand on his shoulder.

"She's comfortable."

"What about her vital signs?" Charlie asked.

"Not as strong as yesterday," Rachel said.

Charlie's heart hurt to the point of physical pain.

"I'm not leaving until she does," he said.

"Understood," Rachel said. "Can I get you anything? Something to drink? A coffee or a soft drink?"

"I'm fine for now, but thank you," he said.

"Just let me know if you change your mind. I will be in and out, but still in the building."

Charlie heard her, but didn't respond. He was too focused on the slight rise and fall of Annie's chest—the only proof he had of the life still within her.

Wyrick drove slowly on the freeway and got off as quickly as she could. Between the rain coming down and the spray from the traffic in front of her blasting at the windshield of her car, she was as close to driving blind as she'd ever been.

Once she was on the city streets, the drive seemed safer. There was still the rain, but not the same level of speed to contend with. By the time she pulled through the gates of the estate and drove around to the entrance to her apartment, every muscle in her body was screaming from the tension.

She grabbed everything in one load and dashed inside, dumped it all on the sofa and then went back to lock the door. Only after she heard the click did she begin to relax, because she knew something about Darrell Boyington that Charlie didn't.

Boyington was a hit man, and Cyrus Parks had hired him.

It appeared she was going to have to send another message to Parks that he wouldn't forget. Something more than shutting down every UT-based facility on the face of the earth for three days like she had before. Something that hurt him where it hurt him most.

But right now, she needed to text Merlin and let him know she'd be working from home for a while. Then she changed into some comfortable clothes and began setting up the temporary office of Dodge Security and Investigations.

It was around 7:00 p.m. when Charlie got a text. When he saw it was from Wyrick, he read it.

You do not go all day without eating. You have food
at the front desk. Sit in the lobby and eat it.

He sighed. How the hell did she know he hadn't
eaten all day? Oh right. Psychic.

Rachel was adjusting the IV drip when he stood
up.

"I'll be back in a few minutes."

"We're good here. Take your time," Rachel said.

Charlie glanced at Annie, then left. Once they
buzzed him into the lobby, he saw a sack on the
counter and pointed.

"Is that for me?"

The night clerk nodded. "It was just delivered. I
was about to send someone to tell you."

"I'm going to eat it outside and get some fresh air."

"There's a courtyard just off the common room,"
the clerk said.

"I'll just sit on the bench out front," Charlie said,
then took the sack and walked out into the night.

It had quit raining hours ago, but the fresh-washed
scent was still in the air as Charlie sat down in the
shadows, opened the sack and unwrapped the roast
beef sandwich au jus. The slices of roast beef were
melt-in-your-mouth tender, and the crusty bun and the
warm jus warmed his belly. He ate without thought
until the food was gone.

As he gathered up the wrappings and sack to throw
away, he felt something else in the bottom of the sack.
It was a Hershey bar. Chocolate was Wyrick's call-

ing card. He peeled off the paper, then sat and ate the whole thing, one small square at a time. By the time he had finished the candy bar, the knot in his belly was almost unwound.

It was with reluctance that he got up, tossed his garbage into the trash can in the parking lot and then went back inside. But this time when he walked back into the residents' quarters, the fresh air and full belly had renewed him enough for the hours to come.

The next morning, Wyrick had the temporary office set up and the office phone on voice mail. Merlin finally responded to her text from yesterday, but his response was a little cryptic.

I'm outside. Come find me.

So she grabbed a jacket and headed outside, but he was nowhere in sight. After a few moments, she thought of the greenhouse. The warm air wrapped around her like a hug as she entered it and then saw him at the back.

"Hey," she said.

He turned at the sound of her voice and smiled.

"Come in! I haven't had a visitor out here in ages. Do you like tomatoes? I love them, and those you get in a supermarket don't even taste like tomatoes. You have to pick them when they're really ripe to get that ripe on the vine taste."

"Yes, I like them," Wyrick said.

"Awesome. Try one of these!" he said, and plucked a small cherry tomato from the plant closest to him.

Wyrick obliged because it was Merlin and popped it in her mouth. Juice filled her mouth at the first bite.

"Umm, so good," she said.

"Told you!" he crowed. "So, you're working from home! What's wrong?"

"Charlie is unavailable to take on new cases for a while, so I'll be working from home, that's all."

He grabbed a little plastic bowl from a shelf, filled it with cherry tomatoes and handed it to her.

"Enjoy. There's more where these came from. And one day, you'll be the one growing them. When you do, eat one for me. I love these things."

Wyrick left the greenhouse with a lump in her throat and the little bowl clutched against her chest. She hurried across the grounds and back into her apartment, then locked the door.

It wasn't until she set the tomatoes on the counter that it dawned on her how much time she spent locking herself inside. Wherever she was, she was always locking doors. But was it only to keep the bad guys out—or was it to keep everyone out?

All she knew was this overwhelming fear began when she thought she was going to die, and then she didn't. The cancer went away, but her fear didn't. And it was all because of Cyrus Parks. He'd called himself her father, discarded her when he thought she was flawed, then stalked her from afar when she didn't die. He kept the fear alive until she scared him, and now he wanted her dead. A whole new sense of injustice rolled through her.

"Well, Daddy dear, it's about time you learn that you don't always get what you want in life."

She went into her little office, opened her laptop and pulled up a file labeled PAYBACK. After shutting UT down before, she didn't think she'd ever have to use this one, but time had proved her wrong.

She opened the file and began pulling up one program after another, her fingers flying over the keys as she entered password after password to get them started. Once she was in, the rest was a matter of her own special skills and then removing the contents.

It took less than two hours to commit the crime of the century and erase every trace of what she'd stolen. She'd tied the knot. Now all she needed was to tie the bow.

She hacked into Parks's personal email and sent one message.

I'm not dead and your hit man, Boyington, is in jail. You should have left me alone.

She hit Send, knowing that the email would disappear within minutes of being opened.

Then she pulled the videos from the office building, found the parts where Boyington had confronted her and sent all of them to the police department, to the officer who had arrested Boyington. Then just for good measure, she added background on the names she already knew of the other men Cyrus Parks had hired to track her, and documented all the times she'd moved because of it since she'd come to live in Dallas. She sent a signed electronic statement and forwarded it, too, and considered her part in that done, unless it ever went to trial, which she doubted. People like Cyrus always paid their way out of trouble.

Ten

Cyrus Parks was at a business lunch, and as it began winding down, he took out his debit card to pay. Minutes later, he was shocked when the waiter brought it back as declined.

"Good Lord! Are you serious? There must be something wrong on their end," he muttered, and pulled out a credit card, only to have it declined, and then the third one he used came up the same way.

One of the men finally took pity on him and paid.

"There's obviously some computer glitch attached to your name. I've got this. No worries."

And the moment his friend said it, Cyrus's heart skipped a beat. *It can't be. Surely not.*

"Yes, obviously," Cyrus said. "I'll get my tech people right on it and hope it isn't some hack job from a disgruntled employee."

"In our level of the world, it happens," another man said, and they soon parted company.

But the moment Cyrus was in his limo, he began

to panic all over again. He checked his phone for messages that would alert him to what was happening, but there were none.

"Where to, Mr. Parks?" the driver asked.

"Home. Take me home."

It took thirty-plus minutes to navigate the traffic, but the moment Cyrus was inside his house, he hurried to his office. The first thing he did was pull up his private email. He recognized all of the senders, except for one. All it said was PAYBACK.

"Oh God, oh God," he muttered, as he opened it and read…

I'm not dead and your hit man, Boyington, is in jail. You should have left me alone.

"No, no, no," he muttered, and logged in to his bank. There was a one-dollar balance. His heart sank, as he began checking into all of the accounts where his money was kept, and one after another, they each had a one-dollar balance.

His rage at Wyrick was nothing compared to his anger at the hit man. He'd just paid him the rest of the contract money to quit the job and leave her alone. The bastard had taken the money and went after her anyway. Obviously, he had failed in the process *and* given up the name of the man who'd put out the hit.

The only good part of this whole shit storm was now Cyrus knew the hit man's name. He'd deal with him first and Wyrick later.

He started to reply to the email, only to realize it

was gone. He grunted. Of course it was. He did not create fools.

The bank had been hacked. They would have to replace the money that disappeared, but that would take time. The other places he'd hidden money didn't have that same insurable feature. That money was gone.

Universal Theorem had a constant flow of income, but this was Cyrus's personal income. It was going to take time to build the accounts back up, and in the meantime, he was, as they say, a little short on cash.

Charlie rested in the recliner next to Annie's bed, but his legs hung off the footrest and he was too tall to stretch out. His eyes burned from lack of sleep, and he was moving on autopilot, but sleep was impossible. There was no way to sleep through the sounds of her breathing or the intermittent moan she would emit.

Doris would raise the head of Annie's bed, and for a while that would ease her labored breathing… until it started all over again.

Doris knew. Charlie knew. Everyone in Morning Light knew. Annie Dodge was in her last days.

He lost track of time, and didn't even know whether it was day or night until he'd get the call that his dinner had been delivered and was waiting at the front desk.

At first he'd felt guilty about leaving her, but even he knew he had to eat sometime. But after a while, that call became the momentary escape he needed.

And every evening Wyrick sent something different.

The second day Wyrick sent a giant barbecue sandwich, steak fries and a beer. He ate with tears in his eyes.

The third day was cold and windy, and she'd ordered kung pao chicken, fried rice and spring rolls. Every day, something different, in the hopes it would strike the right chord and he'd eat enough of it to keep him going.

The fourth night it was a bag full of tacos, churros and Mexican beer.

And every night, the break and the food made going back into Morning Light bearable.

While Charlie was sitting vigil, Darrell Boyington was arraigned and let out on bail. He had retreated to his penthouse like a dog with his tail between his legs. Being booked and fingerprinted had technically brought an end to ever taking another contract job again, because he was now in the system. He'd been really good at his job until he let Wyrick get under his skin, and that was on him. It was the need for revenge that caused his downfall.

His lawyer was talking about getting the stalking charges dropped to harassment, but he was still facing the possibility of a little jail time and a fine. It wouldn't really affect his business activities. He had never been the face of the sports bars he owned, so business would not be affected. But it was the actual fact of serving time that horrified him.

* * *

It was just after lunch, and Darrell was waiting on a phone call from his attorney, but he was too fidgety to sit, so he took one of his favorite cigars out onto the balcony and lit up.

The air was cold and today there was enough breeze to carry away the smoke. And then he heard a commotion going on from somewhere below him, and out of curiosity, he got up and walked to the railing. Within moments, a drone shot straight up from somewhere below. Before he could react to what he was seeing, it was in his face.

The blast from the bomb it was carrying destroyed the living room behind him, and blew him and the balcony into pieces, before dropping all of it onto the street below.

Cyrus Parks had effected his own brand of payback.

Wyrick was sitting in the kitchen with Merlin, going over another set of papers with him and his lawyer, Rodney Gordon, when her cell phone rang.

She glanced at caller ID and then frowned.

"Excuse me a moment. It's the Dallas Police Department. I suppose I'd better answer this," she said, and got up and walked out into the hallway to talk. "Hello?"

"This is Detective Tillman, Homicide Division, calling for Jade Wyrick."

"I'm Wyrick. What can I do for you, Detective?"

"For clarification, you recently filed stalking charges against a Darrell Boyington. Is this correct?"

"Yes."

"What is your present location?" he asked.

"I'm at home. To be exact, I'm in my landlord's kitchen, with his lawyer, where we've been for the past two hours. Now, what's going on, and why all the questions?"

"Darrell Boyington is dead. Someone flew a bomb onto his balcony while he was on it and blew him all to hell."

"I'm not into killing people. That was his hobby," Wyrick said.

There was a moment of silence before Tillman spoke.

"What do you mean by that?"

"Boyington was a hit man. I'd suggest you start looking at the people who hired him, and the families of the people he killed."

"And you know this, how?" Tillman asked.

"I just know stuff," Wyrick said. "Hang on and I'll let you speak to my landlord and his lawyer to verify where I am. They're still here."

She didn't wait for him to agree; she just sauntered back into the kitchen, talking as she went.

"Hey, guys. A detective named Tillman needs to verify my whereabouts for the last two hours. Do you mind talking to him a minute?"

"Not at all," Rodney said. "Put the phone on speaker. Then Art and I can do this together."

"Done," Wyrick said, and laid the phone down on

the table. "Okay, Detective. Arthur Merlin is my landlord. Rodney Gordon is Merlin's lawyer. They're listening."

"Detective Tillman, I'm Rodney Gordon. I believe you have testified in a couple of cases I've tried. If you're asking how long Miss Wyrick has been with us, it's going on a little over two hours now, and before that, she was in her apartment in the basement below."

"I'm Art Merlin, Jade's landlord. She rents my basement apartment, but she's also a friend. She's been here in my kitchen for more than two hours, during which time she has consumed a cup of coffee, one Pepsi and two candy bars."

Wyrick laughed, and Tillman heard her. It was a nice laugh.

"Okay, Miss Wyrick. The recent incident between you and Boyington was why I called, and if I have further questions, we'll be in touch."

Jade picked up her phone, ended the call and dropped it back in her pocket.

"Now, where were we?"

Merlin wiggled a finger at her. "What was the recent incident between you and this dead man that I don't know about?"

"Charlie caught him planting GPS trackers on my car. It was the third time he had shown up at my place of work to harass me, and I filed stalking charges against him."

"Good Lord. Did you know him?" Rodney asked.

"Not until he walked into Charlie's office, demanding to see him, which all turned out to be a ruse to get to me. He is…was…a hit man."

Merlin's expression shifted to one of concern.

"UT?" he asked.

Wyrick sighed. "I don't know why I am surprised you know that much."

He grinned and winked. "I know stuff, too."

Rodney threw up his hands. "Okay, obviously this is a need-to-know basis, and I don't need to know. And considering my workload, that's fine, too. Now, we have one more set of papers to go over, but we won't need you. I think this will be the last of it, until—"

"Until I'm gone," Merlin said, and grinned at the lawyer. "She's gonna take care of my tomatoes, and scatter my ashes in Galveston Bay. Whatever else she does afterward, she does with my blessing."

The thought of Annie and Merlin both living their last days made her sad, and Wyrick, being Wyrick, hid her emotions behind sarcasm.

"Thank God I don't have to go pick out a headstone, then come up with something smart and wise to put on it."

They both burst into laughter.

"I'm going back to the dungeon, Master. Ring if you need me," she said, and left through the kitchen stairwell.

Merlin sighed. "She is a broken child with the heart and stamina of a warrior, and most likely the most brilliant mind on the face of the earth. Treat her well when I am gone."

"Consider it done," Rodney said.

* * *

Sometime around midmorning on the fifth day of Charlie's vigil, Annie's breathing became markedly worse. Doris had been watching her carefully for a couple of hours, noting the change, but it was just now becoming evident to Charlie.

"What's happening?" Charlie asked, as Doris placed her stethoscope on Annie's chest.

"It's sounding like she's developed pneumonia. I want Dr. Dunleavy to look at her," Doris said. "I think he's still on-site."

Charlie stood helplessly by as Doris made the call, listening to her side of the conversation, while watching Annie struggling for every breath. She was already on oxygen, but it was no longer working as it had.

He shoved a hand through his hair and then rubbed the back of his neck. He was so tired he was numb. Over the past few days he'd helped bath her, and when he was at his wit's end watching her struggle to breathe, he'd rub her hands and feet with lotion because he couldn't breathe for her, and he needed to do something.

A few minutes later, Dr. Dunleavy walked into Annie's room. He gave Charlie a quick pat on the shoulder and then moved toward his patient.

His examination was cursory. Annie's instructions were clear. No medicines to prolong her life. No CPR should her heart stop, and so it went. Charlie's wishes would hold no weight here, and the longer he watched her struggle, the less likely he would have been to wish her back. Watching someone die was hard. Watching someone you love dying was hell on earth.

Finally, Dunleavy stepped back and then approached Charlie.

"She has pneumonia. Her lungs are filling with fluid."

"Jesus," Charlie whispered. "She is going to drown, isn't she?"

"I'm sorry, Charlie. So sorry, but her wishes are clear. No extraordinary measures of resuscitation."

Speech was impossible, and so was this, and yet Charlie couldn't leave her. Seeing her out was the last thing he would do with her.

"So what do we do?" Charlie asked.

"Honor her last wishes," Dunleavy said, and walked out.

"I'm going to give you a little time with Annie," Doris said. "I'll be in the hall if you need me."

Charlie sat back down beside Annie and reached for her hand. His voice was shaking, and he was swallowing past tears.

"Dammit, Annie, you never did want to quit on anything. It was one of the things I admired about you most. You are my best friend, and the only woman I ever loved. But I want you to know that whenever you're ready to go home now, just go. You'll be well there. You won't be lost anymore."

He sat there, waiting for her to inhale again. And waited. And waited, then realized he was holding his breath with her. Then she gasped, choked, and when she inhaled, it sounded like she was strangling.

Charlie shook his head and closed his eyes as the struggle for breathing continued. He didn't know how long he'd been sitting there like that, but it wasn't until Doris came back into the room that he realized what he'd been doing.

She walked up beside him, paused for a moment to watch, then leaned over and whispered in Charlie's ear.

"Let her go, Charlie."

"I did. I told her to go," he said.

"No, I mean let go of her hand. Turn her loose… really loose."

"Oh shit," Charlie said, and yanked his hand back. "I didn't think. I just—"

"No, no, it's okay," Doris said. "But we don't really know how much the physical touch impacts the soul's reluctance to leave. I've witnessed many things in my years of hospice care, and we both want her journey out of here to be as easy as possible."

Charlie nodded, and then went a step further and got up and moved his chair to the far corner of the room. If she needed distance, he was giving it to her.

Anything for you, baby. Anything for you.

And for the next four hours, he sat in total silence, unmoving—waiting for his Annie to let go.

Wyrick couldn't sleep. The world was waiting for another soul to leave, and she could feel it. Her heart was breaking for Charlie's grief, because she could feel that, too.

And so she sat within the silence, waiting for the call from Morning Light to tell her Annie Dodge was gone.

* * *

It was a couple of hours before dawn.

Charlie was lost in thought, remembering the year Annie turned thirty years old. At her request, he'd taken her to a little cabin on Lake Texoma. They'd planned to cook out under the stars, but it started raining, so they built a fire in the fireplace in July, and roasted wieners and marshmallows there.

They ate until they were full, and so sticky from sweat and the toasted marshmallows that in the dark of night, they stripped naked and ran laughing out into the rain.

"Charlie."

He jerked, then glanced at Annie.

She was still, and motionless…and there was no more strangling gasps.

Charlie stood. He knew before he asked that she was gone, because he couldn't feel her anymore.

"It's over?"

Doris nodded. "A couple of minutes ago. I kept waiting for her to take another breath, but she didn't. She was a fighter…such a fierce spirit, and now she's at peace."

Charlie moved toward the bed in a daze as Doris stepped out into the hall with her phone. Only moments before he'd been remembering making love to her in the rain. He leaned over and kissed her on the forehead.

"You are forever my Annie. Time won't change that. Death won't change that. Love you, baby."

Doris came back into the room. "Charlie, I'm

sorry, but I need to finish up in here. Dr. Dunleavy was already on the way. He'll be the one to officially release her. If you want to wait in the common room, I'll come get you when I've finished."

He wiped a shaky hand over his face and then walked out. He got all the way to the common room and then sat down in the dark, remembering the times he'd sat in here with Annie, and all the puzzle pieces she would hand him, wanting him to find where they went. And now she was finally whole again. The last piece had been put back into place.

Wyrick was dozing sitting up when her cell rang. She jumped, then fumbled it trying to answer.

"Hello? Hello?"

"Miss Wyrick, this is Morning Light. I'm calling to let you know that Annie Dodge passed away a short time ago."

The ache that pierced her was real. "Ah…damn. Is my boss still there?"

"Yes, ma'am. He's sitting with her until the hearse arrives. It will be another hour or so."

"Thank you for calling," Wyrick said.

She hurried to the bathroom to wash the sleep out of her eyes, then grabbed her purse and left on the run, calling for an Uber to pick her up at Charlie's apartment in thirty minutes. Now all she had to do was get there.

Charlie was going through the motions—sitting with the body, answering questions about her belongings. They had them packed and sitting beside his bag. He wondered when they'd done that, and then realized it didn't matter.

"Can you just donate them?" Charlie asked.

"Yes, of course, if that's your wish," Doris said.

He nodded, thinking as he did that when he left her today, he'd never be back in this place again. There was a sense of relief about that. Annie was free of it, and now so was he.

An hour passed, and then another. Someone brought him a cup of coffee and then carried away the bag with her clothing.

He kept looking for Annie in the body on the bed, but she was gone. It didn't even look like her anymore. How did that happen so fast?

It was going on the third hour when he heard voices, and then people were coming in the door. The men from the funeral home had finally arrived.

"Mr. Dodge, our sincere condolences," they said. "Do you mind stepping out of the room?"

Charlie picked up his bag and walked out into the hall. When they wheeled the body out, it was fully covered beneath a sheet. Everything was becoming impersonal—the separation between life and death painfully blatant.

He walked with her all the way to the exit, and then they went one way with her and he went another. A nurse let him out of the residence area and he found himself standing in the lobby, trying to remember what to do next.

Pinkie was already on duty, and she was in tears.

"I'm so sorry, Charlie," Pinkie said.

"Thank you. Thank you for everything," Charlie said, and then walked out of the building in a daze.

He looked up at the sky. The fucking sun was out. How the hell did it keep shining when his light was gone?

He wiped a hand over his face and then looked for his car and saw Wyrick, arms folded, legs crossed, wearing a sheepskin coat and blue jeans, and leaning against the back of his Jeep.

She held out her hand as he approached.

"Give me your keys."

He handed them over.

She unlocked the Jeep with the remote and took the bag from his shoulder.

"Get in. I'm driving," she said, and tossed his bag in the back.

Charlie slid into the seat and buckled up, then leaned back and closed his eyes.

Wyrick started the engine, and shot out of the parking lot and onto the street like a bullet from a gun.

There was nothing to say that would make anything better, and so she said nothing at all. She wouldn't look at him. Couldn't look at him.

But when he finally put his hands over his face and doubled over in the seat like a broken child, she cried with him, silent tears rolling down her face, feeling every ounce of his pain as if it was her own.

Charlie Dodge's world had come apart at the seams.

Time was the healer, but Charlie's sentence had just begun.

Wyrick drove him all the way to his apartment building and up into the adjoining garage in total silence, then parked in his assigned parking place and got out.

Charlie was red-eyed and silent when he got out, but when she handed him his keys and his bag, he took them.

"Go to bed. Sleep until someone calls you with questions only you can answer. I'm safe. Boyington is dead. Someone flew a bomb onto his balcony while he was on it. It wasn't me. Parks called a hit on the hit man. Don't come back to work until you're ready to kick ass again."

Then she turned on her heel, jumped in her Mercedes and drove out of the parking garage, leaving Charlie and a layer of rubber from her tires.

Eleven

Charlie did what he'd been told, because conscious thought was beyond him, and when he got into his apartment, he locked the door behind him and then stood in the entryway, trying to remember what he was supposed to do.

Oh yes…bed.

Sunlight was streaming through the living room windows. It wasn't time to sleep, but he was weary all the way to his bones, and so he went to the bedroom, stripped and showered, then fell into bed naked, with the water still drying on his skin.

There was no funeral to plan. Annie wanted to be cremated, and their social circle ended when Annie forgot her friends existed. He'd seen her out of this world, and now there was nothing left for him to do. When he finally closed his eyes, the image of Annie still struggling to breathe was in his head, and tears welled and rolled out from beneath his lids.

He fell asleep from exhaustion, then began dreaming that she was drowning, and woke up as she was going under. In anger, he rolled off the bed and strode into the kitchen, banging doors and looking on shelves until he found an unopened fifth of whiskey.

His hands were shaking as he opened it up, then sloshed some into a coffee cup and downed it.

"No more dreams. Do you hear me, God? No more fucking dreams!"

He carried the bottle back to the bedroom and set it down beside his bed, then turned on the TV and drank the bottle dry.

Wyrick dealt with her emotions by going back to work. She went through the emails, sending appropriate responses, and then began sifting through the ones she could handle on her own.

She had already set up an app from Bill.com to accept retainers without coming into the office, so she picked another prospective client to contact and made the call.

"Hello, this is Wanda."

"Mrs. Carrollton, my name is Wyrick, and I'm calling on behalf of Dodge Security and Investigations in regards to your granddaughter, Katrina. Do you have time to speak with me?"

Wanda Carrollton was ecstatic. "Yes, and please call me Wanda."

"Yes, ma'am. Charlie Dodge is unavailable at this time, but I work with him, and will be working on your case, if that's acceptable."

"I don't care who's doing it as long as someone can find my girl."

"Yes, ma'am. I'll send you an invoice via email to pay for your retainer, and then I'll need some background. Your granddaughter's full name, her parents' names, last known addresses, occupations, anything you have on any of them. Even Social Security numbers, because my research is all online."

"Oh, that'll take a bit. Can I gather up what I have and then send it to you in an email, like I did my request?"

"Yes, ma'am. I'll keep you updated as I go, and maybe we'll get lucky. How long has it been since you lost touch with her?" Wyrick asked.

"Twenty years. She was six when my son died and her mother moved her out of state. She stayed in touch for about a year and then nothing. It was like losing my son all over again. I let life sideline my desire to find her, but I'm not getting any younger, and even if she wants nothing to do with me, I'd like to know she's okay."

"Yes, ma'am. I'll invoice you, and then wait for you to send me the info to get started."

"Thank you! Thank you, so much," Wanda said.

"I can't promise miracles," Wyrick said. "But if it's at all possible, I'll find answers."

"That's all I need. Just answers, so I will have a little peace of mind," Wanda said.

Wyrick hung up with a sense of purpose. Work would keep her mind off what Charlie was going through. No matter how lost he got in his grief, he was the only one who could find his way out. She wasn't scared for him, because Charlie Dodge was a survivor, but she was so sad for his hurt.

As for Merlin, his declining health was a reality, but he was still enjoying a measure of quality with it. She had yet to fully take in what she'd been given, but it was far more than a home.

Back in Odessa, the doctor at Medical Center Hospital had been weaning Tony Dawson off sedation a little at a time, and Tony was beginning to show signs of regaining consciousness. When a nurse came out of ICU looking for Baxter and Macie to let them know, they hugged each other, crying tears of relief.

"Can we see him? Has he spoken?" Baxter asked.

The nurse shook her head. "He hasn't said anything, but all of the signs are there that he's becoming aware. If you'll both follow me, I'll take you in."

Macie grabbed Baxter's hand and squeezed it, suddenly anxious. They'd been warned of all kinds of complications—that he'd wake up and not know them, or maybe not know who he was—but right now, just knowing he was coming to was a step in the right direction.

They followed the nurse through the ward, but it was hard not to hurry. As soon as they reached his bed, they began looking for changes—a slight movement beneath his eyelids, the fingers on one hand slightly twitching.

"You can talk to him," the nurse said. "Just quietly, please."

Macie reached for his hand, stilling the twitch with her grip.

"Hi, Tony, darling. It's Mom. Dad and I are right here beside you. We want you to know that you're not lost anymore and you're safe."

Baxter gently patted his son's arm. "Hey, T-boy. Can you hear me?"

All of a sudden Macie gasped. "He just squeezed my hand. Oh, Baxter! He heard us."

Baxter was so emotional he was shaking. "We love you, son. Just keep getting better and come back to us."

Tony moaned, and when he did, the nurse was immediately there.

"It's the pain. He's just beginning to feel it," she said, and adjusted the drip on his IV.

"Just rest, Tony. It's the fastest way to heal. We're just outside in the waiting room and we're not leaving here until you come with us," Baxter said.

Tony's lips were moving slightly, but no sound was coming out, and then he was gone again.

"He's out," Baxter said, and patted Tony's hand. "We'll be back, son. Rest well."

Macie leaned over the bed and kissed his cheek.

"Love you, honey. You're going to be okay."

Charlie suffered the hangover from hell the day after he'd emptied that fifth of whiskey, and to add to his misery, he received flower deliveries from the

Dunleavy family in Denver, as well as flowers from Morning Light.

He didn't want to look at flowers and remember Annie dying. It was going to take years, if ever, before he could think of her without remembering her last days. In sickness and in health, until Alzheimer's parted them and death took her.

So he gave the flowers to the women from his cleaning service, who also did his laundry.

He got a text from the Dawson family, telling him that Tony was regaining consciousness and squeezed their hand when they spoke to him.

It was an affirming thing to know that the kid was healing, and he sent a brief text back, thanking them for the update. Even though that news was good news, it didn't change his focus. He'd known for months now that he was going to lose Annie. He thought he was prepared, and now it appeared he was not.

He had to find his new normal, and to do that, he was going to go AWOL. He needed different surroundings and something different on which to focus, so he texted Wyrick that he was out of town for a couple of days, but didn't bother telling her where he was going. He didn't have to. She had that damn app on his phone that tracked him wherever he went, so if she cared enough to snoop, she'd know.

The next morning, he packed up and left with no destination in mind, and drove north on I-35 into Oklahoma. Somewhere near McAlester, Oklahoma, he saw a sign advertising Robbers Cave State Park, which was somewhere he'd never been, and left the interstate on Highway 270 heading east.

On the way, he called their office and reserved a cabin for a couple of nights. It was almost noon when he drove into Wilburton, Oklahoma, population: 2,843.

It was a tiny town nestled within a beautiful grass-land valley between the San Bois and Winding Stair mountains, both of which were heavily forested.

He already had a cabin rented, so he stopped at Roy's Cardinal Grocery Store on Highway 2 on the way to Robbers Cave Park, to stock up on food. He had been told when he called to make a reservation that there was a restaurant on-site, but he wasn't in a socializing mood.

After buying what he wanted, he stayed on that highway until he came to the park, then followed the signs to the office to sign in and get a key.

The woman behind the counter was reading some-thing on her phone when he walked in. She looked up and quickly put it aside.

"Good morning," she said.

"I'm Charlie Dodge. I have a reservation for a cabin."

"Yes, Mr. Dodge. You wanted one with a view in the old part of the park?"

"Yes."

"Cabin One is empty. It's actually the first one ever built in the park. I think you'll like it. There's not much ground behind the cabin, but the view from there off the back of the mountain is amazing."

"Thanks," he said, and as soon as their business was done, she gave him the key and a map of the area.

"The hike into Robbers Cave is pretty this time of year. They'll bring clean linens to your cabin, so leave whatever you want picked up out on the stoop, and they'll trade you clean for dirty," she added.

Charlie wasn't planning hikes, but he wasn't going to tell her that. He took the map and the key and left.

A short while later, he pulled up in front of the old rock cabin and parked. It took a couple of trips to carry in his bags and the groceries, but once he was inside, he began putting things away, then poked around the one-bedroom cabin, noting the television, the kitchen and the wood-burning fireplace, before checking his phone. He already knew there was no available Wi-Fi and that service was going to be spotty here, but he didn't care. He turned up the thermostat to warm the place up, gave the bathroom a quick look, and then he went into the bedroom, kicked off his boots and stretched out on top of the spread.

The room smelled of pine and lemon oil, and a faint odor of ashes. He heard a scratching sound near the window and wondered if there was a mouse in the cabin, but when he looked, he saw it was just branches from the bushes outside.

The silence lulled him into a sense of well-being. Within moments, he had closed his eyes. In the distance, he could hear the faint sound of children laughing. It was a good sound, and it felt good to stretch out his legs, even if his feet hung off the end of the bed.

The thick walls muffled all but the loudest sounds,

and when the heater kicked on, it added a low hum within the room. Charlie was finally asleep.

It was midday when Wyrick received Wanda Carrollton's information. It was enough to get started, and she needed to stay busy. Getting that text from Charlie had been disconcerting, but not surprising. Charlie Dodge was a grown-ass man who'd gotten himself back from Afghanistan in one piece. If he felt the need to disappear for a while, she understood it.

She went upstairs once to check on Merlin, and found him in the kitchen, having soup.

"Hello, Jade! Are you hungry? There's more noodle soup."

"No, but thanks. I'm working a case and just wanted to check on you. Do you need anything?"

"Crackers. I forgot to get them out of the pantry."

"Done," Wyrick said, and opened the pantry door, then stopped and grinned. The lineup of cracker boxes was impressive.

"Saltine, pretzel, wheat or rye?"

"Old-school saltines, please," he said.

She grabbed the box and slid it onto the table in front of him, then went back to the pantry and got a jar of peanut butter, too.

"Just in case you want dessert," she said.

"You must be psychic," he said.

She grinned. "I must be," she said, and then went back down to start running a search on the info Wanda had given her.

Within an hour, she found out why the mother

quit contacting Wanda all those years ago. She was dead. She had remarried, to someone named Andy Delgado, but they were both killed in a car accident when Katrina was seven. At that point, Katrina disappeared into the foster care system.

Wyrick sighed. This was bad news. Once a kid was logged into the system, the paper trails were often buried, which meant more digging. But Wyrick was a master at research and buried info, so she went back to work. Katrina would be twenty-six years old now. Wyrick knew she could find her, but there was no way to predict the outcome.

Charlie slept all afternoon, and woke up just as the sun was going down. He got up and stepped outside long enough to gauge the falling temperature and the gathering clouds, and got a whiff of burning wood and charcoal, and the scent of cooking meat. The residents in other cabins were making dinner on their grills, but he wasn't cooking.

He went back inside, made himself a sandwich with some cold cuts, opened a bag of chips and popped the top on a longneck beer and settled down in front of the TV to eat.

There was one brief moment when he started to call Morning Light to check in, and then remembered. His vision blurred slightly as he blinked back tears, took a drink of the cold, yeasty brew, then upped the volume on the television and ate his food.

Later that night, after he'd gone back to bed, it began to rain. Charlie roused enough to hear it coming down on the roof, and then rolled over and went back to sleep. It rained off and on all night, and when he woke the next morning, the cabin was cold. He got up to turn up the thermostat, and when he glanced out the window, he noticed the raindrops had frozen onto the bushes.

No wonder it was cold in the cabin. It had fallen below freezing last night. The plus side was that the ground was too warm to freeze, so the only ice was on the trees and the grass.

But it prompted him to think about building a fire. Wood had been laid in the fireplace, complete with kindling below it to start the logs to burning. He took the grill lighter from the mantel and set the kindling ablaze, then went to make coffee.

By the time the logs were ablaze, he was on the sofa with a cup of coffee and a honey bun. He turned on the television again and watched mindlessly as he ate, but it was hard for Charlie to relax. He didn't know what to do with the day. He thought about packing up and driving on to somewhere else, but was beginning to realize there wasn't anywhere to go to get away from his truth, and so he sat, staring into the fire.

By midmorning, he was antsy from doing nothing, and decided to go out and get some air. He put on his coat, then, because he was in the mountains, slipped his handgun into the inside pocket of his jacket and locked the cabin on his way out.

He thought about driving down to the lake, then changed his mind and took off walking up the road, passing other cabins as he went. Some had been rented, but more were standing empty. If this had been summer, they would have been full, with people everywhere.

He soon wandered off the road and up into the trees, crunching leaves and kicking pine cones as he went. Squirrels scolded. A hawk screeched from somewhere up above the canopy. The air was cold on his face, but he was warm beneath his coat.

It wasn't until he began hearing a lot of vehicles, and people talking loudly back up on the road, that he began to wonder what was going on. Then he caught a glimpse of what looked like state police cruisers and realized something serious was happening.

And the moment he walked out of the trees, a vehicle from the park department stopped.

"Sir. Two inmates have escaped from the McAlester Penitentiary and were sighted in the park about an hour ago. We're asking everyone to get back to their cabins and stay there until we sound an all clear."

"Damn," Charlie said. "Are they dangerous?"

"Reported to be armed and dangerous," the ranger said. "What cabin are you in?"

"Number One."

"That's a good distance away. Hop in and I'll give you a ride back."

"Thanks," Charlie said, and got in, glad for the lift.

As soon as they arrived, Charlie got out, unlocked the front door, carried in some more dry firewood, then went inside, locking it back behind him.

He laid his handgun on a table in the living room, added a couple of logs onto the burning embers in the fireplace, then set the alarm on his Jeep and went through the cabin checking windows to make sure they were locked.

After that, he turned on the television, found a local station that was covering the search, and then grabbed a cold pop and a bag of chips for the lunch he'd missed and settled in.

The police factor increased as the ensuing hours passed. He kept hearing choppers flying over, and knew finding them by air would be hard, considering the heavily forested mountains around them. He hoped they found them before dark, because no one in the park would be sleeping tonight if they didn't.

It was just after sunset when Charlie stepped out to bring firewood in for the night. He paused on the steps to check out the area, and then began gathering up an armload. He was just about ready to go back inside when he heard a bloodcurdling scream from up the road.

He dropped the firewood, darted back inside, grabbed his handgun from the table and slammed the door shut behind him as he leaped off the steps.

The woman's screams were getting louder, which meant he had to be getting closer. Three of the nearby cabins were inhabited, but he couldn't tell where the screams were coming from. And then all of a sudden a young girl came running out of the middle cabin, running barefoot in her pajamas.

"The bad men… Mommy told me to run," she sobbed, and pointed back inside the cabin.

Charlie grabbed her by the shoulders. "See my cabin at the end of the road? The door is unlocked. Go inside and lock it. Don't open it for anyone unless it's me or the police. Now run!"

"But… Mommy…"

"Go!" Charlie said. "And don't look back." Then he took his gun off safety.

The little girl ran toward Charlie's cabin as he ran toward the open door. He didn't know what he was going to find, but the woman wasn't screaming anymore.

It was a careless, foolish thing to do, but when Charlie reached their front porch, he didn't slow down. He went up the steps and into the cabin on the run.

There was an unconscious man on the floor in a pool of blood, and the woman was nowhere in sight. Then he heard something breaking in the back of the cabin and a woman moan, and he slipped down the hall, following the sounds.

A bedroom door was ajar, and he could see two men in prison orange, and the missing woman, unconscious and bloody, lying spread-eagle on the bed.

There was a rifle lying on the floor beside the bed, and both prisoners were taking off their orange jumpsuits and tearing through the man's suitcase, trying to find clothes that would fit.

One prisoner was in the act of changing clothes, and the other one was still rummaging through a suitcase. They had taken the cash out of the woman's purse and the man's wallet, and it was lying on the bed beside the unconscious woman.

"Hey, Grover, I found the car keys. Let's get the hell out of here."

"Just a minute, Joe. I'm almost—"

Charlie shoved the door inward, slamming it against the wall.

"Get down on the floor! Down on the floor!" he shouted.

Joe made a dive for the rifle, and Charlie fired.

Joe dropped and screamed "My knee! My knee!" while Grover hit the floor screaming "Don't shoot! Don't shoot!"

Charlie could hear sirens now and speeding vehicles on the road outside. Someone else must have heard the screams and called the ranger station. He kicked the rifle out of their reach and then moved quickly to the woman on the bed to feel for a pulse. She was alive, and with a spreading bruise on her jaw.

Moments later, he could hear footsteps, and men shouting "Police! Police!" as they came running into the cabin.

At that point, he called out.

"Back here! In the back bedroom. I have the prisoners subdued."

The woman was moaning, beginning to regain consciousness as police swarmed the room, and Joe, the prisoner he'd shot, was writhing and screaming in pain. Grover already knew the routine and was belly down with his hands locked behind his head.

Charlie's hands were in the air. "I have a permit," he said, and carefully laid the gun on the floor and stepped back. "I'm down the road in Cabin One. I heard the woman screaming and started running up this way. I met their daughter running out of this cabin, and sent her down to mine and told her to lock herself in. The man in the living room was already on the floor. I don't know what they did to him. The woman was like this, and they were changing clothes when I arrived."

One of the officers took Charlie's handgun, as another one was calling for multiple ambulances. Two state policemen headed down to Charlie's cabin to retrieve the child, while the others on-site handcuffed both prisoners and dragged them out of the cabin.

The first ambulance arrived and took the wounded prisoner, and the second one was right behind it. They took the wounded man from the living room floor, while the third ambulance arrived and began tending to the woman.

Charlie watched from a corner of the room as the woman began talking and mumbling as she came to.

"Ronnie…they hurt Ronnie. My little girl…my Shelby?"

A state police officer pulled Charlie aside.

"Sir, we need to see some ID."

Charlie pulled his wallet from his back pocket.

"I'm Charlie Dodge. This is my driver's license

and my private investigator's license. My military ID and my permit to carry."

"Whoa. This is enough," the officer said. "You're a PI?"

"Out of Dallas," Charlie said. "I was taking a break from the job and walked into this."

When he mentioned his name, a park ranger joined them.

"Are you the same Charlie Dodge who finds missing kids?"

"Yes, missing people in general," Charlie said.

"The same Charlie Dodge who just found that missing hiker in Big Bend National Park?"

Charlie nodded.

The ranger smiled and shook Charlie's hand. "It's a pleasure to meet you! Ranger Arnie Collins, who you worked with on that case, is my brother-in-law. He's stationed in the Chisos Mountains area, and he's still talking about that."

"Small world," Charlie said. "What happened to the man in the living room?"

"Head injury. Looks like blunt-force trauma of some kind."

Charlie pointed to the rifle he'd kicked out of the way.

"Maybe from that?"

They recovered the rifle and gave Charlie back his handgun. Charlie pocketed his weapon, and was walking out with some of the men when two officers came running back.

"The kid won't let us in the cabin. She's crying and thinks everyone is dead."

Charlie sighed. "Ahhh, dammit, I told her not to open the door for anyone but me or the police. And you two aren't wearing uniforms. She'll let me in, and if she doesn't, I have a key," Charlie said, and took off running toward his cabin while the officers got back in their cruiser.

Charlie was already back at the cabin and knocking on the door when they arrived.

"Hey, honey! It's me. Your mama said your name is Shelby. You can open the door now. These men are police."

Charlie heard the lock click, and then the door opened slowly inward.

"Mommy is alive?"

"Yes," Charlie said. "And the officers are going to take you to her, okay?"

She came out sobbing and walked into Charlie's outstretched arms.

"Is my daddy dead?"

"No, but they hurt his head and he's already at the hospital where they're taking your mommy."

The little girl put her arms around Charlie's neck, hiding her face against it.

"Are the bad men gone?"

"Yes, the bad men are gone," Charlie said.

She went limp in his arms. "You saved my life."

Charlie hugged her.

"You were a very brave girl. You saved yourself

when you ran. Now these officers are going to take care of you."

"Okay," Shelby said, and let go of him, then stopped. "I don't know your name."

"My name is Charlie Dodge."

There were tears on her face when she looked up at him unblinking.

"I will remember you forever."

The words were medicine, healing the raw and broken bits of Charlie in a way nothing else could have done. And then they were gone.

He took a slow, shaky breath, then paused on the porch to pick up the firewood he'd dropped and went back inside. He put another log on the fire and then locked the door. The warmth and silence after so much chaos was welcome, but it felt like his time here was over.

He went into the kitchen to make himself one more meal, and then sat down to watch television as he ate. The incident regarding the prisoners being captured and taken into custody was on the news, along with mention of the family who'd been taken hostage, but no mention of his part in it, thank God.

Twelve

Wyrick stopped work during the day to make a food run. She'd cooked all of the frozen pizzas she had on hand, and eaten all of the leftover Chinese food in the fridge. The peanut butter jar was empty and she was out of bread.

Merlin had food and groceries delivered, but she didn't want too many strangers knowing where she lived. After what had gone on with Darrell Boyington, she was gun-shy in a whole new way.

But she'd done all of the ordering online at Whole Foods, including some fully cooked meals requiring nothing but heat and eat. She grabbed her purse and a cold Pepsi, then put on a coat on her way out the door.

But as she drove away, her thoughts were on Charlie. She knew he was taking a much-needed break. There wasn't anything to be concerned about, and Charlie was a grown man. He had taken care of himself and Annie long before she knew him. But she needed him to be okay, so that she'd be okay, and that was her hard truth. Only this was the third day he'd been gone and she missed him.

The afternoon traffic on the freeway was heavy, but it felt good to be out of the apartment. She'd spent so much time at the computer that she didn't even mind the crazy drivers.

What was unsettling was knowing Cyrus Parks had tried to have her killed. It was a big game changer from trying to win her back, then trying to force her to come back.

The fact that she'd been able to shut down Universal Theorem worldwide had obviously scared him. Taking his money in the way she had would only be a temporary aggravation…and she didn't want him to think she'd kept it. She needed to find a project she knew he would hate, and donate all of that money in his name. Then figure out what kind of safeguard to put in place between them that would make him back off for good.

She could have taken care of all of this years ago, but it would have meant revealing her truth, and that would have turned her into a science project. There would have been people wanting to study her, and countries trying to buy her skills, and her existence would have been hell. The day Charlie Dodge hired her was the day she gained purpose again, and she didn't want to lose that.

But that was for another day. Right now she had food to pick up and a lost granddaughter to find.

Her order was ready when she got to Whole Foods, and the pickup went smoothly. She dug a Hershey bar from the groceries and took a big bite as she left, opting out of the freeway to drive through the city, taking backstreets and winding her way through neighborhoods to get back to Merlin's estate.

As soon as she got the car unloaded and everything put up, she put a chicken tortilla casserole in the oven to bake, set the timer and went back to check the latest search she'd been running. When she sat down at the computer and clicked on the screen, she instantly focused. The last search she'd been running had several hits, and there was one that stood out from all the rest.

If Katrina Delgado had even an inkling that her grandmother was looking for her, she would have been over the moon. She didn't remember anything about her birth family, and barely remembered her mother.

Her foster families had been good ones and bad ones, and when she aged out of the system at eighteen, she was on the streets of Philadelphia for a whole year before she made a friend who took her in, and then almost another year before she landed a steady job at a pancake house.

She was so grateful to have a job that she went out of her way to be the hardest-working, most accommodating waitress there. Six years later she still was. She caught a ride to work from a neighbor who dropped her off at the pancake house at 5:00 a.m. Then she rode a city bus home alone when her shift was over.

She hadn't had a boyfriend in two years. The last one went to jail for selling drugs, and she hadn't known he was doing it. Now she was afraid to trust anyone for fear whatever they were doing wrong would take her down, too.

It was nearing the end of her shift when she noticed it was starting to rain. Just great. It would be a wet walk to the bus stop, but it wasn't the first time and it wouldn't be the last.

She grabbed a coffeepot and stopped off at all her tables to top off the diners' cups. A half hour later she clocked out, and was all bundled up against the cold and the rain when Brenda, her boss, called out.

"Katrina! Wait!"

She turned around and saw Brenda running to her with an umbrella.

"You're going to need this," Brenda said.

Katrina smiled. "Thanks, Brenda! I'll bring it back in the morning."

"Keep it," she said. "I have another one."

"Much appreciated," Katrina said, and popped it open as soon as she got outside, then hurried toward the bus stop.

For once, the bus was on time and she didn't have to wait long in the rain. By the time she got home, she was cold and shivering.

First thing she did every day was change out of what she called her pancake clothes and throw them in the laundry. Then she slipped into warm sweats and thick socks, and made herself a cup of hot tea.

She was digging through the cabinet for honey to

stir in it when her cell phone rang. It was a number she didn't recognize, but it didn't matter. Nobody called her, so a wrong number might be the only call she would receive this week. She answered.

"Hello."

"Hello, may I speak to Katrina Delgado?"

"I'm Katrina."

"Katrina, my name is Wyrick. I'm working for a woman who is looking for a granddaughter she lost touch with. I need to ask you a few questions. Is that okay?"

Katrina's heart skipped a beat.

"Yes, I guess," she said.

"Was your mother killed in a car wreck when you were seven?" Wyrick asked.

"Yes. She and my new dad, Andy Delgado, both died."

"But your name was Sharp?"

"Yes, but I went by Delgado after my mom remarried," Katrina said.

Wyrick began going down the list of facts that she'd gathered, checking them off.

"And after their deaths, you were put into the foster care system?"

"Yes, in the state of Illinois. I live in Philadelphia now."

"Is your birthday June 4th, 1994?"

Katrina's heart was starting to pound.

"Yes, it is."

"And your mother's name was Vivian Ray Sharp?"

"Yes."

Wyrick sighed. "Katrina, your grandmother, Wanda Carrollton, has been looking for you."

"Oh my gosh!" Katrina said. "Is she my mother's mother?"

"No, she's your paternal grandmother. Your father was her only son. Are you interested in reconnecting with her?"

"Yes, oh yes. I don't have any family," Katrina said, and started crying. "Where does she live?"

"She lives in Dallas, Texas. It's where you were born, and where you lived until you were six."

Katrina was stunned. "I have no memory of any of that."

"May I give your grandmother your phone number so she can call you? My job was just to find you. However you two decide to begin a relationship or not is for you to decide."

"Yes, absolutely," Katrina said. "But tell her to call me in the evening after 6:00 p.m. I work from 5:00 a.m. to 3:00 p.m. at a pancake house, then ride a bus home. I don't get home until almost 4:00."

"Yes, I'll tell her," Wyrick said.

"What did you say her name was again?" Katrina asked.

"Wanda Carrollton."

"Wanda. Oh my God! I have a grandmother! I have family! Real family!" Katrina said. "Tell her to call. I'll be waiting, and thank you! Thank you for finding me!"

"You're welcome," Wyrick said, and disconnected.

The timer went off on her casserole. She jumped

up from her desk to take it out of the oven, but she was still riding the high from her success. This was the best feeling ever, and as soon as she set the casserole aside to cool, she called Wanda.

She was going to make two women happy tonight. Not a bad day's work, she thought, as she made the call.

When Wanda answered, Wyrick could hear the television blaring in the background.

"Hello?"

"Wanda, this is Wyrick, calling from Dodge Investigations. I have some news for you."

"Okay?"

"I found your granddaughter," Wyrick said, and then heard Wanda squeal.

"Oh Lord, oh Lord…bless you. Is she okay? Does she remember me? Does she want to meet me?"

"Yes, she's okay. She does want to meet you, and I have her phone number, so you can be the one to reach out to her. But she doesn't remember anything from her past. The reason you lost touch is that her mother remarried within a year of leaving. Then she and her husband were killed in a traffic accident. Katrina wound up in foster care and was never adopted."

"Oh no!" Wanda said, and then started to cry. "Where does she live?"

"Philadelphia." Then Wyrick gave Wanda the phone number and filled her in on the best times to call.

"I'm calling her the minute we hang up," Wanda said. "How do I pay the final bill?"

"Your retainer covers all of it. Consider yourself paid in full. I wish you and your granddaughter many happy years together."

"Thank you, Wyrick, thank you."

"Yes, ma'am. You're welcome," Wyrick said, and disconnected.

Katrina Delgado was still overjoyed from the earlier phone call, so when her phone rang again, she thought twice in one evening was nothing short of a miracle. When it occurred to her that it might be the long-lost grandmother, and then caller ID came up with another out-of-state number, she grabbed it.

"Hello, this is Katrina."

"Katrina, I'm Wanda Carrollton, your grandmother. I am so very, very happy that you answered my call."

Katrina dropped down onto the sofa with the phone pressed against her ear, listening to a voice from her past.

"I didn't know I had a grandmother…or any family at all. Thank you for looking for me," Katrina said.

Wanda sighed, thinking of all the time they'd lost. "And you are my only living family, too. We have a lot of years to make up for, if you're willing."

"Yes, ma'am. I am very willing," Katrina said.

"Not 'ma'am.' You called me Grammy when you were little."

Katrina was laughing through tears. "Then Grammy it is. I don't know where to start."

"Just talk to me, sugar," Wanda said. "It doesn't matter what you talk about. I just want to hear your voice."

Charlie went to bed thinking, after all of the chaos and drama, that he wouldn't sleep. He kept remembering the feel of the young girl's arms around his neck, and the intent look in her eyes when she told him she would never forget him.

Then he fell asleep to the sound of wind in the pines, and dreamed of Annie making pancakes for breakfast, and how she always sprinkled blueberries on the batter before she flipped them, and made smiley faces on his plate with the syrup.

He woke up sad, feeling lost and empty…like he would never laugh again, then packed up and left Robbers Cave.

There was no hesitation in his decision as he took the highway out of Wilburton, retracing his journey back to Interstate 35 that would take him home to Dallas. The one positive about what had happened at the park was proof that there was no escaping life. As long as you were breathing, you got whatever was on the agenda.

Tony Dawson was awake and talking. Today they were moving him from ICU into a private room, which meant his mom and dad would no longer be restricted by the visiting hours of ICU.

Macie had gone downtown in Odessa to get her hair done and pick up their laundry, but Baxter was on-site when the move was made. As soon as they got Tony situated in his room, Baxter went in.

Just knowing he and Macie could come and go at will now, and talk without concern of bothering others, was huge. They already knew Tony was aware of his so-called friends' deception for the trip, and that he remembered falling. He'd told them he had vague memories of crawling into a cave because he heard water. After that, he remembered nothing. They'd told him that the rangers couldn't find him, and that they'd hired a PI, who ultimately did find him. But Tony hadn't asked them a single question and they knew he had them.

"How are you with the pain, son?" Baxter asked.

"It's bearable," Tony said. "I'm so glad to have a window to see out of…and see sunshine. Where's Mom?"

"Downtown getting her hair done and picking up our laundry."

Tony glanced down at his leg…suspended in air with all the pins sticking out. His ribs were sore but healing, and it still hurt to take a deep breath. The staples in his head were healing enough that they were starting to pull and itch, and the bruising on his body was fading to faint purple and green. He couldn't help but wonder if he'd ever be whole again.

Then he looked up at his dad.

"I have questions, but I didn't want to ask before because…I think I was afraid of the answers."

Baxter nodded. "Ask away."

"How long did it take to find me?"

"Charlie found you on the fourth day," Baxter said.

"But why, Dad? Randall and Justin saw me fall. They could have led the rangers right to me."

"They lied to cover their asses. Their story, after they were found out, was that they thought you were dead and didn't want to get into trouble."

The shock on Tony's face was vivid, and then his eyes filled with tears. "Who does that shit?"

"Well, they did. Randall was jealous of you. He wanted to hurt you, and Justin went along."

Tony was silent for a few seconds, and then he asked, "Has Trish asked about me?"

Baxter reached for Tony's hand. "Son. That girl has worn out our phones checking on you. She refused to believe you were dead, and then when she found out what happened, completely blamed herself for all of it. She kept saying that if she had told you at the start that she and Randall had once dated, none of it would have happened. Whatever happens between you two is your business. But she told us that all she wanted was for you to be found alive, and that even if you hate her forever, it's okay, because her prayers for you were answered."

Tears were running down Tony's face.

"I didn't blame her then, and I don't blame her now, but that's what made Randall mad. That's why he swung at me."

"All I know is that I'm grateful to God that I don't have a son like him. He's got a bad streak in him."

"What happened to them?" Tony asked.

"They're in big trouble. Out on bail but facing federal charges, and it's up in the air as to whether they'll be tried as juveniles or adults."

Tony blinked. "Federal?"

"All of that happened on federal lands...and then they lied to the park rangers, who are federal employees, and the story goes on. They hid your backpack so it wouldn't be found, and I guess you crawling into that cave was what delayed finding you. They expected your body to be found right off, and when it wasn't, then they were caught up in their own lies."

"Oh my God. What are they going to think about me at school?" he mumbled.

Baxter smiled. "Nothing other than you are one tough dude to have survived what they did to you, and you have your girl to thank for that. We heard through the grapevine that she talked to the principal, who made an announcement at your school that you'd been found—and noted who was to blame for what happened. She wanted to make sure you didn't come back to any troubles."

Tony wiped the tears off his face. "She's awesome, Dad. Really awesome."

"Oh...that thing Justin said about her the night you guys had your fight... It was a lie. He admitted it to his parents and to the people we hired to find you."

Tony sighed. "I already knew it was a lie. I knew my heart...and I knew my girl."

Baxter patted his shoulder. "I'm proud of you, son."

Tony glanced at the time. "I guess Trish is in school right now."

"I don't think so. Macie said the rest of this week is parent-teacher conference."

"Could I talk to her, Dad?"

Baxter grinned. "Yes, and I suppose you want me to leave the room while you do?"

Tony grinned sheepishly. "Just give me a few minutes."

"You got it," Baxter said, then pulled up her number and made the call.

Trish Caldwell was in her room hanging up laundry. She had opted out of going to the mall with her friends, to stay home and help her mom by catching up on household chores.

When her phone rang and she saw who was calling, her heart sank. It was Baxter Dawson's number. Her hands were shaking as she answered, and all she could think was *Please don't let this be bad news*.

"Hello?"

"Good morning, Trish. Baxter Dawson here. I have someone who wants to talk to you. Hang on a minute."

Before Trish could think, Tony's voice was in her ear.

"Hey, you," he said.

"Tony! Oh my God… Tony!" she said, and burst into tears.

At that point, Baxter walked out of the room.

"Don't cry, honey. Please don't cry."

"I'm sorry. I'm so sorry. It's all my fault," Trish kept saying. "I should have—"

"Stop," Tony said. "I'm going to run out of energy fast, so just listen. I don't blame you for anything. None of that shit was your fault, and I never believed what Justin said. That's what made them mad. Because what they planned didn't work. You and I are fine…if you still want it, I mean. I'm pretty beat up, and I may walk with a limp for the rest of my life, but I will be walking, and I still have two arms to hug you. I love you, Trish, and if that's enough for you, then you're enough for me."

Trish was laughing now, and sobbing. "Yes, yes, always…you'll always be enough. I thought I'd lost you, and then they found you, and that was enough. I love you, too, Tony Dawson. I can't wait to see you again."

Wyrick was watching news coverage on an update about the devastation caused by Hurricane Dorian to the northern part of the Grand Bahama and the Abaco chain. There were places that had been completely leveled to the point that they were no longer inhabitable.

And that was when it hit her.

This was what she could do with Cyrus's money. Charity was beyond him…even beneath him, and it was going to piss him off royally to know that was what she'd done with it. It would probably agitate their situation again, but she didn't care. He wouldn't leave her alone, so she felt no compunction in striking back where it hurt.

She was also working on a new file she called FAILSAFE that was going to stop all of this shit. Everything she had, everything she knew and every piece of data she'd ever collected while working for Universal Theorem was going in it, including all of the genetic experiments they had in process worldwide, even videos of some of it, along with proof of their presence within the world of human trafficking, aka the Fourth Dimension, that she and Charlie had helped take down.

She was in the process of writing up a dossier about herself, telling how she was created, how many failures they had before her and what they did to her mother. How she cured herself of cancer, how they hounded her then, wanting her back. She was including names of all the men they'd hired to tail her, then stalk her. And then she named Cyrus Parks as the man who'd hired Darrell Boyington to kill her, which also pointed a finger at Parks as the person who took Boyington out when he failed. It would be up to the law to prove it, but it would also give Cyrus Parks way more to think about besides her.

And the more she worked on this, the more she understood Cyrus's desire to kill her. She was living proof of every illegal thing they'd ever done, and once they lost control of her, she became a threat. Outing UT would end the privacy she enjoyed, but if she didn't, they were going to end her life. It was going to be one hell of a trade-off, but there was no longer a way to hide behind it in safety.

Thirteen

The moment Charlie Dodge crossed the state line from Oklahoma into Texas, it felt right. Shit or no shit, he belonged here. He stopped at Gainesville to refuel, and grabbed a cold drink and some chips before leaving the mini-mart, then ate as he drove, licking salt from his fingers until the bag was empty, and the hollow feeling in his belly was gone.

When he finally reached the outskirts of Dallas, he merged onto the freeway and headed toward his apartment building. As he did, he thought of calling Wyrick, then didn't. There wasn't anything to say, and he'd text her later and let her know he was back.

He was almost home when he got a text from Baxter Dawson, letting him know that Tony was out of ICU and healing well. They thanked him again for giving them back their son.

As soon as he pulled up into the parking garage attached to his apartment building, he returned the text with well-wishes for all of them.

For Charlie, that case was over and done. He grabbed his bag and got out, then entered the building and headed for his apartment.

The modern amenities of his home were a stark contrast to the old rock cabin he'd been staying in, and it felt good to be back in familiar territory. Maybe getting away hadn't been a bad idea after all. He might be missing that wood-burning fireplace a little, but his gas fireplace took a chill off a room just as well, and with less fuss and mess.

As soon as he flipped the On switch and got instant flames, he took his bag to the bedroom. As always, the first thing that came off when he got home were his shoes. After that, he changed into sweats and went to the kitchen in his sock feet to check out the contents of his fridge. Unwilling to settle for half a stick of butter and three bottles of beer for dinner, he picked up his phone and ordered in.

Today he'd make a shopping list.

Tomorrow he'd fill it.

But for now, he was having pizza.

Merlin had a doctor's appointment and was dressed and ready to leave. But he was starting to realize he wasn't strong enough to drive himself there. It was the first time this had happened, and it made him a little sad. As much as he thought he had faced his truth, this was unsettling.

He thought about asking Wyrick, but this was short notice. And the longer he sat, the worse he felt. Even if someone else took him, he wasn't certain he'd be able to get through the appointment and home without a wheelchair. So, he made an executive decision on his behalf, called the doctor's office and told them what was happening. Within minutes, he was on the phone with the doctor's nurse.

"Mr. Merlin, Dr. Willis will need to examine you to see what we need to do next."

"Then I'll need an ambulance to get me there. I will not spend my last days in hospital. I have private twenty-four-hour nursing already in place when the need arises, and I am signed up for hospice care when the time comes, too. So if this is the time, then I need to let them know."

"Let me talk to Dr. Willis about this. Are you okay to be alone right now? If you think you're not, then call an ambulance and get yourself to ER."

"I think I'll call the ambulance," Merlin said. "One way or another, I need to know if this is me on the downhill slide."

"I'm sorry this is happening," she said. "I'll let Dr. Willis know. He'll be in contact with ER to get your test results."

"Thank you," Merlin said. Then as soon as he hung up, he called 911 and asked for an ambulance to be dispatched to his address, then called Wyrick, knowing she'd be freaking out when the ambulance arrived if he didn't let her know.

Wyrick was in cleaning mode. She'd already dusted and vacuumed, and had just finished mopping the kitchen and bathroom when her cell phone rang. She hung the mop up to dry and then wiped her hands on her jeans before answering.

"Good morning, Merlin."

"Good morning, Wyrick. I wanted to give you a heads-up that I've called an ambulance, so don't freak out when you see it coming."

Her heart sank. "What's wrong?"

"Today is a bad day, and I have a doctor's appointment. So I'm going in to ER instead of his office. I'll be back. I'm just not up to driving myself."

Wyrick was sad. She'd known it would happen, but she hadn't expected it to happen like this.

"I can take you," she said.

"I know, dear. But I'm pretty weak today, and I don't think I'd be able to walk anywhere, and neither one of us has a wheelchair."

Wyrick took a slow, shaky breath. "Well, dammit."

He laughed. "That's pretty much what I thought. Don't worry. Please. I need you not to fight the inevitable, because I'm not."

She was blinking back tears now. "Yes, yes, I get it. I promise. Is it time to call your nursing service?"

"Yes, I think so. I can call them from ER if I deem it necessary."

"Okay, but I'm coming up anyway. Where are you?"

"I'm in the den," Merlin said.

"I'll be right there," she said.

"And I thank you for the help."

She dropped the phone in her pocket, put on some

shoes and headed up the stairs on the run. Finding him in the den was easy. But looking at him without registering the shock she felt? Not so much.

"It's cold out and that jacket isn't enough. Where would I find a heavier coat?"

"Is it really? I have a coat in the front hall closet. It's camel-colored."

She turned and left the den, found the coat and came back just as fast.

Merlin had taken his jacket off, and once again, Wyrick was left having to hide her reaction to how thin he'd become. She helped him on with the coat and then sat down beside him.

"I have the number to the private nursing people, don't I?"

He chuckled. "It's probably somewhere in all that crap Rodney gave you."

"I'll find it. As soon as you leave, I'm calling them. I'll have someone here before the end of the day," she said.

"It may take them a little longer than that to set up a schedule, so don't expect—"

"If they can't make it happen, I'll find interim help until they can. I don't want to go to bed tonight worrying if you're going to face-plant while I'm asleep."

He chuckled. "Face-plant. Jade, my dear, your bedside manner is missing a little delicacy."

"There isn't a delicate bone in my body and you know it," Wyrick muttered. "And don't expect me to apologize for it, either."

Merlin laughed out loud. "God, you are good for what ails me," he said. "While you're organizing my world today, don't forget to feed yourself."

She frowned. "Are you insinuating that I'm skinny?"

"I don't insinuate. I state facts."

She shrugged. "I've been busy."

"You've been worrying…about me…and about your boss. And there's that bit about someone trying to kill you, too. I hope you're dealing with that."

"Yes, Merlin, I'm dealing with that."

"Just watch your back. You are your own miracle. You deserve to be happy."

"I refuse to cry, so don't try being nice to me," Wyrick said.

Merlin laughed again.

"I hear the ambulance," Wyrick said. "Stay where you are. I'll bring them back to you."

"Thank you," he said, then leaned back and closed his eyes against the wave of nausea sweeping through him.

Wyrick hurried through the house, and was at the front door when the EMTs came up the steps.

"In here," she said, and swung the door inward.

They entered, pushing a gurney, and followed her through the grand hall to the den.

It was obvious how weak Merlin was when they helped him to his feet, and then they covered him over and strapped him on before taking him out.

Wyrick watched until he was safely inside and the ambulance was gone. Then she locked the house up and went back downstairs to look for info on the nursing situation. When she found what she needed, she made two calls. One to hospice, and one to his private nursing company.

"Can you get someone here by this evening?" Wyrick asked.

"Yes. Mr. Merlin notified us far enough in advance that we've had a tentative schedule in place. I'll have to juggle a couple of nurses to get one there this soon, but after we get the schedule ironed out, he will have regulars."

"And they understand that I will be overseeing his care?" Wyrick said.

"Yes, ma'am. We have all of his instructions and wishes, and they're very clear. All you'll have to do is introduce yourself and give them your contact information. You won't be responsible for any of his medical care. Our nurses will follow his doctor's directives."

"But I will be in and out, to satisfy myself that his care is top-notch and he is comfortable. I promised him I would do that, so that understanding is paramount," Wyrick said.

"Yes, ma'am. Of course. Don't worry. Just let us know if they're bringing him back to his home or if they hospitalized him temporarily."

"I will," Wyrick said, and disconnected.

She'd done all she knew to do for him, but she was still a little anxious. The only other person she felt responsible for was Charlie. In her mind, keeping him safe and in one piece was part of her job. Now there was Merlin, needing care on a level she could not provide. But she would be there to make sure the people who did know how to care for him did it right.

About four hours later, Wyrick was in the main house when the ambulance brought Merlin back. She had a wheelchair waiting. He was weak and nauseated from the pain meds they'd given him, and as soon as they got him situated, they were gone.

"Your nurse is on the way," Wyrick said.

"Thank you," Merlin said. "I had an infusion while I was there and I'm feeling pretty shaky."

"When I was doing chemo, sometimes meds on an empty stomach made me sick. Have you eaten anything today?" Wyrick asked.

"A cup of coffee this morning. I was too shaky for making food."

"How about a little soup?" Wyrick asked.

"I don't want you cooking for me," Merlin said.

"I don't cook for anyone, but for you, I'll open a can of soup."

Merlin chuckled. "You are good for me. Open the soup."

"Because I like you, I will also heat it," Wyrick said, and wheeled him into the kitchen with her.

She'd already looked through his pantry while he was gone, and knew the soups were there, so she chose noodle soup, put it in a bowl and heated it in the microwave, then rolled him to the kitchen table.

But when she put the soup in front of him, his hands were shaking too much to get the soup into his mouth.

"May I?" she asked, and took the spoon out of his hands and fed him.

By then, he was too weak to argue and let her spoon little bites into his mouth until he was full, then cried when she wiped a drip of soup from his chin.

"Dammit, I'm sorry. I hate being helpless," he said.

"Don't ever apologize to me again," Wyrick snapped. "You didn't ask for this. Nobody asks for this shit. I am doing this because I know exactly how you're feeling, and because someone once did this for me."

Merlin sighed. "Then thank you. Can I ask you something?"

"Ask away."

"How long did you do chemo before you were cured?"

Wyrick took a deep breath and then turned and faced him.

"They didn't cure me. They told Cyrus Parks they'd done all they could for me. The fiancé I had said he didn't want to watch me die and dumped me, and Parks considered me a failure because of some defect they had not detected in my DNA, and let me go."

The shock on Merlin's face was telling.

"Dear God. Monsters," he muttered. Then it hit him. "But wait! Then how are you still here?"

"I healed myself. I think it was rage at what they'd done that triggered something within me. I don't know the full range of my capabilities. All I know is every so often, something new turns on inside of me and I just know stuff. Or I can do things I couldn't do before. I guess I'm the ultimate time-release capsule in human form. Charlie knows some of this, and now so do you."

Merlin sighed. "Well, I'm dying, so your secret is safe with me."

Wyrick threw a dish towel at him, which made him laugh.

"That soup perked you right up, didn't it?" she said. "Just for that, you're going to your room."

Suddenly serious, he nodded. "I could do with a nap."

Wyrick pushed him through the house and down the main hall to his room, made sure he got himself safely onto the bed, and then pulled off his shoes and covered him with a blanket.

"Where's your phone?" she asked.

"Here," he said, and pulled it out of a pocket.

She put it beside his bed. "Sleep well. Your nurse should be here soon."

As soon as he closed his eyes, she left.

An hour later, his nurse arrived with an overnight bag. Her name was Ora Jones, a sweet forty-something woman with a soft voice, and the bluest eyes Wyrick had ever seen. She brought a little cold air and so much confidence into the house that Wyrick finally relaxed.

"You must be Wyrick," Ora said. "Just call me Ora. If you'll show me where Mr. Merlin's room is, and leave me your contact info, then I can officially relieve you of worries."

"All of my contact info is on a pad in the kitchen, but my apartment is just downstairs, so if you need help quickly, just call or text, and I'll come running."

"Thank you," Ora said.

"Follow me, and I'll introduce you to Merlin," Wyrick said, and then took her through the house, pointing out features and rooms as she went, until they were in another wing.

"This house is huge," Ora said.

Wyrick nodded, then pointed. "This is Merlin's room." She pushed the door inward without knocking. He was still in bed, but he was reading.

"Merlin, your nurse is here."

He smiled, then put down his book as they approached.

"Ora, this is Merlin. Merlin…this is Ora. I'll be downstairs if anyone needs me."

"We'll be fine," Ora said.

Wyrick glanced at Merlin. "Do you need me to bring you anything?"

"Next time you get a chance, I have a taste for some of my tomatoes."

"I'll get you some," Wyrick said.

"Thank you, darling," Merlin said. "Now go make your magic happen and find another lost soul."

Wyrick took a deep breath and left the room, then went out the back door of the kitchen with a small bowl and straight to the greenhouse.

The air was cold, so she ran all the way, welcoming the warmth and the earthy scents of all things growing as she walked into the greenhouse and shut the door. She paused a moment to orient herself again, then headed for the tomato plants at the back, loaded with tiny green and red tomatoes.

She picked the bowl full, checked the watering system to make sure the timer was on, then ran back to the house and left the tomatoes on the cabinet.

Once she was back in her apartment, she pulled up the tracking app she had on Charlie's phone. When she realized he was back in Dallas, she breathed a quiet sigh of relief. For the moment, the two men in her life were in their homes, and that was as safe as she could keep them.

Next thing on her agenda was tying a tighter knot in Cyrus's tail, so she headed to her computer. She had everything ready to go, including a press release. It would be acknowledging Cyrus Parks, the director of Universal Theorem, making a personal donation of forty million dollars toward the rebuilding of the Grand Bahama and the Abaco chain after the devastation of Hurricane Dorian.

She'd already hacked into Cyrus's personal computer system so that everything she was about to do would appear to have come from his IP address. Then she wired the money she'd moved from his personal accounts into the specific charities involved in rebuilding, knowing they would show up as donations in his name, and then sent the press releases to every major news outlet.

This was going to accomplish two things.

The first, a reminder to him that she could cripple him in a heartbeat with a few clicks on a keyboard.

But the other aspect of this publicity would become a safety factor for her.

Cyrus Parks's name and face were known only in certain circles for a reason. The more powerful people were, the less they wanted to be known. Now the world was going to know the name, which would generate all kinds of research and poking into his life in a way he was going to hate…and make it far more difficult to put out another hit on her when the world was watching.

He was a cold, heartless bastard, and she wasn't going to waste a moment of guilt on him. For a man who'd devoted his entire career to trying to create a new race of humans, he had no regard for human life as it existed.

Now that she'd enacted her own retribution for trying to kill her, she shifted focus back to Dodge Investigations, updating the file she'd made on Wanda Carrollton's missing granddaughter, then updating the file on Tony Dawson. Once she was finished, she closed them.

After that, there were dozens of new messages to go through, and phone calls to return that had been left on their voice mail. It was business as usual.

It took less than twenty-four hours for Cyrus's "donations" to make the news, but he wasn't aware of it until he got a phone call at work. His secretary buzzed him on the intercom.

"Mr. Parks, there is a call for you on line one. It's a reporter from the *New York Times*."

Cyrus frowned. "Thank you," he said, and took the call.

"This is Cyrus Parks."

"Mr. Parks! I'm Ed Warner, a reporter for the *Times*. We want to interview you regarding your generous donation to rebuilding on the Grand Bahama and Abaco after Hurricane Dorian. What prompted you to donate so much money? Forty million dollars is an amazing amount. Do you have personal connections there? Or was it a favorite holiday retreat for you?"

Cyrus gasped. Forty million dollars? And then it hit him! That was what Wyrick did with his money. *She gave it away. To a bunch of nobodies.*

"I have nothing to say," he said, and hung up.

Within seconds, his secretary was buzzing him again.

"Mr. Parks, there are dozens of calls coming in from media. Some of it worldwide."

"Tell all of them I'm not making any statements or granting any interviews."

"Yes, sir," she said.

Cyrus lurched from his chair and strode to the windows. The leaves were beautiful in Richmond this time of year—a veritable color wheel of reds and golds, with patches of evergreens throughout. He should have been thinking of roaring fires and mulled wine, of hot chocolate in his mother's kitchen on a cold day. Instead, he was still picking at the sore Jade Wyrick was on his ass.

He knew after the three-day shutdown that she was dangerous. And then finding out she'd been a part of shutting down Fourth Dimension had been the last straw. He hadn't said a word to anyone at UT about that, but there was only one person on earth who could have taken down the security that was in place there, and that was the person who'd built it. Then when he found out Charlie Dodge was involved, he knew she'd been there.

He accepted his part in why she shunned them now, but her existence was a threat to his life's work. At first, she had cheated death, and he wanted to know how. But that desire had long since passed. Now she was that thing he'd left undone.

He watched a single red leaf come loose from a branch, then float toward the ground. When it finally landed, he sighed. Having witnessed the death of something beautiful, he was uncertain of how many more seasons he would see. It made him nostalgic for his youth all over again.

He could hear the phones ringing in the outer office. His poor secretary. Maybe hiring a hit man hadn't been the best idea, but he couldn't figure out how Wyrick knew what he was before he'd even made an attempt. Something else had to be going on with her now. It was almost as if she was psychic.

And then it hit him. One of the DNA donors they'd

used in the experimental lot from which she'd come was a psychic.

Crap. What was she turning into next?

He already knew she was a mathematical whiz, and a tech genius, and her scientific understanding of everything was beyond human comprehension. She healed herself of cancer. And if she also attained psychic skills, it would explain how she'd outed Boyington.

"Why do we yearn to create that which will destroy us?" he muttered, then picked up the coffee cup on his desk and threw it across the room.

It shattered against the wall, leaving coffee splatter on the wallpaper and shards of pottery all over the floor.

His secretary heard the noise and came running.

"Mr. Parks! Are you okay?" she asked, staring at the mess in disbelief.

"No, I am not. Get the janitorial service in to clean this up. I'll be out for the rest of the day, and I am unavailable. Period."

"Yes, sir," she said, and hurried away.

Cyrus took a back exit out of the building and headed home. Just thinking of all the power brokers who kept UT's donations healthy made him anxious. They weren't the kind of people who bought into the "it's the thought that counts" mindset. They gave money to make it back many times over. Even if it was his personal money, they would not be impressed.

At first, he didn't know how he was going to sell

this, and then it hit him. The men he'd been dining with when his money first disappeared knew he'd been hacked. If he could make them believe it was the hackers who'd done this, too, then the rest of this would all blow over.

Except for Wyrick, who wasn't going to go away.

Charlie sent Wyrick a text the next morning and got an instant reply.

I'm back in town.

I know.

Fine, but since I'm not tracking you like a lost dog, are you okay, and are you still working from home?

Yes, and yes. Found a missing granddaughter for a client via internet. Case closed. Merlin is failing. 24-hour nursing at his home and Hospice involved. I am his heir. As if I wasn't rich enough already. Life is a joke on all of us.

Charlie read between the lines of her text. Maybe because he'd just lived it, he saw the fear and sadness, but he couldn't empathize. She would slit his throat before she'd let him say he was sorry for her in any way.

No more trouble from daddy dearest?

He just donated 40 million dollars to survivors of Hurricane Dorian. A real bighearted guy.

Charlie blinked. A forty-million-dollar hit for siccing a hit man on her? He couldn't help but grin. Damn, but he did like the way Wyrick rolled.

Fourteen

Three days later

It was late afternoon when Charlie left Dallas with Annie's ashes. She hadn't ridden in the car with him since the day he moved her into Morning Light, and this ride was going to be their last. He glanced at the box in the passenger seat and then back at the highway, blinking back tears.

"So, lady…why do I feel like you're really here? Maybe because the best part of you came along for the ride?"

He wasn't expecting an answer, so he wasn't disappointed by the silence. Instead, he turned on Sirius XM to the Willie Nelson channel and caught the end of "Seven Spanish Angels."

"Ah…missed one of your favorites, honey. But it doesn't matter now, does it? You're a real angel now, even though you were always mine. Oh hey, here comes my favorite…'You Were Always on My

Mind'…and that's the truth, Annie. No matter where I was, or what I was doing, you were always on my mind. I don't know how the hell to function without you. Even when you forgot me, then forgot you, I remembered us. I don't want this to be over, but it already is, isn't it? I'm the one who's still struggling."

And so he and Annie drove for two and a half hours to Lake Texoma, with Willie singing background. After he reached the lake, he wound around it to the turn leading to "their" rental cabin down by the water. He had a sack of groceries in the back seat, and Annie riding shotgun— just like they'd done so many times before.

He pulled up at the cabin just in time to watch the sunset, then got Annie and the groceries and went inside. He set everything on the kitchen table and turned up the thermostat.

"Damn, but it's cold in here. I'll get a fire going before we roast the wieners and marshmallows. Remember the last time we were here? We came to have a little cookout, only it was July and pouring rain. Remember that fire we built in here? It was the middle of the summer, and despite the rain, I have never been so hot or had as much fun in my life."

He talked as he worked, because the silence was painful, and when the wood finally caught and the logs began to burn, he went back to the kitchen.

"Gonna be a full moon tonight, Annie…and no rain predicted."

He found the roasting forks in a cabinet, and put three wieners on one and carried it to the fireplace.

The fire crackled as he put the fork into the flames, and soon the fat from the meat began dripping into the blaze, smoking it as it roasted. When the wieners were all blackened on one side and dripping on the other, he pulled them out.

"Looks about right to me," Charlie said, and carried it back to the kitchen and made himself three hot dogs with mustard. He popped the cap off a bottle of beer, and carried it all back to the fire, then sat and ate in silence.

Another hour passed until the beer was gone and the hot dogs eaten. At that point, he got up and went back for marshmallows. He put as many as he could get on another roasting fork and then held them into the flames, turning them as he did until they were brown and toasty, on the verge of turning black.

"Just like you like them," Charlie said, and pulled them out of the fire, then carried them and Annie outside onto the porch.

He set the box with her ashes down beside him, then, one by one, pulled the marshmallows off and ate while watching night come to the lake.

It was too cold to hear frogs or crickets, but the night birds were out. The hoot from an owl sent something small and furry scurrying into the underbrush nearby, and the silhouette of a loon floating majestically in the path of moonlight was otherworldly.

Charlie popped the last marshmallow into his mouth, then licked his fingers.

The moon looked blue, just like Charlie felt, but

putting this off wasn't going to make it easier, so he wiped his hands on his jeans, then looked down at the box.

"Let's do this, baby. Our last hurrah."

He picked it up, and as he started walking toward the shore, he began hearing the gentle lap of water against the rocks.

He stopped at the edge and looked up, gazing into the moonlight and to the billions of stars above him, holding Annie in his arms.

He stood within the silence until the view before him blurred from welling tears. Then, swallowing past the lump in his throat, he took the lid off the box.

"Always in my heart…always on my mind," he said, and flung the ashes out across the water in an arc.

Some of them caught on the wind—some seemed suspended in midair, as if they'd just performed a delicate jeté—and then they were gone.

Charlie had done the impossible.

He'd finally let her go.

Charlie locked up the cabin and left for Dallas before sunup, and the farther he drove, the lighter he felt. The sadness was still there, but that heavy weight in his chest was gone.

One day, one thing, one step at a time.

He smelled like smoke, or he would have gone to the office just because he didn't want to be home. He wasn't quite ready to jump back into the world of lost people, but he needed something besides himself on which to focus.

So he went home and cleaned up, then drove to work.

It was the first time he'd ever been there without Wyrick, and opening up and turning on lights as he went made him realize how much her presence there meant.

The computers were off. The coffee wasn't made, and there were no sugar-crunch bear claws under the glass dome in the coffee bar—and no bossy woman at the front desk telling him what to do.

He strode into his office, hung his Stetson on the hat rack and his coat in the closet, then popped a little pod of coffee in the coffee maker to make himself a cup.

While it was brewing, he turned on his computer and went straight to personal email. There were over four hundred messages to wade through, so he went to get his coffee, then settled in, going through them one by one until he was done.

By then it was midafternoon and his belly was rumbling. He shut everything down and walked out, locking the door behind him. Just like he used to do before Wyrick came to work for him.

She had been the game changer. He could never have solved the cases he'd solved later without her. She was a royal pain in the ass to deal with, but she was his royal pain.

He stopped at a steak house on his way home and ate an early dinner. By the time he got back to his apartment, he felt better. Today had been productive and his belly was full of beef. It was enough.

Cyrus Parks was still battling the media's curiosity. By his not giving any kind of interview, or making any public statement, the media was creating their own version of the truth, using various photos of him taken throughout his life, and writing stories with vague hints of who he was, and what Universal Theorem was about, and assumptions of his wealth.

He was pissed, and some of the shadow figures in his organization had backed off from him, because they did not want to be dragged into the publicity of his existence.

And, if that wasn't bad enough, two agents from the FBI showed up at his home. He was horrified to find out that his name had been mentioned as the man who'd put out the hit on Wyrick, and they were investigating him in a possible connection to Darrell Boyingon's murder.

"Gentlemen, I can assure you, I have no connection to some hit man's demise," Cyrus said.

"But you have a connection to Jade Wyrick. She used to work for Universal Theorem."

"Well, yes, I know her. But she was let go after she became ill from cancer. She hasn't worked for UT for years. I have no idea where she's even at."

"Well, we know that's not true, because during the statement she gave when she filed charges against Boyington for stalking her, she mentioned the names of a couple of private investigators in Dallas who you had hired in the past to keep tabs on her. We have spoken to them, and they corroborated her statement."

Cyrus's chin came up. "Do I need to call my lawyer? Am I under arrest for something?"

"No, sir, but we may have further questions."

"Not without my lawyer present we won't. We're through here," he said, and rang for his housekeeper. "Ruthie, these gentlemen are leaving now. Will you please see them out?"

"Yes, sir," she said. "This way, please."

As soon as they were gone, Cyrus called his lawyer. His life was spinning out of control and he didn't know how to stop it. Mistakes had been made. Big ones. There had to be a way to rein this in.

Wyrick hadn't heard a thing or sensed even the slightest disturbance from Cyrus Parks since she'd dropped her bombshell on him. But she knew he was likely being inundated by the media from the number of times he was showing up in the tabloids.

She didn't care how uncomfortable she'd made him. It was nothing compared to what he'd done to her, and she had more important things upon which to focus, like her friend who was upstairs, dying.

Even though Merlin had given her carte blanche to move up into the main house whenever she wanted and do whatever she wanted to do to it, she wasn't about to disturb him. She wanted him to see what was his, in the places that he wanted it, for all the days he had left.

The cleaning service kept it spotless, and the nurses who came and went kept Merlin as comfortable as possible.

As for her, she spent evenings with him after his dinner. And on the days that he felt like it, playing cards in his bedroom—usually poker—and beating him every time because she could.

Merlin loved it.

"Wow. No pity for a dying man here," he said when she laid down a royal flush.

Her eyes narrowed as she leaned across the table to rake in the chips.

"Money won't get you into heaven, so don't expect me to feel sorry for you. If you hadn't been watching that nurse's backside as she walked out of the room, you wouldn't have lost count of the cards."

Ignoring the fact that she'd alluded to his sexual interest in a woman's backside, he rubbed a hand over his rapidly thinning hair.

"Are you insinuating that I count cards?" he asked.

"I insinuate nothing, Arthur Merlin, and you know it."

Merlin threw back his head and laughed, then stopped and thumped his chest when he started to wheeze.

"Ah, God, don't make me laugh. I can't breathe and laugh at the same time anymore, and I do not want to die on a losing hand."

"Then beat me," she said.

He shook his head and tossed in the cards he was holding.

"You are unbeatable, unabashed, unconcerned and unforgivably brilliant, and if I have to lose to someone, I pick you," he said.

"Thank you," she said. She kept picking up the cards and then stacked them into a neat pile, putting them back in the box. "It's past your bedtime, and there's no need playing another hand tonight and watching you lose. I'll bring the Old Maid cards up tomorrow. Maybe you can beat me at that."

Merlin grinned.

"Sleep well," Wyrick said, and then leaned over and kissed his forehead.

"Bring me some more tomatoes!" he said.

"That's something you can do better than me," Wyrick said. "I've never grown anything successfully."

"Have you tried?" he asked.

She paused, then shrugged. "No."

"Then you don't know what you can do until you've tried," he said.

"Is that fatherly advice?" she asked.

"No. Dr. Phil," Merlin said.

Wyrick walked out laughing.

Merlin swung his legs back up on the bed and stretched out, smiling to himself. He could count the number of times he'd heard her laugh like that on one hand. It was satisfying to know he'd been the cause of it.

"He's all yours," Wyrick said as she walked through the kitchen, where Ora was making a cup of tea.

"I heard you both laughing. Laughter is good medicine," she said.

"It won't cure Merlin," Wyrick said.

Ora paused. "Honey, I've been doing this kind of work for a really long time, and there's one thing I've learned. When it's our time, it's our time. My job is to make every day count for them in whatever way they need. After that, the rest is up to them and God."

Wyrick felt the words like a caress. No one had ever said anything to her quite like it, and it made her wonder about her own healing in a whole new way.

"Thank you," she said. "I'm going to my apartment now, and I'll be going back to the office in the morning. So if you need to contact me through the day, just call or text."

"I will do that," Ora said. "Sleep well, honey. We've got Merlin's best interests at heart, always."

"I know that," Wyrick said. "But I'm still just a call away."

Her steps were slow as she went downstairs. She wrote a note to herself to get some tomatoes for Merlin before she left for work tomorrow, and then she sent a text to Charlie.

Done hiding. Opening up the office tomorrow. You do you.

It was that kind of night for Charlie—kicked back in his recliner watching football and eating tacos, happy with the moment. Then his phone signaled a text.

He read it and frowned. Damn woman. She was going to make him get back in the swing of things. If he left her on her own and Cyrus Parks tried something new, then he would have to live with the guilt of not being there to help. But going back meant peopling again. And putting up with her bossy ways.

He took another bite and chewed, thinking of the plus side.

Sugar-glazed bear claws.

Her coffee was better than his.

And he didn't have to take a case that he didn't have a feel for.

So, instead of telling her what he was going to do, he just sent her a thumbs-up emoji and went back to his tacos and the game.

No way would he ever leave her on her own. He could never do enough to repay her for how it felt when he'd walked out of Morning Light the morning Annie died and seen her leaning against his Jeep. She gave *backup* a whole new meaning.

Wyrick set the alarm for thirty minutes earlier than usual to go get Merlin his tomatoes, so when it went off the next morning, she sat straight up in bed, wondering why the hell she was awake before daylight.

"Oh. Tomatoes," she muttered, and jumped out of bed.

A few minutes later she was running across the grounds toward the greenhouse with a little plastic bowl, her tennis shoes untied and her bathrobe belted against the cold.

"Crap on a stick, but it's cold," she muttered, as she reached the greenhouse and then slipped inside.

The grow lights cast shadows that weren't obvious in daylight, shadows that took on the shapes of skeletal arms and legs. Shadows with no heads and only bodies. Basically, creepy as hell.

"Okay…tomatoes, tomatoes, tomatoes," she said, and headed for the back.

It didn't take long to fill the box with the tiny cherry-red globes, and as soon as she was finished, she headed for the door. It was an eye-opening experience for Wyrick to find out she could be spooked like this, and by the time she left the greenhouse, she was running.

She took the tomatoes up to the kitchen and left them on the counter, then went back down to get ready for work. She hadn't been to the office in days and days, and felt like making a statement.

After a quick scan of her closet, she chose glitter-gold lamé pants, a red V-neck sweater and a white leather blazer. Her white leather half boots had gold metal tips and taps on the heels. An attention getter she didn't really need. No matter what she was wearing, wherever she went, she was noticed. On anyone else, adding glitter-gold eye shadow and fire-engine-red lipstick would have been overkill, but on Wyrick, it worked.

She already had everything bagged up and ready

to take back to the office. All she had to do was stop on the way and get bear claws. Just in case.

Charlie got up with the sun and turned up the thermostat on his way to make coffee, then headed for the bathroom to shower and shave.

It felt like a normal day as he got dressed. And when he settled his Stetson on his head as he headed out the door, he was ready for Wyrick and whatever else the day might bring. The traffic that usually pissed him off just made the day feel normal, and he needed that.

When he got to the office and pressed the button in the elevator to go to the office, his pulse amped up just a little, like it always did before he used to go out on patrol. Maybe this was a sign that he was ready for this after all.

He smelled coffee in the hall outside the door and sighed—his home away from home—then walked in.

Wyrick didn't bother to look up, and as usual, her fingers were flying over the keyboard.

"Cinnamon roast coffee. Bear claws. Messages on your desk."

"Good morning to you, too," he said.

"Don't push it," she muttered.

He sighed. Yes…he could do this shit.

He walked past her desk, grabbed a cup of coffee and a bear claw in the coffee bar and then put them on his desk, before hanging up his hat and coat.

Wyrick closed her eyes and took a deep breath.

Charlie Dodge is back. Today, she would ask for nothing more, and went back to sorting through emails.

A half cup of coffee and a bear claw in his belly later, he began going through the messages, and the day began.

Cyrus Parks had given the phrase *lying low* a whole new meaning. He took a brief leave of absence from his office in Richmond, but only after he had convinced his associates that the big charity donation in his name had been done by the same hackers who'd recently drained his personal bank accounts.

That satisfied them, but Cyrus was far from satisfied. He had a job to finish, and needed time and information. He realized now that his big mistake had been just assigning one man to follow her. One man to harass her. One man to take her out.

What he needed was a tag team to trace her every step until he found the weak spot in her routine. That would be the opportunity he needed to end her existence for good.

One week later

It was just after 2:00 p.m. when Wyrick got a text from Ora and wasted no time in responding.

If you want to say goodbye to Merlin, come home.

On my way.

Even as she was getting up from her desk to tell Charlie she was leaving, there was a knot in her stomach.

Charlie looked up when she walked into his office, and knew immediately something was wrong.

"I have to go home. Merlin is dying."

He stood. "Do you need me?"

She shook her head. "I don't know when I'll be back."

"We're good here," Charlie said. "Go do what you have to do, but if there's anything I can do to help, let me know."

She turned on one heel, went back to shut down her computer, and within a couple of minutes, she was out the door.

Charlie got up and went to the window, watching for her to leave the building.

She came out running.

His stomach turned. He knew that frantic, won't-get-there-in-time feeling. He watched her take off out of the parking lot like the world was on fire and she was trying to outrun the blaze, then said a prayer for her safety, and another prayer for anyone who might get in her way.

For Wyrick, the drive home was a blur. When she got back to her apartment, she tore off her leather and put on jeans and a sweatshirt, then washed the mask of makeup from her face, scrubbing frantically to remove everything that wasn't her.

She tore up the stairs with the water still drying on her skin, then emerged into the kitchen and ran.

Ora was at Merlin's side when Wyrick appeared. She got up to give Wyrick her seat.

"He's been holding on...waiting for you. I notified his doctor. He's not in pain," Ora said.

Wyrick pushed the chair aside and reached for Merlin's hand. It was cold and nearly lifeless, only a slight twitch of his fingers as she held them.

"Merlin. I'm here."

His eyelids fluttered and then opened enough to see her. His lips moved, but no sound came out. She thought he said *Thank you*, but she wasn't sure.

"No, thank *you*, Merlin—for being my friend, for giving me a safe place to be, for having my back. You honored me in a way no one ever had before, you crazy man. You with your searchlights on the roof, and your wizard mind, and your hothouse tomatoes." Her voice broke. "I love you, and I will treasure what you have given me for the rest of my life."

He squeezed her fingers as he took a deep breath, gathering everything within him to utter his last earthly words.

"Give 'em hell, Jade. Make me proud."

"I will," she promised, and then stood witness as life left him in one last exhalation.

Ora stepped up beside Wyrick and reached for his wrist, holding it, feeling for a pulse.

Wyrick was motionless...waiting. A minute passed, but he never took another breath.

Ora checked for a heartbeat with her stethoscope, then looked up at the clock.

"Time of death, 3:18 p.m."

Arthur Merlin was gone.

"What do I do?" Wyrick asked.

"The immediate things are my responsibility," Ora said. "I'll call his doctor, and I will notify the funeral home. Once his body leaves the premises, my business here is done. You might want to notify his lawyer."

"Yes, I'll call Rodney," she said, but when Ora turned away to make the calls, Wyrick smoothed the wisps of what was left of his hair away from his face. "Go do you, magic man. I've got this."

She went back to the living room, then stood in the doorway looking at all of the old elegance, remembering the first time they'd met.

That one online notice of a group meeting on a Mensa site right after she first moved to Dallas. Cyrus Parks had taken pride in the fact that she'd had a perfect score in every IQ test she'd ever been given, including the tests to belong to Mensa. Before, it had never mattered to her like it had to him. It was just who she was. But back then, after UT, she was looking for a connection to something...or someone...to fill the void of what had happened to her, and she thought maybe being around people like her would be the answer.

She arrived at the meeting, thin and bald, with a scarf tied around her head, and a tall, thin man with long white hair and a long white beard welcomed her into the grand mansion with a smile and a cup of tea.

It was winter then, and she sat in the big over-stuffed chair beside the fireplace, drinking her tea and listening, and knew within minutes that while they were nice enough and accepted her, they weren't like her. She was still the exception. She was always going to be the odd one out.

But back then she didn't care. She just wanted human companionship and was just getting settled into the routine when Cyrus Parks found her again. After that, she separated herself from the group. She didn't want Parks to know her routine, and she didn't want to think about any of them becoming caught up in his web.

Then she found Charlie Dodge and the work that came with him, and a year passed, and then another, and Parks was always on her tail, and she was always moving from one address to another.

When Parks began pushing her boundaries even more, she remembered Merlin, and the basement apartment, and once again, his place became her refuge—the one place where the security was better than the men Parks put on her tail.

And now, because of Merlin, it was hers.

She walked across the room to that same over-stuffed chair and sat down beside the fireplace. It needed a fire. She pulled up the lawyer's phone number and made the call.

"Gordon Law Firm."

"I'm calling on behalf of Arthur Merlin. May I please speak to Mr. Gordon?"

"One moment, please," the secretary said, and put her on hold.

Wyrick leaned back in the chair and closed her eyes, waiting.

"Hello? Wyrick, is this you?"

"Yes. Merlin died a few minutes ago. I'm supposed to let you know."

"Oh dear…bless his heart and yours. I'm so sorry. I'll get the ball rolling on my end, but in the meantime, is there anything I can do for you?"

"No, but thank you. As you know, he didn't want an obituary posted or a memorial service. I will claim his ashes at a later date, and scatter them according to his wishes."

"Yes, and thank you for calling," Rodney said. "If you don't already have your own lawyer, I'll be happy to stay on as yours when the transfer of property goes into your name."

"Thank you," Wyrick said. "In the meantime, let me know if there's anything I need to do."

"Yes, I will…and again, my condolences," he said, and hung up.

Wyrick laid the phone aside and thought about going to make coffee. Instead, she turned on the gas starter in the fireplace and lit the kindling beneath the logs. Flames flared, licking the logs above them, and soon there was a fire.

She sat in silence, staring out the window, watching for Merlin's ride out, and thought about her life, wondering how it would end.

She wouldn't ever marry.

She couldn't have children.

Likely, she would wind up like Merlin one day— old, alone and rich as sin. But as long as Charlie Dodge outlived her, she wouldn't ask for anything more.

An hour passed, and it was moving toward the end of the second hour when a long black hearse appeared at the gates and then came up the drive.

They were here.

She sent Ora a quick text to let her know, then waited. She wouldn't ever want the job of collecting the dead, even though she accepted that someone had to do it, but watched as they got out with the gurney, rolling it toward the house and up the steps.

The doorbell signaling their arrival tolled throughout the mansion as Wyrick got up to let them in. One of the men introduced himself, and the funeral home for which he worked, but it all went over Wyrick's head.

"This way," she said, and led them through the foyer, then down the grand hall to Merlin's room, where Ora was standing at the door to oversee Merlin's exit.

Wyrick watched them lifting him from the bed onto the gurney, then covering him from head to toe before fastening the straps across his body. When they were finished, the same man nodded at Wyrick and gave her his card.

"Our condolences for your loss. We will be in touch."

Wyrick led the way back to the door, silently held it open as they rolled him out, then watched as they carried him down the steps to the hearse.

A few minutes later, Ora came up the hall with her bag over her shoulder.

"My work here is finished. You may get a survey from the company later, but I just want you to know that, in spite of the sadness of our meeting, it has been a true pleasure to get to know you. I understand why Merlin was so fond of you. You are genuine, which is a rarity in this world."

"Thank you, and thank you for all you did for him," Wyrick said. "You have a kind and gentle spirit…a good fit for your calling."

Ora smiled.

"I'll see myself out. Have a good life here, and make this place your home now. He said you'll do wonders with it."

Wyrick felt a spurt of joy. "He did?"

"Oh yes. He talked often about what you might do with it. I suspect he'll be looking over your shoulder now just to see what magic you create."

Wyrick liked the thought of that.

"Then I guess I'll have to wow him," she said.

Ora left, and now Wyrick was alone. She'd only ever been in a few rooms in this place, and now it belonged to her. In a day or two, she'd take a tour, but right now she just wanted to go back downstairs to what was familiar.

Fifteen

It was almost sundown when Wyrick went back upstairs to make sure the security system was set, then turned on a couple of lights in different rooms so that the mansion did not look empty.

She locked the doors to the stairs after she went down, and then locked herself in below. Before, she'd known Merlin was upstairs, and now there was no one on the whole estate but her. It was a disconcerting feeling she was going to have to conquer.

She turned on the television for company, then puttered around in the kitchen, dragging out cartons of leftovers until she settled on what was left of Chinese takeout and reheated it.

As was her habit, she ate in front of the TV in the living room and thought about calling Charlie just to hear his voice, but she didn't, because that wasn't their relationship.

No matter how much their lives had changed in

the past month, with Annie's death, Boyington's murder and cancer finally claiming Merlin, that part of their lives was still the same. Keeping him at arm's length and pissed off at her was how she rolled.

Charlie thought about Wyrick all evening, wondering what was happening, wondering if the old man was still alive. He didn't know anything about their relationship other than he was her landlord, and someone she'd known for a while. But he knew from the reaction she'd had today that she cared about him.

He thought about texting to check on her, then thought better of it and let her be. But if he'd known she was alone on that estate with Cyrus Parks still lurking in her life, he wouldn't have been as certain she was okay.

Wyrick slept with a handgun under her pillow and a can of Mace on the table by her bed, then woke up before 4:00 a.m. and couldn't go back to sleep.

The house above her was an unknown, sitting like a weight upon her shoulders, and it pissed her off beyond words that Cyrus Parks had taken away even an iota of her confidence.

Then, just to prove to herself that Cyrus could kiss her ass, she got up and started turning on lights and turned up the thermostat, then stomped up the stairs.

"I'm not hiding from shit," she muttered, as she strode through the main floor of the house, turning on lights as she went. "I'm here, house! Merlin gave you to me, so don't go freaking out at my long legs and bald head. I'm not afraid of you, so don't go freakin' out on me, okay?"

She got all the way to Merlin's bedroom, then stopped. The door was closed, and there was a part of her that didn't want to go in, but she wasn't harboring ghosts, no matter how charming, and pushed it open.

The huge sleigh bed had been stripped, but everything else was in place. She took a deep breath and then entered.

"I'm here…just like I promised. I'll give your girl a new lease on life and make new memories here, okay? And in the meantime, I need to feel safe. So no surprises."

After that, the rest of the tour was anticlimactic.

The second floor was all bedroom suites, and the attic above that was almost as large as the basement apartment in which she'd been living. Part of it was storage, and part of it were the tiny rooms from generations past, when the family still had live-in staff.

It was almost 6:00 a.m. before she'd seen it all, and she went back downstairs to get ready for work.

Charlie wouldn't be expecting her, but Merlin no longer needed her, so she was pleasing herself.

She didn't feel like an in-your-face outfit for the day, and reached for a pair of hip-hugger bell-bottom jeans, a pair of blue suede half boots and a royal blue V-neck sweater.

Once she was dressed, she moved to the mirror and looked at her face—really looked—then put the eye shadow aside and reached for a tube of blue lipstick, the same shade as her jeans. Her eyes hid what she was thinking. Dark eyes were like that, but there was still something missing.

She dug through her makeup drawer, found a sheet of face gems and peeled one blue-colored gem in the shape of a starburst off the page, then stuck it on her forehead like a Hindu bindi.

Then she looked at herself again. Brown eyes so dark they almost looked black. The sky blue starburst on her forehead, and the slash of metallic blue on her mouth. It was still her, but without the costumes of leather and the mask of bright paints. She wouldn't exactly say she was in mourning, but it was her version of paying respect.

She grabbed her bag and locked up on her way out, then took off out the main gates, taking care to close them behind her.

Charlie's steps were dragging as he approached the office door, but when he saw the lights already on and smelled fresh brewed coffee, he sighed.

She's here.

He opened the door and then froze when she stood and faced him. She'd never come to work this stripped down, and he wasn't sure how to take it.

Then she started talking, and he got it.

"Merlin died yesterday. I got there in time to say goodbye. Ironic, isn't it? I treasured the friendship, and the last thing I needed was more money. But I got more money and a mansion, and lost my friend. Life's a joke and then we die."

Charlie felt the gut punch of that last sentence,

and for the first time since he'd known her, he saw her for the lonely child she'd been, and the lonely woman she was. But before he could respond, she changed the subject.

"Are we here to work a new case?"

Charlie shrugged. "Depends on the requests, but I'd like to stay away from national parks for a while."

Wyrick frowned. Something must have happened while he was at Robbers Cave that she didn't know about.

"I'll go through the emails and send you some notes. They were out of bear claws. You have Danishes this morning," she said. Then she got the coffee cup from her desk and went to refill it, before going back to work.

Charlie went into his office, hung up his hat and his coat, and then got a cherry Danish to go with his coffee and sat down at his desk.

He could hear Wyrick's keyboard clicking, assumed she was typing up the notes, and took a bite of the sweet roll.

But he was wrong. Wyrick was looking for recent stories relating to Robbers Cave State Park in Oklahoma, and when she found the one with the escaped prisoners and then realized they'd shut down the park with everyone in it during the manhunt, she rolled her eyes.

God only knew what he got himself into while all that was going on, but whatever it was, it was over and he'd come home in one piece.

So she exited that screen and then pulled up the

info on two of the six requests that had come in, and began typing, and then the phone rang. The call was for Charlie. She put it through and then kept working until he came out of his office and handed her a piece of paper with some notes on it.

"Just put a hold on starting anything new," he said. "I'm going to be deposed regarding my part in the cases against Randall Wells and Justin Young. The prosecution wants the videos we have of your interviews with both boys during our search. Can you make copies and email them to their office?"

"Yes."

"They're going to have a pretrial hearing to decide whether the cases stay in juvenile court or if they'll be turned over and tried as adults. I wouldn't want to be their parents," Charlie said.

Wyrick glanced down at the paper he handed her, then nodded.

"Something went wrong somewhere for them to be so unemotional about human life. I'll upload the videos to the prosecutor's office now."

"I'm going to run a couple of errands," Charlie said. "I'll be back in a few."

Wyrick glanced at the clock, then got a cheese Danish from the coffee bar and went back to her desk. Now that he was out of the office, she dug back into the incident at Robbers Cave, and then found a story in the local paper about the family who'd been taken hostage, and found the rest of his story within the telling of theirs. She read it, then read it again.

So Charlie Dodge saved a ten-year-old girl named

Shelby, then took the convicts down and rescued the parents. Now she understood why he said no more jobs involving parks.

She had finished her sweet roll and was cleaning up her desk when the office door opened. Two fifty-something women with the same faces walked in, both with hair in varying shades of blond and both wearing diamonds and fur-trimmed coats.

Identical twins, and Wyrick already had a read on them. They were also competitors with each other, and had been all their lives.

They stopped in the doorway, staring without apology at her lack of hair, blue metallic lipstick and the blue starburst gem on her forehead.

Wyrick stared back at them without blinking.

"Ladies, if you stare at me any longer, I am going to have to charge admission, so maybe you should introduce yourselves and tell me why you're here?"

They both inhaled at the same time, then rushed her desk.

"I'm Portia Carlyle."

"And I'm Paula Carlyle," the other one said.

And then they both began to talk at once, speaking in almost perfect unison.

"Our mother recently passed. She had a four-carat yellow diamond that Daddy gave her for their fiftieth wedding anniversary, and it's disappeared. We need to hire Charlie Dodge to find it."

"We're just devastated," Portia added.

"Yes, devastated," Paula echoed.

"Mr. Dodge isn't that kind of investigator," Wyrick

said. "His cases involve missing people, not missing things."

"We have money!" Portia cried. "We'll pay whatever he charges."

"We want to speak to him personally," Paula added.

"Well, he's not here at the moment, so—"

"We'll wait!" they echoed, and then took themselves over to the sofa and sat, glaring at Wyrick and muttering beneath their breath about secretaries getting above themselves, and needing to wear a wig... and no self-respecting woman would put jewelry on her face instead of her fingers.

Wyrick ignored them.

But the longer they sat, the more they fussed, until somehow they were fighting with each other.

"You were the last one to handle it. I know because I saw you trying it on!" Portia cried.

Paula gasped. "I can't believe you're accusing me of stealing my mama's special ring!"

"She was my mama, too," Portia screeched, and shoved her.

Paula shoved her back, and then the wrestling match was on. Wyrick rolled her eyes and called Charlie, who was already on his way back to the office.

"Hello. What's up?" he asked.

Wyrick put the phone on speaker. "Can you hear all this nonsense?" she asked.

Charlie's pulse kicked. He could hear women

screaming and thumping. It sounded like the place was on fire, and people were scrambling to get out.

"What the hell is going on?" he asked. "Are you okay?"

"You have two prospective clients who have gotten into a fight while waiting to talk to you, because they aren't having anything to do with me. They're sisters. And they are, at the present time, on the floor of my office fighting like trailer trash. How long before you'll be back?"

"Oh good Lord," he muttered. "I'm about ten minutes out."

"So, either I'm calling the cops, or you deal with them. Your decision," Wyrick said.

"Keep the phone on speaker and put it in their faces," he said.

Wyrick took the bottle of water off her desk, walked over to where the sisters were rolling and screaming, and emptied it on them, shocking them into momentary silence.

"Ladies…and I use that term loosely… Mr. Dodge wishes to speak with you."

They were flat on their backs now, staring up at the phone in Wyrick's hand. And then Charlie's voice came down upon them.

"Both of you! Get off the floor. Shut the hell up and wait quietly for me to arrive, or I'll have Wyrick call the police and have you arrested for disturbing the peace."

There was total silence as the sisters glared at Wyrick and then at each other.

"I don't hear you!" Charlie shouted. "Do you two understand me?"

"Yes," they said, and got themselves off the floor and back into their seats before glaring at Wyrick for tattling on them.

"I'll be there shortly," Charlie said, and disconnected.

Wyrick dropped the empty water bottle into the trash and sat back down at her desk.

"You have ruined our hair and makeup. Where is your ladies' room?" Paula asked.

"You ruined yourselves," Wyrick said, then pointed at the door. "Out the door. Down the hall on your right."

"A public toilet?" Portia cried.

"You made public fools of yourselves," Wyrick said.

They got up in silence and hurried out of the office, and were gone only long enough to dry themselves off. Their appearances upon returning were far less dramatic than their initial arrival, and so were their demeanors.

They sat down at opposite ends of the sofa, continuing to glare at Wyrick, who ignored them.

Then Charlie Dodge walked in, and when he did, the door slammed against the inner wall. Both women jumped and then shrank back. They hadn't expected anyone that big or that intimidating.

He stared at the sorry state in which they now sat and then looked at Wyrick.

She shrugged.

He bit the inside of his lip to keep from grinning and then walked over to where they were sitting.

"Talk," he said, and when they both started to talk at once, he bellowed, "One at a time!"

Paula shuddered. "We want to hire you to find our mama's missing ring. It's a four-carat yellow diamond."

"Did you ask her when she had it last?" Charlie said.

"Mama's dead," Portia said, then pointed at Paula. "She had it last."

"I do not settle family disputes. I do not find missing articles, only missing people. File a police report. If someone stole it, they will check the pawnshops."

Then all of a sudden, Wyrick was standing beside Charlie.

"Who's Jehru?" she asked.

Paula frowned. "He's our spiritual guide. How did you—?"

Charlie glanced at Wyrick. She had that faraway look in her eyes he was beginning to recognize, and Wyrick was still talking.

"His real name is Gregory Foster. Which one of you gave him access to a checking account?"

Portia gasped. "How did—?"

"I think my partner just solved the mystery of the missing ring. It'll be up to you and the police to get it back…if you file a police report. And I'd advise you to change the PIN on that account as soon as possible," Charlie said.

The twins were in shock. "Yes, well, this is not

what we thought…uh, not how it…" Then they looked at Wyrick anew. "How did you know all that?"

Wyrick ignored them. "I think we're through here."

Charlie went in his office and shut the door.

They left the office in silence.

Moments later, Charlie came back out, glanced at the wet spots on the rug and then grinned at her.

"I wish I'd seen that."

She shrugged. "Easiest way to end a catfight is spray them with water."

"And you know that how?" Charlie asked.

"Read it in a book once."

"Did you ever spray down a pair of fighting cats?" he asked.

"Not until today," Wyrick said.

Charlie laughed all the way back into his office, and it wasn't until he was sitting at his desk that he realized it was the first time he'd laughed in weeks.

So the healing had begun.

After what Wyrick considered a wasted day, it finally ended. With a deposition looming and testimony to give, Charlie backed off starting another case until that was done.

He went home first, and Wyrick stayed to lock up. She had her bag on her shoulder as she rode down in the elevator, and when she got in her Mercedes, she paid no attention to the panhandler standing at the end of the street.

She didn't see him taking a picture of her in the

car, or know he was sending it out to the catering van in a driveway five blocks down.

She paid no attention to the catering van as it pulled out of the drive and moved into the flow of traffic behind her, nor did she realize that the roadside service truck she passed on the freeway was on the phone with the woman in the pink Volkswagen bug who picked up Wyrick and her Mercedes at the exit ramp, following it to the quick-stop where Wyrick stopped to fuel up her car.

When Wyrick paid and left the station, she barely noticed the utility truck in the lane beside her, and when she finally turned into her neighborhood, it turned one way while she turned another.

There was a small white Ford Focus behind her now, with an old man behind the wheel, when she turned up the drive and aimed the remote to open the gates to the estate.

The old man drove past as Wyrick drove through, closing the gates behind her, unaware of the choreography Cyrus Parks had set in place.

For the next nine days, the same people, using different vehicles every day, trailed her everywhere she went.

It was Saturday when Wyrick received a text that Merlin's ashes were ready to be picked up, so she put aside the designs she'd been working on to renovate the upstairs and made a quick trip to the funeral home, still unaware she was being followed—unaware that

Cyrus Parks was receiving daily reports on her activities.

When she got back, she set Merlin's ashes on her coffee table, then sat down and sent Charlie a text.

Taking the chopper to Galveston tomorrow to scatter Merlin's ashes. Leaving in the a.m. Back before noon.

Will you let me know when you get back?

Yes.

She'd already talked to Benny about servicing the chopper while she was driving home, so now two people would know where she was going and when she would be back.

She leaned forward, her elbows on her knees, and then glanced at the box.

"Okay, old friend. We're going to Galveston tomorrow, but in the meantime, I'm going to make a sandwich and have some of your awesome tomatoes with it. Better than chips, any day."

Later, as she ate, she kept fiddling with the little drone she'd come up with that would release the ashes from below the chopper. She'd been working on it for days, and had everything about ready to go. Once she reached Galveston, all she had to do was land somewhere long enough to fasten it to the struts, and then take off over the bay.

So as soon as she had it ready, she tested the release on the drone several times until she was satisfied, and then packed it and the box with his ashes into a bag and carried it to the counter.

She went to bed but couldn't sleep, so she sat up and watched TV, unable to relax. Her thoughts were in free fall and unsettled, and she didn't know why. Maybe when this last request was granted, she could let go.

Finally she slept.

It was just after daylight when she woke abruptly, imagining she'd heard someone calling her name. But the apartment was silent, except for the sound of a slight dripping in the showerhead she'd been meaning to fix. She got up to make coffee.

Thinking about the upcoming flight, she opted for buttered toast and nothing more, but tossed a couple of Snickers in her bag. Benny would have an ice chest packed with water and Pepsi bottles, and she'd be good to go.

It took a couple of trips to get everything into the Mercedes, and then she was off to the private airport where she kept her chopper, unaware of the tag team of trackers behind her at every step of the trip.

The last pair, a couple named Ed and Alma, were in a delivery van, and far enough behind her that she didn't notice, but close enough they followed her turn off the highway toward a small airport, and the drive up to a hangar near the gates.

They parked on a nearby hill, then watched her and a man in coveralls walk out together and load up some items into a chopper. When they realized she was about to take off, there was a quick moment of panic. Nobody told them she was a pilot, and they had not prepared for this. There was no way to know where she was going, and no way to keep track of her. So they watched in frustration as she took to the air, made one circle, then flew off in a south-eastern direction.

"What are we going to do?" Alma said.

Ed pointed at the mechanic, and then started up the van and headed for the hangar.

The mechanic was walking back into the hangar when they drove up and parked.

"I've got this," Alma said, and jumped out carrying an envelope, pretending to be in a panic.

"Miss Wyrick! Miss Wyrick! Is she still here? She was supposed to take this with her and left it behind."

Benny was taken aback by their arrival. He knew her landlord had died, and where she was going, but he knew Jade Wyrick forgot nothing, and the only person who knew to look for her here was Charlie Dodge.

"She's gone," Benny said. "Sorry."

"Oh my God, this is a disaster!" Alma cried, and then turned in a little circle with the envelope clutched against her chest. "Where did she go? Maybe we can messenger it to her?"

Benny frowned. "I don't know where she goes. My job is to fuel up the chopper. That is all."

Alma sighed. Dammit, it didn't work. Then she looked at Ed and shrugged.

Benny thought that was going to be the end of

that until the driver got out of the van and started toward him.

The man was twice his size and armed.

"Oh man," Benny muttered, and turned to run, just as the man tackled him from behind.

Ed rolled until he had the mechanic on his back and pinned to the ground.

"You can tell me now, or I'll beat it out of you," Ed said.

"I have nothing to tell you," Benny said. Then when he saw the fist coming toward him, he winced.

The impact broke his jaw and the man kept shouting, but he was past answers. Then everything went black.

Sixteen

"Don't kill him!" Alma cried.

But Ed kept pounding on Benny's head and body, until Alma slapped him on the back of the head.

"I said...don't kill him, dammit!"

Ed flinched, then rolled off and got up.

"Is he dead?" she asked.

"I don't know. Go look in the hangar and see if you can find anything to tell us where she was headed."

Alma glanced around at the other hangars, then at the small office in the distance, and moaned.

"I can't believe you did that. We need to get out of here!"

Ed grabbed her by the arm. "I said, go look for clues in the hangar!"

She ran inside, then into the small office, and began shoving papers off the desk, and then tearing through the drawers, but found nothing until she saw a clipboard hanging on the wall. It was the memo clipped on top that caught her attention.

Fuel to Galveston

"Okay, okay," she muttered, and grabbed the memo from the clipboard and ran.

"I found something!" Alma cried, as she ran outside. "She's going to Galveston."

"Good work," Ed said. "Get in the van. We'll notify the boss on the way back to Dallas."

Alma glanced back at the mechanic, lying motionless and bloody on the tarmac.

"What about him? Shouldn't we call an ambulance or something?"

Ed slapped her across the face. "How stupid are you? No, we shouldn't call an ambulance or something. He saw us."

Unaware of the ensuing drama behind her, Wyrick was focused on the flight ahead and keeping a promise. The day was clear and cold in Dallas, but she was heading to warmer weather. Merlin didn't like the cold, and he'd really felt it after he began chemo. Maybe that was part of why he wanted this to happen in Galveston, and she was happy she'd been given the task.

The trip was without issue all the way there, and as soon as she reached the helipad at Fort Crockett Boulevard, she set down to refuel and shut the chopper down. Once the tank was full for the trip back, she got out the drone she'd modified, then Merlin's ashes, and crawled beneath the chopper to fasten it to the struts, checking it over and over to make sure it was in the right place to come free. Once she was satisfied, she climbed back into the cockpit and started up the engine, revved it to liftoff and went up, and out over Galveston Bay, then flying farther, out over the Gulf of Mexico.

Sunlight caught on the water's surface like glitter strewn from the hand of God. It was so beautiful, and so serene in that moment it brought tears to Wyrick's eyes. She pressed the power button on the remote, releasing the drone from the strut at the same time she took the chopper upward. Then she flew it in a wide circle back to watch the drone skimming only feet above the water. She could almost hear Merlin's voice. *Do it, Jade, do it.*

She pushed the throttle forward on the remote and held her breath, watching as the drone nosed down into the glittering water, taking Merlin with it.

Watching it disappear beneath the waves was the finale to a life well lived. She was blinking back tears as she headed back toward shore. By the time she reached flying altitude, she was on her way back to Dallas.

Wyrick was a little over a hundred miles north of Galveston and flying over the Sam Houston National Forest when she caught a flash of movement to her right. With only seconds to react to the helicopter coming at her, and the man with the rifle hanging out of the cockpit, she made a sharp turn to the left trying to get out of the line of fire.

She was already on the radio calling out an SOS, relaying her call sign and coordinates, when the first bullet hit the cockpit. Then two more shots hit the chopper, sending it into a downward spin she could not control.

She kept repeating her coordinates and call sign, then finally added, "Call Charlie Dodge, my next of kin. Dodge Investigations out of Dallas." Even though the transmission was beginning to break up, she kept relaying the SOS until the glass shattered in front of her, a searing pain tore through her shoulder and then her leg, and everything went black.

Wyrick was unconscious and the cockpit was tilting sideways when the rotors tore through the treetops, then hit the ground and broke apart like heat-seeking missiles, slicing through everything in their paths.

She came to still strapped into her seat, lying on her side within a growing cloud of smoke, with the electrical wiring sparking and popping as it began to catch fire. Her shoulder was burning, and one leg was gushing blood. When she tried to unbuckle herself, she almost passed out.

The fact that she had not died in this crash was a miracle, and she didn't intend to let it go to waste. She had to stop the bleeding or she would die before she got out. She didn't know how it worked, but she knew thinking about herself whole and healthy worked, and so she did.

She waited, afraid to move, and then the smoke got worse and she was beginning to choke and cough. Left with no choice, and even though she was still strapped into her seat, she began trying to release all the straps holding her into the seat, with only one good hand and arm.

Gritting her teeth against the waves of pain-filled nausea, she finally found the release. As soon as she was free, she fell the rest of the way down onto the ground floor of the forest. Blocking out everything but making her body move, she finally got to her feet, with one arm dangling at her side. She could feel a bullet hole on the front of her chest, but didn't know if there was an exit wound. What she did know was that the bleeding had stopped, but she didn't know for how long. At this point, her choices weren't good. Burn up, bleed out, or get out.

She was coughing nonstop now, and her eyes were watering so badly she was left to feel her way out. The windshield was shattered, but the heat was greatest there, so she began climbing, using the seat backs as steps, pulling herself up with her one good arm, until she felt the door handle above her.

She turned it and pushed up, but it didn't budge. Bracing one foot on the instrument panel and her other foot on her seat, she bent over, bracing her back against the door, then pushed upward again, and all of a sudden it was open.

She was gasping for breath as she pulled herself up, and then crawled out onto the overturned cockpit. But once out of the cockpit, the smoke around her was dispersing enough that she could see. She started to slide off the side and fell. Landing on her wounded shoulder, she passed out from the pain.

It was heat from the flames that woke her again, but when she tried to get up and run, her leg wouldn't hold her, so she started dragging herself with one arm, grabbing anything she could hold to pull herself along, and crawled away from the crash site until she could go no farther, then rolled over onto her back.

From what she could tell, she'd come down in thick forest, somewhere near a creek, because she could hear running water. She'd lost all track of time. The bits of sky she could see through the canopy told her there was still daylight, but she didn't know for how much longer, or if it was even the same day.

If they tell him, Charlie will find me...alive or dead... Charlie will find me.

The blind faith she had in him was constant, and it was the last thought she had before she lost consciousness again.

An airport employee found Benny Garcia and called an ambulance and the police. By the time they got him to a Dallas hospital, the police had confiscated the video from the security cameras with some good shots of the license tag on the van, and of the assailants who'd been in it. They were running facial recognition on the man and woman, and had a BOLO out on the van when Benny came out of surgery. He had not regained consciousness, but he was alive.

* * *

Charlie was kicked back in his recliner watching football when noontime came and went. But by the time it was nearly 2:00 p.m. and he still hadn't heard a thing from Wyrick, he was beginning to worry. He sent a text she didn't answer, and his call went to voice mail. And then twenty minutes later, his phone rang.

"Thank God," he muttered, assuming it was her.

Then he realized he'd left the phone in the kitchen and got up running to answer it. His relief was short-lived when he saw it was the FAA instead.

"Hello?"

"This is Loren Franklin. I work for the FAA. May I speak to Charlie Dodge?"

"This is Charlie."

"Mr. Dodge, we got an SOS from a chopper pilot named Jade Wyrick. She was in distress and going down, and said to notify you as next of kin."

Charlie's mind went blank. She was his last anchor to sanity and this couldn't be happening. He'd just lost Annie. He couldn't lose her, too.

"No," Charlie groaned, and dropped to his knees. "Where did it happen? Where did she go down?"

"We haven't found the crash site yet. Her voice was breaking up during her last communication and we aren't certain of her final location."

He rocked back on his heels as if he'd been sucker punched.

"Are you saying she isn't dead?"

"Oh! I'm sorry. I didn't mean to give you that impression. But the last thing we heard clearly from her was to notify you it was happening, and that you were her next of kin."

All of a sudden, his world rocked back in place. He was on his feet and reaching for a pen and paper.

"I'm flying down. Can you tell me where they're setting up the search?"

"Yes, but—"

"Just tell me," Charlie said, and then took down all of the information she could give him, along with some contact numbers for rangers, and then disconnected and ran to his office to do an online search for charter pilots.

He called two before he found one who was available—a pilot named Billy Wright, who also ran a flight school.

"When do you need to go?" Billy asked.

"Now," Charlie said. "It would take me about thirty minutes to get to your location."

"I'll fuel up. We can leave as soon as you get here."

"I'm on the way," Charlie said, and ran to change. He couldn't believe this nightmare was happening, or that the search for her would be in another national park.

He grabbed his camping pack, dumped the tent, added clothes, shoved a couple of bottles of water and some protein bars in beside the gear, and left on the run.

Once he got out on the freeway, he thought of Benny waiting for her at the hangar. But when he called that number, the man who answered wasn't Benny.

"Hello."

"Uh, hello… I need to speak to Benny," Charlie said.

"Who's calling?"

"This is Charlie Dodge. It's important that I speak to him. Who is this?"

"I'm Officer DuPlane, Dallas PD. Benny Garcia was found badly beaten and unconscious at this location, and has been taken to a hospital. How do you know him?"

Charlie's gut knotted. This didn't feel like a coincidence. "Through Jade Wyrick, who owns that hangar and the Bell Jet chopper she keeps in it. Benny is her mechanic. I'm a private investigator, and Jade works for me. I was just notified that her chopper crashed today. I needed to let Benny know, but now I obviously can't. I'm on my way to the crash site. I don't know anything more. Sorry."

He disconnected to concentrate on his driving and arrived at the flight school in just under thirty minutes.

A short, stocky man in his late forties was standing in the doorway of the office when Charlie parked and got out.

"I'm Charlie Dodge. Are you Billy?"

"Yes, sir. Pay the lady in the office and we'll be good to go."

Charlie hurried inside, then came out running.

"This way," Billy said, and then led the way out to the chopper sitting on a helipad.

Charlie handed him the coordinates, and within minutes, they were in the air and flying south.

It felt like an eternity trying to get there, and every minute that passed, Charlie kept thinking of the few times he'd seen her smile, the love affair she had with Snickers candy bars and Pepsi, the things she did to make his life easier, the true brilliance of her mind, and her unwavering loyalty.

He kept picturing her alive somewhere and waiting for him to find her. She knew he wouldn't quit until he did, but he didn't know if he'd find her in time.

When they finally began approaching their destination, Billy pointed.

"We're almost there. Are you gonna need a ride back?"

"I don't know," Charlie said. "It all depends."

"You've got my number. I'll make time to pick you up if you need it," Billy said.

"Thanks. I'll call if I do."

As soon as they landed, Charlie was out and running toward the command post, and stopped the first ranger he saw.

"I'm Charlie Dodge. The pilot of the downed chopper works for me. Are searchers already out?"

"Yes, sir. There are three different teams. They left about twenty minutes ago."

Charlie groaned. "I'm going in. What are the GPS coordinates?"

"Mr. Dodge, I would suggest you just—"

"No. I'm a private investigator. I specialize in finding people who've gone missing. She knows I'll come looking for her. It's what I do. So give me the GPS coordinates, or I'm going in cold."

The ranger nodded. "Understood. This is what we were given."

Charlie entered the coordinates into his GPS, then followed the ranger into a tent and to a large map of the forest they'd spread out on the table.

"This is the general location of the last coordinates, and this is where we are. Take the trail up past this tent and head north by northeast. You might catch up with some of the searchers. Do you have a two-way with you?"

"Yes."

"Then tune in to this channel and frequency and you'll hear feedback from the other searchers as you go."

"Thank you," Charlie said, as he set the frequencies, then shifted his backpack and started running, carrying the two-way as he went.

He ran full out along the trail in an effort to catch up with a search party, splashing through creeks and sending small animals scurrying into the underbrush.

He'd been on the trail for almost fifteen minutes when he began hearing voices and stopped, his heart pounding as he tried to locate the sounds. He checked his GPS to see how far he still had to go and then left the trail, heading into the forest until he walked up on a group of searchers. Once he introduced himself, he began peppering them with questions.

"Has anyone found debris?" Charlie asked.

The team leader, a man who went by the name of Tulsa, shook his head.

"Not yet," he said, and then eyed Charlie closer. "I know who you are. You're the guy who finds missing kids."

Charlie nodded. "Missing people in general, but yes. And the woman you're all looking for works for me. She's my partner and office manager."

"Damn. Really sorry," Tulsa said.

"Don't be sorry. Let's just find her. If anyone can live through a chopper going down, it will be her."

They took off with renewed energy. The search had become personal and time mattered.

It was going on twenty minutes later when one of them shouted and then radioed.

Found a piece of the tail section.

Charlie's heart skipped a beat. They had to be closing in on the location now if they were finding debris. He began moving at a faster pace again, moving forward, keeping an eye out for more debris, looking up in the trees as well as on the ground.

And then someone else radioed.

Found a piece of one of the rotors.

Then another one radioed.

Found a cockpit door.

And every piece they found was giving Charlie a clearer picture of the last seconds of Wyrick's fall.

It took everything he had to stay focused and keep moving.

He smelled the smoke first, then the scent from a crash site that a soldier never forgets, and started running, unaware others were running with him.

They found the cockpit lying on its side, and still smoldering. But it was the bullet holes that stopped his heart.

"Son of a bitch! They shot her down!"

He grabbed an upended strut and began climbing to the open door. He was afraid to look inside. Then when he did, his heart skipped.

"It's empty! She's not here!" he cried. Then from where he was standing, he spotted boot prints off to the side and jumped down. "I've got footprints. She got out!" he said, and started looking for a trail.

But when he found it and realized she was crawling, he knew she couldn't be far. He started following the drag marks, shouting out her name.

"Jade! Jade Wyrick!"

Jade was spinning, going around and around on the merry-go-round, and every time she passed her mother, she waved.

Her mother kept snapping pictures and waving back. Then the music started playing louder, and the merry-go-round was spinning faster and faster, and there was pain—so much pain.

Jade was crying now, and calling "Mama, Mama," and holding on to her horse with all her strength.

*"Hold on, Jade. Hold on, baby, hold on. Mama
loves you. Hold on! I won't leave you alone."*

Jade was crying... Help. Help. Somebody help me.

And then the voices in her head became reality
as consciousness returned.

Someone was shouting her name, but it wasn't
her mama. She could hear a man's voice shouting,
"Jade! Jade! Where are you?"

Tears rolled out from beneath her eyelids.

Charlie. I'm here, Charlie. Help me.

But the thought was never voiced, and she couldn't
stay conscious long enough to tell him where to look.

Charlie saw her boot and then her leg and pushed
through the brush to get to her, then dropped to his
knees beside her, feeling for a pulse.

It was there.

"Thank you, God," he muttered, and grabbed his
radio. "This is Dodge. I found her! She's alive."

Searchers came running, and then radioed their
location as Charlie was checking her wounds. She
had a cut on her head, and another on the side of
her neck. But it was the bloodstains on her shirt and
pants that led him to the injuries. When he found
the bullet wound in her shoulder, and then another
one in her upper thigh, blood loss became an issue.

He dumped his backpack, grabbed a pair of surgical scissors to cut through her sweater to get to the
shoulder wound, revealing the red-and-black dragon

on her chest. To his surprise, the wound was barely seeping.

He pulled out the first-aid kit and began tearing open gauze pads to field dress the wounds.

"Unwrap these!" Charlie said, and tossed a couple of rolls of self-adhesive bandages to one of the men while he felt for an exit wound.

There was none, which meant that bullet could have ricocheted off bone and be anywhere inside her. He pressed the gauze pads onto the bullet wound, applying pressure while another man used the stretch bandage to keep them in place.

Once that was done, Charlie cut the leg of her jeans to get to the other wound, discovered it was a through and through, but the bleeding appeared to have stopped, which made no fucking sense. He applied more gauze pads and self-adhesive bandage to hold them in place, and then looked up.

"Do we have a stretcher coming?" Charlie asked.

"About a mile away!" Tulsa said.

Too far. "That's time she doesn't have to give. Jade! Can you hear me?" Charlie asked.

She moaned.

"It's me, Charlie. Can you hear me?"

"Hear you," Wyrick mumbled.

"Did you see who did it?"

"Chopper…rifle," she said, and then grabbed hold of his hand and opened her eyes. "Cyrus…don't leave."

"I'm not leaving you. I promise," Charlie said.

Wyrick sighed, remembering that was what her

mama had told her, and let go, falling back into the shadows.

But Charlie wasn't waiting for that stretcher to arrive. "Since she got herself out of the cockpit and crawled here, I'm taking a chance that moving her isn't going to make anything worse," Charlie said, then scooped her up into his arms.

Her head rolled toward him, her cheek resting against the bicep on his arm as he pulled her close.

"Lead the way," he said.

After that, it was a scramble to get her to the stretcher and then to the waiting chopper from Medi-Flight.

Charlie was one of the men with the stretcher when they slid her into the back bay, and then he climbed in behind her.

One of the paramedics reached out to stop him.

"Sir, you can't—"

Charlie shook his head.

"Sorry, dude. I not only can, but I am, so move out of my way. Someone shot her down. She took a bullet in the shoulder and another one in the leg and still survived the crash before crawling out of a burning cockpit into the brush. The last thing she said was 'Don't leave me.' So move the hell over, because I am not letting her out of my sight."

"Fair enough," the medic said. "Just stay out of the way."

Charlie crawled all the way past where she was lying, then settled in cross-legged and held on to the stretcher as the chopper lifted up and took off.

He watched in silence while one established an IV and another began to cut away the rest of her shirt and jacket to get to the field dressing. That was when they saw the dragon where her breasts used to be.

A paramedic looked up.

"Holy shit."

"She's already survived her own kind of hell. Don't let her die," Charlie said.

"On it," he said, and started the drip.

"Where are we going?" Charlie asked.

"Memorial Hermann Med Center… It's a Level II trauma center in the Woodlands."

Charlie nodded.

They were on the way to Houston.

Seventeen

Wyrick kept fading in and out of consciousness. The sound of the rotors made her think she was still in her chopper—thinking she was still flying. And every time she'd reach for the cyclic stick, only one arm would work, which sent her into a panic, flailing her hand all about, trying to find the stick.

Finally, Charlie grabbed her hand.

"Wyrick! Wyrick! You're safe. Just hold on to me. We're on the way to a hospital."

She moaned. "Shot at me...couldn't—"

"I know, baby, I know." Charlie.

"Cyrus...found me. How?"

Charlie wasn't going to tell her about Benny, and for the first time ever, he lied to her.

"I don't know. Lie still. You're covered in blood."

"Bleeding... I stopped it," she mumbled, and then went quiet.

Charlie didn't say anything. If they'd heard her, they wouldn't believe what she'd said. But he knew she was capable of creating her own miracles, and he was in awe.

A short while later, they were flying over Houston, and when Medi-Flight finally landed on the helipad, a trauma team was waiting.

Charlie came out of the chopper with her, then ran beside the gurney, staying with her all the way until they took her into surgery. At that point, he stood in the hall as the door closed behind them, and flashed back on Annie's body being taken away from Morning Light.

He walked down the hall to the waiting room, still trying to wrap his head around this day, wishing he had his hands around Cyrus Parks's neck. He'd thought when Annie died that his life couldn't get much worse, but he was wrong. This was bad. It was beginning to sink in how desperately he did not want to lose Wyrick, too.

The Dallas police found the white van Benny's assailants had been driving, abandoned in a parking lot at a mall. They'd parked in a location without video surveillance, so they had no idea what the vehicle they'd left in looked like, and the registration on the abandoned vehicle came back stolen over two months ago.

As for Ed and Alma, they were long gone.

Benny's family was at the hospital when he came out of surgery, and so was the detective who had caught the case.

When the surgeon came in to talk to them, they all stood up at once, including the detective.

"Benny Garcia family?" the doctor asked.

"That's us," his father said. "How is my son?"

"He's stable and in recovery, but he's still unconscious. His nose was broken, but has been reset. He has a broken jaw, which has been repaired, but he'll be drinking his meals for a while. We removed his spleen, reinflated a collapsed lung and reset some broken ribs. His eyes are still swollen shut, so we'll have to assess them at a later date."

His mother started crying. "Thank you, Doctor! Thank you."

"He'll be in recovery for another hour or so, and then they'll move him to his room. You can see him then, but keep it low-key."

"Yes, Doctor, we will," his father said, and then the family hugged each other with joy as the doctor left.

"Good news," the detective said, and handed them his card. "When he gets strong enough to talk, would you let me know?"

"Yes, sir," his mother said, and put it in her purse.

Cyrus Parks was at home, pacing the floor with an eye to the clock. Once he learned she had flown out of Dallas, he'd seen this as his chance.

He had people in the air at Galveston, waiting for a sighting, and then once they spotted her flying out over the bay, they circled at a higher elevation, waiting to see where she went next. When she headed back to shore, and then kept flying north toward Dallas, they began pursuit.

He had no idea the strike had already happened, or that they'd waited to contact him until they were on the ground.

And then his phone rang.

"Hello."

"The bird went down in smoke, full of lead. We're done."

Cyrus exhaled as the call disconnected.

That was a hard call to make. She'd been the success story they'd always wanted, only to become a problem they couldn't control, but he was smiling as he put down the phone.

It was over.

Charlie spent three endless hours in the waiting room before a surgeon appeared.

"Anyone here for Jade Wyrick?"

"I am," Charlie said, and stood as the surgeon approached. "Is she—?"

"She's stable and in recovery. The bullet in her shoulder had lodged against her collarbone. We removed it and patched her up. The wound in her leg was a through and through. No major arteries impacted. She has a concussion and multiple contusions and some major bruising. And that is one hell of a tattoo she has. We did our best to keep it intact. The damnedest thing... I've never seen it before, but there was next to no bleeding during surgery. It was like every cut I made cauterized itself. She's in pretty good shape, considering she was shot down. I hope they catch who did it."

"She's an amazing woman," Charlie said. "When can I see her?"

"They'll be taking her to a room on the fourth floor."

"Okay," Charlie said. "Just make sure it's a private room large enough for a place for me, because I'm not leaving her alone. Someone tried to kill her, and it's not the first time. When they find out she's not dead, they will try again."

The surgeon frowned. "We can move her to a private hospital for recovery if it will make it easier to keep her under guard."

"How long do you think she'll be hospitalized?" Charlie asked.

"It's hard to say right now, but I'd guess at least three days minimum."

"Then leave her here. Just make sure your staff knows. And I'll be contacting Houston PD about it. They may or may not choose to get involved, but I'm with her all the way."

"As long as there's no danger to other patients, it's your call, but if that changes, we'll be moving her," he said.

Charlie understood their situation, but his focus was on Wyrick, and as soon as the surgeon was gone, he picked up his things and headed for the elevator.

Wyrick came to in a room full of people talking and machines beeping and sounds of moaning.

And like before, someone was calling her name—this time, a woman.

"Jade! Jade! You're out of surgery and in recovery. My name is Susie. Can you open your eyes for me? Wake up, Jade. Wake up, honey."

Wyrick tried to answer, but it came out as a moan.

"Good girl," Susie said. "Open your eyes now. You can do it."

And so she did, catching a fleeting glimpse into a world of lights, and the scents of antiseptic scrub and ammonia, orchestrated by a dozen different beeps in different stages and rhythms. She knew this kind of place… She'd been in one before, when they took off both her breasts. But why was—?

Oh shit. The crash.

Wyrick sighed. "Charlie…"

Susie patted her arm. "Is Charlie your guy? Does he know you're here?"

She sighed.

"Knows…"

"Do you remember what happened?" Susie asked.

Wyrick's lips were dry, and when she started to lick them, she realized her lower lip was swollen.

"Hurts," she said.

"Your lips?" Susie asked.

Wyrick blinked. "Yes."

"I can fix that," Susie said, and swabbed them with something slick and cool.

Wyrick closed her eyes. The urge to slide away was real, but Susie wouldn't let her, and a short while later, they were rolling her out of recovery and taking her down back hallways to an elevator. Everyone she saw was a stranger. She couldn't relax for fear Cyrus's people would find her and finish the job.

Then the orderlies were pushing her bed into a doorway and into a room. When they began moving her from the gurney to a bed, and there was a nurse standing nearby holding her IV, and a shadow suddenly moving on the wall, she panicked.

"No! Don't—"

All of a sudden, Charlie was standing at the foot of her bed. Her Charlie—dark hair with the tiniest wisps of gray at the temples. The biggest shoulders, the kind that hold the weight of the world. The man with the broken heart was here for her.

"I'm here. You're safe," he said.

And just like that, her panic was gone.

"You found me," she said.

"Barely, and when you get better, you're putting one of those damn tracking apps on my phone so I can keep track of you, savvy?"

"Savvy," she mumbled, and closed her eyes.

And for the next three days, Wyrick's sleep was haunted by scenes from her past that came and went with the pain and the meds that dulled it. She didn't know she talked in her sleep, but now Charlie did, and with every nightmare he witnessed, leaving him to read between the lines—the shock of her existence rolled through him.

What they'd done to her as a child, leaving her care to people who were little more than scientists keeping records of her progress, ignoring the childhood she should have been living in an effort to study and utilize every second of her mind and skills, was a crime and a tragedy.

As for Wyrick, each dream was a reality until she woke up in a panic. And each time she awoke, she had to readjust the reality of where she was, to where she'd been. Then Charlie would be right beside her bed, shaking her awake, or just holding her hand and telling her she was safe.

The sound of his voice was enough.

And so the days passed, while Wyrick healed faster than her doctor could believe, and neither she nor Charlie saw fit to tell him why. She wanted to go home. She was vulnerable here, and the sooner she got home, the sooner she could bring all of this to an end. It was going to cost every bit of privacy and anonymity she had, but Cyrus Parks was going down.

Wyrick was sitting up in bed with the tray table across her lap, poking at what passed for her lunch. Meat loaf with ketchup, scalloped potatoes cooked without salt and a little salad in a plastic bowl with one cherry tomato on top. The tomato made her think of Merlin and his greenhouse, which made her want out even more.

"This stuff is awful," she muttered.

"It's not so bad," Charlie said, happily eating the food from his tray.

"You'll eat anything," Wyrick said.

Charlie popped the tomato from his salad in his mouth and chewed.

"You're just pissy because they don't serve Snickers and Pepsi," Charlie said.

It was the truth, but she glared at him, just the same.

"I'm not pissy, and they're releasing me tomorrow," she said. "I want to go home."

"They're letting you go tomorrow if you have someone to stay with you until you're more mobile, which means hiring a nurse for a while," he said.

Wyrick frowned. "No nurses. I don't trust anyone. Cyrus will find out I'm alive, and some nurse who's supposed to take care of me will poison me instead. I'm going home and that's final, and if I have to, I'll check myself out against doctor's orders. I have to get home. I have something I have to do."

Charlie pointed at her meat loaf.

"You gonna eat that?"

Wyrick rolled her eyes. "No, I'm not going to eat it. Help yourself."

He raked it onto his plate and kept eating, talking around the bite he was chewing.

"Calm down, woman. Nobody's going to do anything to you again."

"Oh! What…now you turned psychic, too?" she muttered.

"I know because I'm taking you home, and I'll stay with you in your home, until you feel like kicking ass again."

Breath caught in the back of her throat, and for the second time in her life, she was speechless.

Merlin had cared enough for her to make her his heir, and Charlie, in the middle of his grief, cared enough about her to keep her safe.

"Well?" Charlie asked.

"Thank you," she said.

He nodded. "You're welcome. Uh…are you going to eat your pudding?"

"Yes."

"Oh. Well, that's okay. Just thought I'd—"

"Kidding," she said, and handed it to him.

He poked a spoon into the pudding. "At least the smart-ass part of you is back," he said, and took a bite.

It was a beautiful day in Houston, but there was a storm heading to Dallas. It wasn't due to arrive before midafternoon, and they were due to fly out at 9:00 a.m., giving them plenty of time to get back and settle in before it hit.

Charlie had gotten special permission for Billy Wright to land on the hospital helipad to get her home, and they were checked out and waiting in her room when a nurse came hurrying in, pushing a wheelchair.

"Your ride just radioed that he's inbound with a fifteen-minute ETA. Hop into this hot rod, Miss Jade, so we can get you up to the roof," she said.

Wyrick was wearing scrubs and a zip-up hoodie that belonged to Charlie. She slid off the bed, bal-

ancing on her good leg, and hobbled to the wheelchair. She couldn't use crutches or a walker because
of her injured arm and shoulder, but Merlin's motorized wheelchair was still in his room. Once she got
home, she would manage.

Charlie shouldered his bag and walked beside her,
judging every curious look they got as a possible
threat. They rode the elevator up, and then were in
the shelter waiting for the chopper to arrive.

To Charlie's relief, Billy Wright was early. He
landed, then jumped out and opened the door as they
approached.

The sound of the rotors and the whipping wind put
a knot in Wyrick's gut. This was going to be a tense
flight back, trying not to relive the crash.

Billy gave Charlie a quick pat on the shoulder. "I
see that was a successful search." And then he smiled
at Wyrick. "Ma'am, if you would rather lie down on
the flight back, I have a new sleeping bag, or we'll
buckle you up in a seat. It's your call."

"Sitting," Wyrick said, shouting to be heard over
the noise. Then before she could think, Charlie lifted
her out of the wheelchair and into the cockpit.

She grabbed on to a seat to steady herself, and he
climbed in behind her.

"Sit in the outside seat so you don't have to bend
your leg," he said, so she settled into the seat behind
his and let him buckle her in, appreciating the time
he took to adjust her headset and seat straps to ac-
commodate her shoulder wound and the sling she
was wearing.

"Are you okay?" he asked.

She nodded.

Satisfied, Charlie loaded his gear. Then both men climbed in and they were gone.

Wyrick was sick to her stomach, scared that another chopper would appear out of nowhere and kill them all. She couldn't sit still for looking out and then leaning forward, looking up and looking down.

Then all of a sudden, Charlie's voice was in her ear.

"Wyrick, close your eyes. I've got this."

Once again, the panic she was feeling subsided as she looked up at the man in the seat in front of her. He was a physical presence between her and danger, and her trust of him was implicit.

She closed her eyes, and the next thing she knew, they were landing.

"Rise and shine, sunshine… We're here," Charlie said.

Wyrick woke just as the chopper was making its descent.

"We're in Dallas?"

"Wright's Aviation… It's on the outskirts," Charlie said.

"Any relation to Wilbur and Orville?" Wyrick asked.

Billy laughed. "No, ma'am. Just my daddy, Delroy, who taught me how to fly."

He was shutting everything down as Charlie got out.

"Sit tight. I'm going to drive the Jeep up to get

you," he said, and took off running toward the office where he'd left his Jeep days earlier.

It reminded Wyrick that her car was still at the hangar. Even though it would be a while before she'd be allowed to drive again, she wanted it home.

Then Charlie pulled up beside the chopper.

"Do you want front seat or lie down in the back seat?" he asked.

"In the front," she said, then held her breath against the pain as he scooped her up in his arms and moved her from the cockpit to his Jeep.

"Oh crap, that hurt," she said.

"Pain meds are wearing off. Hang on a sec," Charlie said, and got a blister pack out of his pocket, popped out a couple, then got a bottle of water from his backpack and opened it for her.

She swallowed the pills, then leaned against the seat, willing herself to relax as they drove away. They were back on the highway and heading into Dallas when she mentioned her car.

"All this time, I never once thought about my car still at the hangar," Wyrick said. "I'm going to call Benny and see if he'd be willing to drive it in for me."

Charlie shifted slightly in the seat. "Uh, Benny won't be able to do that. I'll figure something out and get it back to you," he said.

She frowned. "What do you mean, Benny can't do it?"

Charlie took a deep breath. There wasn't any way to sugarcoat this.

"Right after you took off, a couple drove up in a

van and began trying to get him to tell them where you went. He kept telling them he didn't know, and the man beat him up pretty badly, but he wouldn't tell. The cops said the office had been ransacked, though, so if anything had been written down, they found it. We think it's how the sniper in the chopper found you."

Charlie was watching when Wyrick went pale. When he saw her jaw set, and then her nostrils flare, he felt the anger.

"It's not your—"

She held up her hand, her voice shaking with rage. "Like hell, it's not my fault! Of course it's my fault. He'll take anyone down to get to me. This just confirms I am right in what I am going to do when I get home. And I'll tell you now—if you don't want the shit that's going to become my life to bleed over onto you and your business, I will understand. I can still do research for you and will do so gladly, but I can do it anonymously. No one has to know we're associated."

Charlie frowned. "What the hell are you talking about? What are you going to do?"

"Tell the world the truth about Cyrus Parks and Universal Theorem—about what they do, what they're involved in, which includes shit like Fourth Dimension, other levels of human trafficking, and experimenting with human life trying to re-create me. I'm the proof of their illegal experiments and the people they've made disappear to make it happen, and that's why he wants me gone."

There was a knot in Charlie's gut that was getting tighter by the moment. She was going to destroy herself to take them down.

"I've got your back. I'll always have your back. You do what you have to do," Charlie said, and kept driving.

Wyrick absorbed the vow in a way Charlie would never understand. He could have said *I love you*, and it wouldn't have touched her any deeper.

She tried to thank him, but knew if she opened her mouth she would cry, so she nodded instead, and the tears came anyway, rolling silently down her face as they drove.

A short while later, they were on the freeway and eyeing the darkening sky in the north, remembering there was a winter storm coming in, when Charlie broke the silence.

"I know the area you lived in, but I've never been there. You're going to have to direct me."

"Oh…okay," she said, and then proceeded to do so until they were approaching the estate. "It's the four-story brick with the black iron gates."

"Holy shit!" Charlie said. "That's a mansion."

"I know," Wyrick said. "Merlin was very wealthy, but I live in the basement apartment. Unfortunately, the remote to the gates is in my car back at the hangar, so you'll have to key in the code."

Charlie drove up to the entrance and rolled down the window.

"What's the code?" he asked.

"Seven, three, four, three," Wyrick said.

Charlie punched in the code and the gates swung inward.

"Drive around to the back," Wyrick said. "That's the ground-floor entrance to where I stay."

"Do you have an extra house key?"

She sighed. "Inside."

"If I pick the lock, am I going to set off an alarm?"

"No. I didn't set it because I was coming right back."

Charlie pulled up to the back entrance, then opened the glove box and got out a set of lock picks.

"Give me a couple of minutes, and then I'll come back and help you inside."

She nodded, then watched him striding to the door. He paused to check out the lock, then opened the wallet of lock picks. She saw him take out a couple and squat down in front of the door. Less than two minutes later, he stood up and opened the door, then came back for her.

"That was too easy," Wyrick said, thinking of all the months she'd spent sleeping here, feeling safe.

He shrugged. "Or I'm just good."

She rolled her eyes.

He grinned. "Are we hobbling, or do you want a ride?"

"Probably the ride," she said.

He leaned in, scooped her up into his arms and carried her inside, kicking the door shut behind him as they went.

She'd left lights on in the front part of the apartment, but she wanted to get into her bed.

"My bed's down the hall. I've been thinking about sleeping in it ever since that first night in the hospital."

Charlie carried her to the bedroom, then eased her down onto the side of the mattress. He took off her boots and the jacket she'd worn home.

She lay back with a groan, and when Charlie pulled the covers up over her, she sighed.

"I just need to rest for a little bit and then I'll be in the office, bringing UT down around their ears."

"Is the thermostat set okay for you?" Charlie asked.

"Yes. If you need to go home to get some things, now's the time to do it. That winter storm watch said the front would hit Dallas by midafternoon and it's really dark in the north."

"I don't want to leave you."

"Then get my gun. It's in the top drawer of that dresser."

He stared. "You have a gun."

"Yes, and it's bigger than the one you carry," she said.

Charlie opened the top drawer.

"Look under the bras."

There weren't any bras there, just a variety of colored socks, and then it hit him. She didn't have boobs, therefore she didn't have bras. He turned and glared at her.

"Your sense of humor is weird as hell," he said, then shoved the socks aside and put the gun on the table beside the bed.

"Go do what you need to do. There's a remote for the gate and a spare key to my apartment in the kitchen upstairs. Go up the stairs at the end of this hall. You'll come out in the kitchen. They're in the drawer next to the sink."

Charlie left the bedroom, curious as to what was above her, and hurried up the stairs, then came out into a huge kitchen. The design was old-fashioned, but the appliances were state-of-the-art. He couldn't imagine what the rest of the mansion must look like, but that was for another time. He found the remote and key, then ran back downstairs.

"Got them," he said. "I'll lock you in, and I won't be long, so don't shoot me when I come back."

"You're safe," she said. "I'm not a very good shot."

"With a gun that size, you don't have to be," Charlie muttered, and left on the run.

Wyrick heard him leave, and then his car driving off the property. She closed her eyes and concentrated on the pain in her body. She didn't quite understand how it worked, but in the same way she'd stopped herself from bleeding out, she could also block out pain. She needed to be clearheaded and at ease when she kicked the first block out from under Cyrus Parks. After that, it would be like a house of cards. It was all going to come tumbling down.

Eighteen

Charlie took all of the shortcuts to get to his apartment, then grabbed a suitcase and started packing. He didn't know how long he was going to be there, and he didn't expect it to be easy. They got on each other's last nerve on a regular basis, but she was, by God, worth the hassle. And after what he'd learned about her these past few days, all he wanted to do was fix every damn thing they'd broken in her.

He tossed in his laptop and iPad and a handful of charging cords, his favorite old sweats and his toiletries kit, then ran into the kitchen and put his entire candy stash into a plastic bag and packed it, too.

Chocolate.

It was what tamed the dragon in her.

He could hear the wind changing as he carried his suitcase out of the apartment into the parking garage and put it in his Jeep. Even as he was getting in, he could feel the temperature dropping. Damn, it was cold—cold enough to snow, as he headed back to the old mansion.

Wyrick conquered the pain, but she still had to get from her bedroom to the office without face-planting. She threw back the covers to get up, then gasped. Putting weight on her leg was hell.

Damn you to hell and back, Cyrus Parks, for doing this to me.

Then she hobbled out of the room, grabbing on to furniture as she went to steady herself, then into the hall, holding on to the wall to balance herself until she got to the office.

She slid into the seat with a sigh of relief, booted up the computer, then took her arm out of the sling, wincing as the muscles pulled.

The first thing she opened was the FAILSAFE file. She'd thought long and hard about how to do this, and who to tell first. Part of her concern at the outset had to do with who might be involved that would squelch the revelations of what she was about to unveil.

Her solution was to become the whistleblower, and she began sending the same information to every media outlet in the free world, including the Associated Press, and then to the judicial side, the FBI, the CIA and to the US attorney general, uploading the proof of her claims by sending file upon file, with data and test results of using humans as guinea pigs for their tests, and all of the failures—the bodies buried in doing it—then files with proof of the illegal testing and research they'd used to accomplish what they'd done.

It was an avalanche of information that, once released, could no longer be hidden, and the people guilty of collusion would fall along with them.

She sent proof of Cyrus Parks and UT's involvement in human trafficking to the FBI, to the attention of Special Agent Hank Raines, who had been in charge of taking down the Fourth Dimension, explaining that the very high-tech security installed at that place was from a system she had personally designed and created for UT when she still worked there, and that the only person who would have had knowledge of that specific system would have been Cyrus Parks. Then she linked the file she'd sent to the FBI to Hank's file, as well.

But the denouement—the final proof was her. Her personal story, from the time they'd experimented with the DNA of four scientists, to the gene-splicing and gene manipulation they'd used on the harvested eggs of the women who were their surrogates, to replanting the viable embryos, trying to create a race of geniuses.

All of her story was in that file…including her mother, who'd carried her and raised her until the age of five, her own kidnapping and her mother's murder meant to keep her from fighting UT for custody.

The file detailed her life in UT, and how she became an experiment they studied, using her abilities, testing her mental acuity daily, and pushing her constantly to see what she could do. Then she delineated, in detail, why they threw her away when she got cancer, then why they wanted her back when she survived, and why they now felt threatened by what she knew when she refused them.

It was all there...why they wanted her dead, and what they'd done in an effort to make that happen. Jade Wyrick was giving up all the secrets of her life to stay alive.

And when the last file was sent, she was too sad and exhausted to cry. This was the last day she would ever call her own again.

She was about to get up when she remembered Benny. Her shoulder was throbbing, but she couldn't rest until she made things right. She always paid him monthly by direct deposit, so she logged in to one of her local bank accounts and sent half a million dollars into his checking account, then sent him an email.

Benny, I just found out what happened to you. There are no words for how sorry I am that you were hurt because of me. I just want you to know that all of your medical bills will be taken care of, and I have deposited a sum of money into your account to offset any financial hardships as you are recovering. If anyone asks, I'm just someone you work for, and you know nothing about my life. It's safer for you that way.

She signed off, then hit Send.
The room was silent. The showerhead was still

dripping. But she could hear the wind rising, and it felt like the temperature was dropping.

She opened her desk drawer and pulled out a cell phone. It was a duplicate of the one she'd lost in the crash. The texts from her old one wouldn't be on it, but she still had all of her contact info, so she put it in her pocket, slipped her arm back into the sling and turned up the thermostat as she hobbled her way back to bed. She made it to the bathroom, and when she came out, she got in between the covers, pulled them up to her chin and closed her eyes.

Benny's wife discovered the email, which led her to check their bank account. When she saw the deposit, she screamed out in disbelief and began to cry. Her children came running, thinking she'd received bad news about their father. By the time she explained, they were all celebrating. Benny would be coming home tomorrow, but she couldn't wait to tell him the news.

Unaware of the magnitude of demons Wyrick had unleashed, Charlie returned to the mansion. He entered her apartment carrying a suitcase, and with a duffel bag slung over his shoulder. He dumped it all on the living room floor and then went to check on her.

"You're awake," he said.

"I know."

He sighed. "Let me rephrase that… I hope I didn't wake you."

"No. I heard you drive in. What's the weather doing?"

"Nothing yet. Can I get you anything?" Charlie asked.

"Chocolate?"

He made a U-turn and bolted back down the hall.

Wyrick thought she'd scared him off until he came back carrying the candy he'd brought from his apartment, along with a bottle of Pepsi he'd gotten from her refrigerator.

He dropped the candy onto the bed beside her, opened the bottle of Pepsi and set it on the table by the gun, then turned on her TV and handed her the remote.

"You don't have an extra bedroom," he said.

"I have eight of them," she said, and pointed at the ceiling.

"Sorry. Too far away. You own this monster. I'll bunk on your sofa tonight, but tomorrow, you're moving up a floor."

"I was going to remodel," she said.

"Instead, you got shot out of the air. You are a phoenix, Wyrick, but don't push your luck. Heal first. Remodel second."

"I pulled the trigger on Cyrus Parks. Be prepared."

He looked at her closer, then sat down on the side of the bed, dug out one of his candy bars and started eating it.

Wyrick stared. He was sitting on her bed like he

had a right to be there, eating candy he'd just given to her.

She frowned. "What are you doing?"

"Getting prepared," he said. "If you started a war, you don't get all the chocolate."

When Special Agent Hank Raines saw the email from Wyrick with a subject heading of Fourth Dimension, he immediately opened it.

It took a few moments for shock to set in, and then he began opening file after file, reading in disbelief. But then he opened the file on her personal story and nearly fell out of his chair.

"Holy shit!" he muttered, and grabbed his cell phone.

He didn't know what had happened to prompt this or even how to take it, but he knew someone who would. He called Charlie Dodge.

While Wyrick was resting, Charlie was upstairs exploring. He found the empty bedroom downstairs, and when he saw the wheelchair, he guessed it must have been Merlin's room. He didn't know how she would feel about sleeping there, but it was a logical choice.

Then he found the elevator and rode it up to the second floor, and found the seven other bedroom suites, each one elegant in its own way. It reminded him somewhat of the Dunleavy castle in Denver, but on a smaller scale.

The elevator was the turning point. If she wanted

to be upstairs, then there was a safe way for her to get up and down from the second floor while she healed.

Then he went through the kitchen, checking to see what was in the refrigerator, but it had been completely cleaned out. It was cold, but sitting empty. The butler's pantry was huge, and the food pantry a separate thing altogether. This way of living was so out of his comfort zone that he was almost intimidated by the opulence.

It wasn't something he would have ever aspired to, and the Wyrick he knew didn't really fit in here, either, but then he reminded himself—he'd only seen one tiny part of the amazing creature she was, and had no idea of how she'd lived before she went into hiding.

He was about to head back downstairs when his cell phone rang, and when he saw it was Hank Raines, he paused to answer.

"Hey, Hank. What's up?"

"I have no freaking idea. That's why I called you. What the hell is going on with Wyrick?"

Charlie frowned. "Uh…she's home and healing."

"Healing from what?" Hank asked.

"She was in her chopper last week, flying back from Galveston, when a sniper in another chopper intercepted her and shot her down. She crashed in Sam Houston National Forest with a bullet wound in her shoulder and another in her leg. I was with the search party that found her. She's been recovering in a hospital in Houston up until today, when I brought her home."

"Jesus…why would anyone do that?"

"To shut her up," Charlie said.

"Might that someone be a consortium called Universal Theorem, headed by a man named Cyrus Parks?" Hank asked.

"Yeah, why?"

"She sent me some information that I didn't quite know what to do with, but now it's beginning to make sense. I need to contact the director and—"

"Uh… I don't think you'll have to," Charlie said.

Hank frowned. "Why not?"

"Unless she changed her mind, that same information is already in his hands, and a multitude of other nationwide agencies, maybe worldwide. I don't understand all of what it entails, but this wasn't the first attempt on her life, and I guess she sees this as her only recourse to staying alive. Tell the truth of how she came to be, and take down the people who are still trying to play God. They've been trying to silence her to protect themselves, but doing what she's doing is a huge sacrifice to her personal privacy. She's giving up her sovereignty to save herself."

Hank's voice was beginning to shake. "By nationwide, do you mean local authorities? State level? National level? Don't you think that's overkill?"

Charlie frowned. "First of all, *overkill* is a poor choice of word considering what I just told you. And we're talking Wyrick here…who trusts no one. Why would she trust people who could help bury her and hide the crime?"

"Okay, I should have chosen a better word, but dammit, there are good cops, too," Hank said.

"Not in her world," Charlie said. "She sent the same thing to the media, too. There's not going to be any secret whistleblower. She gave herself up to prove it, and I made her a promise to keep her alive to see it happen."

"Holy shit," Hank muttered.

"Well, I'd say you guys have some scrambling to do. Get some warrants ASAP, before Cyrus Parks and his people start disappearing or destroying their own evidence."

"They can destroy all they want," Hank said. "I don't know how she did it, but the files she sent are hard proof. There are even videos of lab experiments and people doing them. How the hell she got hold of all this stuff is beyond me, but we have it, and if you're right, so does every other motherfucker in the nation. It's going to show up on every news outlet, at which time there will be religious groups after UT for trying to play God. There will be people after them for human trafficking. And another branch after them for medical malpractice and experimentation on human embryos—the freaking list goes on and on. Even the companies attached to them are going to be in deep shit."

"From your lips to God's ears," Charlie said. "Now, all of you, get off your butts and start picking them up for questioning, or whatever you call the tap dance you do with criminals these days."

"You sound a little bitter toward the justice system, too," Hank said.

"Maybe if there was real justice in this world, I wouldn't be," Charlie countered. "I gotta go."

"Okay...and give her my best. Tell her thanks, and to get well soon. It's not going to take long before the world comes after her, too, just to see what she looks like, so if you need federal protection at any time, let me know. I'd consider it an honor to be one of her bodyguards."

The intensity in Hank's voice was proof of how moved he'd been by Wyrick's story, and it occurred to Charlie that he might need to know what she'd turned loose, too.

He went downstairs, dreading the conversation, and found her in the kitchen, leaning against the counter and eating peanut butter out of a jar, her arm out of the sling.

"Hey, you're not—"

"Did you know that the heat register in the kitchen leads right down into the one here in the ceiling above my head, and that I heard every word of your conversation with Hank Raines?"

"Good. Then I don't have to repeat it. So, did your psychic-self hear his side of the conversation, too, or just me?"

"Just you."

"Then you need to know that he sends his wishes for you to heal quickly, and then if you have to travel anywhere to testify, or need protection at any time, that he would consider it an honor to be one of your bodyguards."

Wyrick's eyes widened. She licked the peanut butter off the spoon and then put it in the sink, and screwed the lid back on the jar. When she looked up, there were tears in her eyes.

The world shifted under Charlie's feet when he saw them. Dammit.

"Don't you dare cry," he muttered.

She glared. "I don't know what you're talking about."

"Fair enough. I don't know what everyone else is talking about, either, so do you think it would be okay if I read the stuff you turned loose on the world?"

She shrugged. "You signed up for my war. I agree you need to know what you're fighting for. Did you bring your laptop?"

"Yes."

"I'll send you the same links that everyone else received. You can read to your heart's content."

She started to hobble down the hall, and then he came up behind her, picked her up and carried her to the office.

"You can't keep doing this," she said.

"I won't have to, once I get your ass upstairs and in that motorized wheelchair I saw."

"It was Merlin's," she said.

"I guessed. Was that his room?"

She nodded. "And now it's mine."

Surprise showed in his voice. "You're going to pick that one?"

"The only people trying to hurt me are alive. I'm not afraid of the dead. Besides, I've already had a talk with the house."

He blinked. "You talked to the house?"

"Yes. Now go away so I can send you the files. I can't think when you're standing here."

Charlie turned to leave and then stopped.

"Since when does my presence disturb you from doing anything? You always shut everyone out when you're working."

"I don't know. Since I fell out of the sky? Now, do you want to read the stuff or not?"

He walked out, thinking about what she'd said, and then the files began coming. He started reading and fell into the hell into which she'd been born.

He read for hours, and when he finally glanced up and saw the time, he realized she must be starving. He set the laptop aside to go check on her and found her back in bed—this time, sound asleep.

He stood there a moment, looking at the healing cut on her head and the bruising all over her face and neck, and then walked out before she woke up and caught him staring.

He didn't have words for what he was feeling, but it wasn't pity. She'd become an integral part of his business life, but seeing her like this, and knowing what she had endured in her short life, hurt his heart in a different way.

The media outlets were the first to react to what she'd sent. They'd just had the story of the century handed to them. Journalists and editors went ballistic, thinking they had been the sole recipients, and started scrambling to verify it.

But then the first story broke in an online paper only a day later, and then another one from another news outlet, and then another from a different paper in a different part of the country. At that point, it became apparent that everyone had been given the same information and, in the current mode of the day, were running with what they'd been given without verifying anything or anyone. In the long run, it wasn't going to matter, because the God's truth of Universal Theorem—and Jade Wyrick's life—was in every file.

Ironically, the first story the media broke was the one about her. The media dubbed her the Genesis child—the only one of her kind, created by an updated version of mad scientists, in a place called Universal Theorem, headed by a man named Cyrus Parks.

And then someone in the media made the connection between Cyrus Parks the mad scientist and the Cyrus Parks who'd recently donated forty million dollars to hurricane-ravaged islands, and the hunt was on as to which interview they'd score first— the one with the mad scientist or the Genesis child he'd created, but as it turned out, the Feds got to Parks first.

It was snowing in Virginia. The flakes were the kind Cyrus's mother had called "duck feathers." So big and so soft that they floated, landing with wet splats on windshields, melting upon impact.

He was in the company limo and on his way home from work when he got a call. He recognized the number—an informant he had within the justice system—and answered quickly.

"Hello."

"Your target went down, but she didn't die and she's back in Dallas."

For a few moments, Cyrus felt faint. He couldn't believe what he was hearing.

"And you know this, how?" he asked.

"I know because she just unloaded proof of everything you and your people are about upon the world. File upon file of data, readouts of testing, names, places, even videos of experiments. And then she gave herself up as proof. I got word that it went nationwide in the media, as well. You can't bury this. It's never going to go away. I can't protect you anymore."

Cyrus still had the phone to his ear when the call went dead.

She was shot and crashed and she's still alive? What the fuck? Is she turning into some comic-book immortal?

As for leaking the stories, it was his worst fear coming true. He'd pushed too hard, and then failed twice in taking her down. She was giving herself up to destroy him. He'd gambled and lost, and he knew it. His days as a free man were numbered.

He'd thought about running, but there was no way

he'd get out of the country, and he wasn't sure if there was a safe place for him to be. Jade hadn't just set the hounds on him and UT. The collateral damage from this was going to be massive, and there were a lot of powerful people who were going to be caught up in the sweep. The evidence was so complete and so damning, there was nowhere to go and nowhere to hide.

Even if he had his people scrub every computer on the premises at UT, he knew there were people skilled enough to retrieve it. But from what he'd just been told, the files she'd turned over were so massive and so detailed that copping a plea was never going to be an option. He thought of putting a gun to his head and then shelved it. He was too big a coward to take himself out.

It took two days before the FBI arrived at his office unannounced. Cyrus stood as they flashed their badges and laid a handful of search warrants on his desk.

"You knocked?" he drawled.

"Search warrants, sir. You and Universal Theorem have been accused of illegal medical practices involving human embryos, hiding the deaths of surrogate mothers and the babies they were carrying, human trafficking…"

The agent was still talking, but Cyrus tuned him out. He already knew the charges. He was trying to wrap his head around the fact that this was really happening.

"Am I under arrest?"

"You're being taken in for questioning," the agent said.

A cold shudder ran through him. Someone was reading him his rights as another was patting him down. He looked around at the opulence of his office and the view of Richmond from the windows, and as the handcuffs locked shut upon his wrists, he had a feeling he was never coming back.

As they walked him out of his office, he locked eyes with his secretary and uttered his last order.

"Roberta, call my lawyer."

It was just after breakfast and Wyrick was in the office scanning through the online news feeds. It had been days since Wyrick pulled the trigger on Cyrus Parks. She'd read the stories that came out. She knew Cyrus Parks was being detained, and that other arrests had been made. She knew the media was looking for her, and the sooner she gave her first interview, the sooner the pressure would be off.

The first thing she had to face were the emails she'd been ignoring. When she'd sent the files, she'd sent them from her public email account, giving all of the recipients the freedom to contact her. So the barrage of waiting mail to be read was inevitable. At last count, there were over four thousand. It made her skin crawl just thinking about it. She'd been an oddity to people who saw her out and about, but an anonymous oddity. But like her hair and her boobs, that part of her life was gone.

The good part was she was healing—really fast.

The bad part was she didn't really need Charlie's help to take care of herself anymore. And she was getting antsy. Sitting around waiting for the other shoe to fall wasn't like her. It was time to come out of the shadows. So she put her laptop aside and went to look for Charlie.

Nineteen

Charlie had fallen in love with this old mansion. He loved the dark wood and the grand hall with the marble floor—all the high tray ceilings and the ornate decor carved into the massive fireplaces of the living room and the den.

The den, which was right across the hall from Wyrick, had become his room. The oversize, overstuffed chairs were made for a man his size, and the massive sofa where he'd been sleeping was long enough for him to stretch his legs.

A high-tech television mounted on the wall had obviously been Merlin's newest toy, and there was a wet bar with a mini fridge where he stashed his midnight snacks. More than once, he was reminded that his entire apartment would fit inside this den with space left over. There was a half bath for the sake of convenience, but he used one of the bathrooms upstairs to shower and shave.

He knew Wyrick was in a holding pattern. She

had to get over the shock of what happened, as well as the healing. But he also knew she was priming herself for the first public appearance she would have to make.

Being dubbed the Genesis baby was like being a human hybrid—a sideshow freak. He was angry on her behalf with no way to help other than keep her safe.

When she went to the office after breakfast, he went up to the third floor. Part of it was attic storage, but there were small empty rooms that Wyrick told him had once been the living quarters of house servants. There were no fireplaces up here to warm the area, and only one small window per room for cooling in the summer. It would have been a very uncomfortable place to sleep and a hard life to live.

He was poking through old boxes when he heard her calling him. He ran out of the attic to the head of the stairs and looked down through the stairwell.

"I'm up here! I'll be right down," he said.

She was waiting at the foot of the stairs, holding her coat.

"What's up?" he asked.

"I want to go get my car."

"You're sure you're up to it?" he asked.

"Yes. Will you take me?"

"Yes, but since your right shoulder and right leg were the main injuries you suffered, you have to promise to drive the speed limit."

She didn't hesitate. "Agreed."

"Was your driver's license in the crash?" Charlie asked.

"I left it in the Mercedes."

"Then you're good to go. Give me a second to get my coat and car keys," he said, and took off running at a lope. He came back wearing a flannel-lined jean jacket and his Stetson.

He helped her on with her coat, then walked her to the back door.

"Wait here," he said, and went out back to the detached four-car garage to get the Jeep.

The wind was sharp, but the sky was clear. It felt good to be outside. When he drove back to pick her up, she was also outside waiting, wrapped up in her white faux fur coat with the hood pulled up over her head. There was a look of expectation on her face as she got in and buckled up.

Charlie glanced over to make sure she was settled and then drove away, closing the main gates behind them as they went. They hadn't gone far when Wyrick started talking. Casual conversation was not her chosen form of communication, so he knew what she had to say was important.

"Has anyone from the federal justice level contacted you about wanting to talk to me?" she asked.

"Yes. I told them you were still healing, but would make yourself available when you were physically able."

"Who was it?"

"Someone from the Department of Justice," Charlie said.

"Then when we get back, tell them I'm ready."

"Okay," Charlie said. "Do you want to talk to them at your home?"

"No. I think I need to have a lawyer present. Merlin's lawyer, Rodney Gordon, offered his services, but he's mainly an estate lawyer. I don't know who to ask."

"I do. Will you trust me to get one?" Charlie asked.

She nodded. "Yes. And there's something else. I have over four thousand emails I haven't looked at, but I'm going to have to allow some kind of televised interview to get the pressure off people trying to hunt me down for one."

"I agree," Charlie said. "What are you thinking?"

"I'm not going to do it at just one news outlet and then have to appear at each one separately, telling the same story, answering the same questions over and over. But I will pick a venue for all media only and, after a brief statement, answer all of their questions. But it has to be live. I'm not giving anyone the chance to manipulate my words later."

"You've thought this through, haven't you?" Charlie said.

She answered abruptly, but with no emotion.

"I have handed my personal privacy to the world on a fucking plate, so, yes, I thought it through long and hard before I did it."

He knew detachment was part of her wall, and it was obviously back up.

"Then we'll make it happen," he said.

Satisfied, she focused on the freeway traffic as

they headed for the private airport. But arriving at the hangar and seeing the crime scene tape set her in a mood again. Then going inside and seeing the chaos in the office was a brutal reminder of what had happened to Benny.

Charlie heard her mumble something about "the bastard" beneath her breath and knew she was talking about Parks.

"Benny is home and healing, just like you," Charlie said. "I checked on him the other day He's over the moon about what he called 'your generosity.' What did you do?"

"Nothing he didn't deserve. Will you please shut the hangar doors after I back out?"

"Yes, and I'm following you home, so don't speed. I'm not going to consider you safe until all of this has passed and the guilty are permanently behind bars."

She got in the car, retrieved her key from a hidden compartment in the console, and when she started the engine and buckled herself in, she sighed.

She was mobile again.

She backed out, then sat with it idling, waiting for Charlie to shut the hangar doors and get back in the Jeep before leaving. A promise was a promise.

And when they got back to the mansion, she parked in one garage stall, and Charlie pulled into the one beside her.

They walked inside in mutual silence, then paused in the kitchen.

"Are you ready?" Charlie said.

Wyrick nodded. "I'm starting with email and

looking up a public venue here in Dallas to hold the press conference."

"And I have to call a Fed about your deposition, and call a friend to get you a lawyer. So let's do this."

They went their separate ways with purpose—Wyrick to the office, and Charlie to the den, and at 2:00 p.m. Charlie knocked on the office door and walked in.

There was an empty Pepsi bottle on her desk and a candy wrapper near it, and her dark eyes looked haunted. He had a momentary urge to put his arms around her and just hold her, and then the thought startled the hell out of him, so he frowned instead.

"Quit what you're doing and come to the kitchen. I have pizza."

She stood, picked up her trash and followed him. She tossed the trash, then sat down at the kitchen table where she'd sat with Merlin, planning his earthly exit. She wiped her hands across her face.

"Don't talk yet. Just eat," Charlie said, and so she did.

She downed two pieces of the hamburger-and-mushroom pizza and drank the glass of sweet tea he had waiting, then got a chocolate chip cookie from the plate between them.

At that point, Charlie started talking.

"Your lawyer's name is Judd Perry. He's a shark and a friend. He'll protect you. Is that okay?"

She nodded.

"Then I'll let him know later. The DOJ is hedging about setting a day and time to talk to you, which leads me to believe they may be working on plea agreements in lieu of trials."

She nodded. Whatever happened, she had to deal with it. She crumbled the cookie she was holding onto her plate and then put her hands in her lap.

"I have received, at last count, eighty-five death threats. Proposals of marriage from twenty-two men and three women. I have hundreds upon hundreds of requests for winning lottery numbers. A good number of churches tell me I'm a child of the devil. A few others offered to save my soul for a generous donation. Every major newspaper wants an interview. I have invitations to appear on every major talk show, from all of the big networks. If circus sideshows still existed, I would be the freak show's main attraction. Some people have given statements to the press saying they've known me since birth and that I'm from another planet."

She picked up a piece of the cookie she'd crumbled and put it in her mouth. She was crying as she chewed and didn't know it.

"It was harder than I expected to find the right venue for the press conference, but I've reserved the Innovation Ballroom at the Hyatt Regency DFW International for eight days from now. They had an event cancellation, or I wouldn't have been able to get it. I hired the media company they work with to set it up. It will be by invitation only, so no media will be allowed in without a pass. There will be facial recognition software at the main entrance, and guards between the main entrance and the one into the ballroom stopping anyone who doesn't pass inspection. If I'm assassinated, it's on my own terms."

Charlie came out of his chair, circled the table and pulled her up, wrapping his arms around her so fast and so tight that she didn't have time to resist.

"Don't! Just don't fucking say that. You might feel like you're alone in this shit storm, but you're not! Understood? I've got your back. You have friends in the FBI who have your back. You just got a dose of the nutcases, but there are way more people who will think you're God's gift to the world, and see you as a victim of what UT did, not as a part of it."

Wyrick was in shock that she was in his arms, but everything he was saying was burying the panic.

Charlie rocked her where they stood, holding her close. He couldn't stand by and let her think she had to hurt alone. She was Wyrick. She was his friend and his partner. And she was breaking his heart.

For the longest time, neither spoke, and when he finally turned her loose, she looked up at him.

"In the movies, this is where the hero runs his fingers through the heroine's hair and tells her it's going to be okay, but we're shit out of luck here. I'm bald, and you're my boss, and so I'm just going to say thank you once, and trust you to remember that still stands, even if I never say it again."

Charlie blinked, and then he grinned.

"Lady, I cannot wait to witness the ass-kicking you're going to unleash on the world. Give me the dates and times, and I'll let Special Agent Raines know that his offer of bodyguard services has been accepted." Then he glanced back at the last piece of pizza in the box. "Are you going to eat that?"

"Nope. It's got your name all over it," she said, and went to refill her tea.

Cyrus Parks did not get bail, nor did he get a judge who would even consider a plea agreement for less than life in prison. It had to do with all the collateral damage of using humans for guinea pigs and the ensuing deaths of failed testing. And they hadn't even gotten to the charges involving him with human trafficking, kidnapping and a list of medical malpractice charges as long as his arm. His choice was a guilty plea and life in a federal prison with no possibility of parole—or a court trial and the revelation of Jade Wyrick's testimony. It was his own damn fault. He should have left well enough alone.

He'd heard through his lawyer that more than thirty people in five different facilities had been arrested with charges similar to his, and more were pending. Employees of all of the facilities were making deals to lessen their sentences, and their testimonies were adding to what Jade had unleashed.

He was afraid of the future. But there was a light at the end of this tunnel. There was always the chance he wouldn't be alive to suffer it.

The past seven days were a nightmare of logistics. Just when Wyrick thought everything was settled and in place for the press conference, another problem would arise. But she dealt with it, using the same skill and concentration she gave to Charlie's agency. The press conference was tomorrow. But today, a prosecutor for the federal attorney general's office was coming to Dodge Investigations to take her deposition.

She'd dressed down on purpose, wearing a black leather jacket and pants, with a white satin vest beneath. The red dragon's head was visible above the V-neck of the vest, and the silver eye shadow below her brow ridge drew attention to her dark eyes. With no other color, not even lipstick, she was a monochromatic version of the feminine mystic. A Picasso portrait-in-waiting for a long-dead master.

She drove herself to work with Charlie on her tail. It was how they rolled these days, and when she pulled into the drive-through bakery to get the sweet rolls for their coffee bar, he was in the parking lot waiting. They got to the office building in unison and went in together in silence.

Charlie knew she was dreading the interview and he dreaded it for her, but the lawyer she had yet to meet was going to be there an hour early so they could talk.

They arrived at eight, and by the time she'd gone through the motions, she was at ease. The only difference between what had been and what was now was the video camera above the door, and the buzzer they'd had added with the sign above it.

Ring to be admitted.

There would be no surprise visits from unexpected visitors, whether they were clients or not.

Judd Perry arrived on time, but when he reached for the doorknob and then saw the sign, then the video camera, he was taken aback. The whole concept of Jade Wyrick's safety was brought home in those moments. So he pressed the buzzer and looked up, knowing they would be looking to identify him.

"Judd Perry to see Ms. Wyrick," he said.

"I'll get it," Charlie said, and let him in. "Hey, buddy. Thanks for this."

"I'm happy to help," Judd said, and then saw Wyrick, and came toward her with an outstretched hand. "Ms. Wyrick, Judd Perry at your service. It is a pleasure to meet you."

Wyrick liked his vibe, and immediately tuned in to his bulldog nature, which was exactly what she was going to need. Someone who wasn't afraid to bite. Someone who wouldn't let go of a truth.

"Thank you for coming," Wyrick said.

Charlie pointed to his office. "We have an hour before the lawyer from the DOJ arrives. Why don't the two of you come into my office and do whatever you need to do to prepare."

He got them seated at the small conference table at the far end of the room.

"Can I get anyone a coffee…or a Pepsi?"

Judd smiled. "I'll take coffee."

Wyrick shook her head. "What do I need to know?"

They were getting set up when Charlie got a call. He walked out of the room to take it, and when he came back, he was grinning.

"The deposition has been canceled. Cyrus Parks isn't going to trial. He took the plea agreement. Life without parole in a federal prison. So no opposing counsel is needing testimony."

"What a pity. I was prepared for my close-ups," Wyrick said, and strode out of the room.

Judd's first impulse was to laugh, but the line was delivered with such a straight face, he wasn't sure. Then he saw Charlie grinning and smiled.

"Is she always like that?"

"You mean, the cut-your-throat wit where you bleed out before you know it? Yeah, she's always like that."

Judd nodded. "I like that. Is she seeing anybody?"

The question took Charlie off guard.

"Uh...no."

"Do you think she—?"

"Right now, I wouldn't give any man on earth a snowball's chance in hell of even getting a smile out of her. She's in a fight for her life, Judd."

Judd flushed.

"You're right. Hell, I'm sorry. But she's such a unique woman, I couldn't help but—"

"You go do you, but I warned you."

Judd nodded. "Got it," he said, and packed up his

briefcase and followed her to the outer office. "It was a pleasure to meet you. If you're ever in the—"

It was the look she gave him that sucked up the last part of what he was going to say, and saved him from a humiliating turndown.

"...as I was going to say...if you ever have need of a lawyer again, you have my number."

"Yes, I do," she said, and then pressed the button at her desk to let him out.

"So, that's the end of that for today. Wanna go home?"

She nodded.

"Then grab those sweet rolls. I'll get the lights," he said.

Within minutes, they were back in their respective vehicles, with Charlie bringing up the rear to make sure she wasn't being tailed.

Charlie stayed out of her way the rest of the day, doing some research work for a client, while Wyrick did a follow-up on all of the details for tomorrow. The media company sent her video of the setup, including the big screens behind the podium and the rows of seats out in the ballroom.

They had the cameras set up for facial recognition, so Wyrick went in and linked her own FR program to their systems. There would be no crowd swarming in for seating. Instead, entering one by one, presenting the passes they'd received.

Hank Raines was all about the security for her, and had a team set up to man it all and verify the passes, and then other agents who would stand guard both on the stage behind her and down on the floor at either ends of the stage.

Charlie already knew his place. Beside her and two steps to her right—within her peripheral vision so she'd know he was there. The security level was presidential.

The rest of it was up to her.

Once he stopped by her office and set a Pepsi and a Snickers bar on her desk and left. The next time he saw her, she was in the kitchen, digging through the refrigerator.

"Do we need to order groceries again?"

She turned, then took a deep breath. Charlie was standing in the doorway in his sock feet wearing a pair of old gray sweatpants and a red long-sleeve T-shirt. The word *outstanding* came and went, and then she regained her focus.

"There's food. I just don't really want what's here."

"I can order. What sounds good?"

"Ribs."

He grinned and gave her a thumbs-up.

"Good call. I'll order. Want fries?"

"Yes, but that's all. No slaw. No beans."

"Meat and potatoes… My kind of woman," Charlie said, and walked out without realizing what he'd said.

She knew he didn't mean it the way she heard it, but it was a reminder not to get too comfortable with his presence. Once the shock and newness of her existence leveled off in the media, she would find a new normal and he would be gone.

And now that the decision of what to eat had been settled, she wandered back into the hall and then looked up.

The circular mural of naked nymphs romping with satyrs among a woodland setting had always intrigued her when she'd come here for the Mensa meetings. She had tried to imagine Merlin as a little boy growing up here, passing under this somewhat salacious artist rendering daily, but she never could see it. He would always be Merlin—the ancient wizard—to her.

Dinner came and went, and after the kitchen was clean, Wyrick uttered a terse good-night to Charlie and went to bed.

The press conference was for 2:00 p.m. tomorrow. She was tense and in despair that this was happening. She had puttered around for an hour, preparing herself for a sleepless night, when the security alarm at the front gates suddenly went off, and all of the searchlights and strobe lights and floodlights came on, lighting up the grounds all the way around the house and up into the sky.

Charlie was dreaming about Annie when the alarms went off. He came flying across the hall into her room with a gun in his hand, barefoot and wearing nothing but a pair of sweatpants.

"Stay here and lock your door," he said, and slammed it shut behind him.

She grabbed her gun and took off after him.

Charlie was all the way up the hall when he heard her running up behind him and turned around.

"What do you think you're doing?" he shouted.

"I'm always your backup."

"Jesus. Then stay out of sight. The cops should be here shortly."

The place was lit up like Christmas as Charlie slipped out of the house. The cold air was a rude awakening to the fact that he was only half-dressed, but when he saw a man running across the grounds toward the back of the house, he leaped off the end of the porch to cut him off, then took him down in a flying tackle.

"Don't shoot! Don't shoot!" the man kept shouting.

Charlie rolled him over onto his back, saw the camera hanging around his neck and yanked it off.

"Idiot paparazzi? What the hell kind of pictures did you hope to get in the dark?"

"I was going to hide in the bushes and get some stuff tomorrow when you came out for the press conference."

Charlie dragged him to his feet, picked up the camera and started walking him toward the gate.

"You're gonna get pictures all right, but they'll be your mug shots."

"Aw, man…just let me go and—"

"Your ride is here," Charlie said, as a police car came flying up the street with lights flashing. The officer pulled up on the other side of the gates and got out with his gun in his hands.

"We're good!" Charlie said. "I'm bringing him out." Then he punched in the code and walked the man out to the cop.

"Intruder on the grounds. We're pressing charges," Charlie said.

The officer handcuffed the man and put him in the back of his cruiser, then glanced at Charlie.

"Do you have a permit for that gun?" he asked.

"Yes. I'm a licensed PI, but I don't wear my identification to bed. If you need it, I can go back—"

"I thought you looked familiar," the cop said. "You're Charlie Dodge, aren't you?"

Charlie nodded. "Guilty. Want the ID?"

"Naw, we're good," he said.

"Then I'm going back inside. If you need info, you know how to reach me."

The cop left with the photographer as Charlie shut the gates and made a run for the house.

Wyrick was standing inside the door with the gun in her hands when he returned.

"Are you okay? Who was it?" she asked.

"Paparazzi. No gun. Just a camera. I'll reset the security alarm. You go back to bed."

She put a hand on her heart and then looked at him long and hard before walking back down the hall.

Charlie watched her go, thinking how this huge house made her look so little. She was so tall and so in charge that he'd never thought of her like that before. He thought about stopping by to make sure she was okay, but by the time he got everything reset, she was back in her room with the lights out.

He paused outside her door, then shook his head and went back into his room, pouring himself a shot of whiskey.

One sip to warm him up.

The second sip to settle the thunder of his heart.

Twenty

The media invited to the press conference had been slowly gathering at the Hyatt since before noon. The stage and sound systems were set up and working. The big screens behind the podium would allow perfect viewing, even from the seating in the back of the ballroom.

They began letting them into the foyer outside the ballroom at noon, and as soon as they had passed through the checkpoints, they drifted toward the buffet tables set up inside, filling plates with appetizers and fruits while music played in the background. As they began recognizing familiar faces, they gathered in little groups, discussing the shocking revelations of the Genesis baby's existence.

Finally, the last of the invited guests had arrived, and the checkpoint was shut down. The guards shut the doors into the ballroom, and then four of them stood guard outside while the men Special Agent

Raines had brought with him were inside and set up at their specific points around the ballroom.

Wyrick and Charlie were already there, waiting in a small room just off the stage, and she'd been sitting in total silence with her hands folded in her lap ever since their arrival, gathering herself for what was coming.

Charlie wished he had words to ease her.

He glanced at the clock. It was almost time.

And then Hank came knocking on the door.

He got up and opened it.

"It's time," Hank said.

"Is the live feed set up?" Charlie asked.

"It's all a go. I haven't seen this much detail since my last assignment with the president. You did good, Wyrick."

She stood up, then lifted her chin in a familiar gesture Charlie recognized. She was ready for battle.

"Just trying to stay alive," she said.

Hank grimaced. "Would it help if I mentioned you look like ten million bucks?"

She shrugged. "It's all about the mask you present to the world—and I'm about to spill my guts in front of it."

"You did a damn fine thing," Hank said. "We're taking down human trafficking rings by the hour. We've shut down more illegal research labs, and there's so much more that's coming down with it. God only knows how many lives you're saving."

Wyrick glanced at Charlie.

"Right beside you," he said.

She nodded. "Then let's go."

Hank led them across the hall into the backstage area of the ballroom.

The journalists had already taken their seats, so when Hank gave a signal for the sound crew to stop the music, the room fell silent. All eyes were focused on a spotlight sweeping across the stage. When the curtains began to open, the hush deepened—and then she appeared, pausing a moment in the light.

The fact that she was bald seemed to go with her otherworldly appearance. She was unusually tall and whip-thin, and wearing formfitting pants in black leather, silver over-the-knee boots with three-inch heels, silver glitter eye shadow framing eyes so dark they looked black. Her lips were red, which then drew the eye to the red-and-black dragon on her chest, visible through a white shirt so sheer that it shimmered.

When she started walking toward the podium like a panther stalking prey, the people in the front row leaned back in their seats.

Then Charlie Dodge appeared behind her. Taller than her six-plus feet by five inches, wearing dark slacks and a Western-style sport coat with a white open-collar shirt beneath, he matched her stride all the way to the microphone.

Within seconds, three agents from the FBI, including Special Agent Hank Raines, took their places onstage a distance behind her. There was no mistaking the level of security she'd brought with her or why it was there. They'd all read the files. They knew about the continuing arrests that had ensued since the files were released, and they thought they knew Jade Wyrick. But they were wrong.

Jade was stone-faced and focused when she reached the podium. She paused until she caught a glimpse of Charlie to her right, noted the location of the television crews scattered about the room that would be filming live, and then she turned her attention to the audience before her.

"My name is Jade Wyrick, and this press conference is a one and done. I won't be available for interviews later. There will be no personal appearances on talk shows. I am not available for your entertainment. After being stalked for years, then tailed everywhere I went, there were two attempts made on my life. The last one less than two weeks ago. After being shot out of the air, I crawled out of a burning chopper, bleeding out with two bullet wounds. My boss, Charlie Dodge, who stands here with me, was with the search team who found me before I died, and I am still in recovery from that. I knew then that as long as Universal Theorem was still in business under Cyrus Parks, my life wasn't worth a shit. I'm going public purely to save my life."

Then she glanced at all of the cameras.

"You've all read varying stories about the people who made me—and what they did afterward. How many women died. How many embryos were genetically and medically manipulated trying to re-create me. You all named me the Genesis baby—the only one of my kind in existence. The crazies already hate me just for breathing. The religious zealots want to pray the devil out of me. But I am not to blame for how I came to be. They continued to fail in re-creating me, because when they murdered the woman who was my mother, they lost their chance to ever re-create me again. I have the DNA of four of the greatest scientific and psychic minds in the world in me. But I have the blood and DNA of Laura Wyrick in me, too. I came from one of her harvested eggs. I am a science experiment that worked, and they wanted me back. She didn't agree, and they killed her to make me theirs."

Jade took a deep breath and looked down at the podium, at her hands, gripping it as tightly as they'd gripped the pole she was holding on the merry-go-round, and when she looked up, her dark eyes were blazing with a rage she rarely let herself feel.

"They kidnapped me from a merry-go-round, on a beautiful, sunny Sunday afternoon. There were men in clown masks who grabbed me. I heard her scream. And I heard the shots that killed her. But UT had their experiment back, and I lost the rest of my childhood in labs, performing like a monkey on a chain for pieces of candy. Can Jade put this piece of electronics back together? Can Jade work these mathematical equations? Does Jade know how jet propulsion works? Does Jade understand the stars? See how long it takes Jade to crack a code, to hack a computer, to not leave any tracks in doing it. What they didn't know was that in doing all that, I also found the files to me...and I purposefully began failing little bits of the tests they gave me, because I didn't want them to know that my skills, knowledge and power were growing at an alarming rate... even to me."

She paused to take a drink of the water from the glass beneath the podium when Charlie swept it out of her hands.

The audience gasped.

"Sorry," he said softly, then leaned into the mic and pointed at the servers manning the buffet tables. "Someone bring me an unopened bottle of water."

Wyrick looked at him then, realizing why he'd done that, then looked back at the audience.

"I am an important commodity in Charlie Dodge's world, too. I bring bear claws to the office every morning."

And they erupted into a roar of laughter, shifting shock to humor at just the right time.

A waiter came running to the foot of the stage with two bottles of water and gave them to the agents on guard. One handed them up to Agent Raines, who tossed them to Charlie.

"Good catch," he said, and went back to his post.

Charlie opened one of the bottles and then handed it to her. She took a couple of quick sips and then handed it back to him.

"Just a few more comments for those special people who are claiming I am an alien, and that they know because they went to school with me. I've never been in a school in my life. I look like this because I had breast cancer. UT decided I wasn't so special after all because my body got sick, so they fired me. I took myself home to die. Only I didn't. Something inside me turned on, and my body healed itself. But my hair never grew back, which pissed me off, so I rejected the idea of wigs, and in defiance, which Charlie will tell you is one of my best traits, I opted for a badass tattoo instead of new boobs. I never have bad hair days. I threw away my bras, and when I look at my naked self in the mirror, I don't see a victim of anything. I see the dragon, and I see the warrior that life made me become. UT wanted me back after I didn't die. They wanted to study me again. And that's when they came after me again. When I wouldn't comply, they stalked me, and then decided I knew too much and tried to kill me.

"The first time they tried and failed, it cost Cyrus Parks forty million dollars of his personal money, donated in his name, of course, to a charity for hurricane victims."

This bit of info created a ripple of murmurs across the ballroom, but she kept talking.

"The second time was what I just told you. I crashed in Sam Houston National Forest and woke up alive and crawled out, and in retaliation for the second attempt, this happened, and Cyrus Parks is in prison for life with no chance of parole and, knowing what I can still do to him if I chose, happy to be there. I will answer questions for thirty minutes unless they offend me, in which case one of my friends in the FBI will escort your ass out of here, or if they're too stupid to discuss, we will all say a prayer for your mama's grief in raising an idiot. So pick your topics wisely. And do not hound me anywhere in the days to come. Even though I have revealed my truth, my life is not your business. You may not have forty million dollars to spare, but I will make you sorry. Forever."

She didn't know people had been crying throughout her statement. And she hadn't seen the constant shock and disbelief on their faces. She took the silence that ensued afterward as disinterest or disapproval, and at this point, she was too numb to care.

And then a man in the front row stood up and started to clap, and then another in the back of the room stood and joined him, and then one by one, everyone present was on their feet, clapping. And they kept clapping and clapping as the waves of emotion washed through every inch of Wyrick's body.

Then she looked at Charlie.

"I want to go home."

"After you," Charlie said.

She nodded. But when she turned around to walk off, there was another moment when the audience realized there was more of the dragon tattoo on her back, and below the waistband of those black leather pants, as well. And the mental images of her naked made their hair stand on end.

And then she was gone.

The agents followed her and Charlie out, and then formed a convoy around them as Charlie loaded her into the Jeep. He took a cold Pepsi out of the cooler, wiped it dry and opened it up, then handed it to her.

"You rocked that, lady. This should be champagne, but the Snickers in the console will make up for it," he said, and then got in.

"About the water," Wyrick said, referring to the glass he'd knocked out of her hand. "I didn't think. Thank you."

"Like you said, it's all about the bear claws," he said, then put the car in gear. They drove home, surrounded by Feds.

As far as the media was concerned, the press conference worked. They saw her in person. They got her on film. And after that parting shot she gave them about making them sorry, no one had the guts to push her further. The applause they'd given her was far less than she deserved, but it was all they had.

The impact of the press conference was felt around the nation, then, as it spread, around the world. And the sight of her had been far more than what they'd expected. She was a beautiful oddity in a fascinating way. And every person who'd ever had a tattoo was in awe of what she'd endured to wear that red-and-black dragon.

Tony Dawson and his parents had watched from their home, amazed that this woman on television had been instrumental in saving his life.

Trish Caldwell and her mother clung to each other as they watched, weeping for a little girl's tragedy.

Wanda Carrollton cried for the childhood Wyrick

lost, and the granddaughter Jade Wyrick had given back to her.

Every cop in Dallas who knew her from Charlie Dodge's office had a whole new appreciation for the badass she was, and were now impressed that Charlie wasn't scared of her.

The Dunleavy family from Denver they'd helped before had come to love her odd ways while she and Charlie were their guests, and after watching the live feed, they wept for the loss of a life she'd never known.

But it was Jordan Bien, the young girl Wyrick and Charlie rescued from the cult of the Fourth Dimension, who was the most affected by what she'd seen.

Jordan's psychic powers were continuing to develop, but she'd never "seen" any of what Wyrick had just revealed, and she was in awe of Wyrick's bravery in the face of all she'd endured.

The mental image of Wonder Woman had given Jordan the mental strength to endure the cult until she was rescued, but Jade Wyrick had just become her new idol.

And Jordan wasn't alone in her awe.

Thousands upon thousands of women who had lost their hair due to their ongoing cancer treatments, or from other diseases, began taking off the scarves they wore to hide their bald heads, while others threw away the wigs they were afraid to be without.

If that Jade Wyrick woman could go bald and flat-chested and tell the world to kiss her ass, then so could they.

Her fierce spirit scared some and intimidated others. But that was just today's viewing public.

Wyrick knew none of this, and it wouldn't have mattered if she had. She just wanted her life back, and to go to the office with Charlie, and go home to Merlin's tomatoes, and the mansion and its secrets she had yet to uncover.

As for Charlie, he knew his days with her at the mansion wouldn't last forever, but he had a gut feeling it was too soon to leave.

That night, as they were sharing Chinese takeout, and debating the wisdom of which case to take next, he brought up the subject.

"How do you feel about being here alone?" he asked.

She didn't answer immediately, which told him she wasn't all that comfortable. Then she shrugged it off.

"It doesn't matter how I feel about it. I've been alone for years. This just happens to be the biggest place I've been alone in."

He reached for another spring roll and dipped it in duck sauce.

"I don't have any reason I can't stay…if you want to give this some time. I mean, this press conference could stir up some more crazies."

Wyrick's heart skipped a beat. *Okay. How do I say yes without making a fool of myself?*

"You think?"

He nodded. "Yeah, this is all pretty new. I mean, you're still the best news of the day, and they're still arresting people. I'm not trying to scare you. Just make you aware...kind of like the water today."

"This place is so big that you could have your own wing if you wanted," she said.

The relief he was feeling was real.

"But being that far away from each other kind of defeats the purpose of a bodyguard," he said.

She frowned. "Then at least move upstairs into a bedroom suite where you'd be more comfortable."

"Then you're down and I'm up. Stop trying to organize me. I'm fine. Do I stay, or do you want me to go?"

"Fine. Stay," she said, and picked up a fortune cookie and broke it apart.

She put a piece of the cookie in her mouth and crunched as she read the fortune she'd pulled out.

Charlie could tell by the expression on her face that the fortune surprised her.

"What does it say?" he asked.

"I don't believe in fortunes coming true."

"That's not what I asked," he said.

She tossed it toward him.

"I'm tired. I'm going to bed."

"I'll clean up," he said, as she strode out of the room. Then he picked up the fortune, curious as to what it was that had set her off.

You are on a journey of discovery. Be ready to embrace the joy.

He laid it aside and then broke his cookie open to see what his fortune said.

What was always before you, you will see anew.

He thought about it a minute, then got up and began throwing away the refuse from their meal.

As soon as he was finished, he checked the security alarm, only to find she'd already set it. Then he began turning off lights and turning on night-lights as he went.

He was walking down the hall toward his room when Wyrick emerged from her room wearing pink leggings and a white flannel shirt with pink flamingos on it.

The whole outfit took him aback. She looked like somebody's teenage kid. Not the fierce warrior from the press conference, and she obviously didn't see him in the shadows as she headed toward the elevator.

"Hey, where are you going?" he called out.

"Up," she said, and kept walking.

"Do you need help?"

She punched the button to open the car, then turned around.

"Charlie. If I know how to go up, then I can find my way down."

The snarky tone in her voice grated on his last nerve.

"Last time you came down, you were on fire and bleeding. Try to do better," he said, and went into his room, letting the door slam just a little to punctuate the retort.

Then the elevator door opened and she stepped into the car.

"Smart-ass," she mumbled, and pressed the Up arrow.

If he was going to stay, then she was moving herself upstairs, which would force him to follow.

Stupid man.

All she wanted was for him to be comfortable.

While downstairs, Charlie was going through the motions of making up his bed on the sofa.

Hardheaded woman.

All he wanted was for her to be safe.

* * * * *

"Two cops broke into your house?" He didn't bother to take out the skepticism. "Did they have a warrant? Did they ID themselves?"

Ashlyn shook her head. "They were wearing uniforms, badges and all the gear that cops have. They used a stun gun on me." She rubbed her fingers along the side of her arm, and the trembling got worse. "They took Cora, but I heard them say they were working for you."

Eli's groan was even louder than the one she made. "And you believed them." The look he gave her was as flat as his tone. He didn't spell out to her that she'd been gullible, but he was certain Ashlyn had already picked up on that.

She squeezed her eyes shut a moment. "I panicked. Wasn't thinking straight. As soon as I could move, I jumped in my car and drove straight here."

The drive wouldn't have taken that long since Ashlyn's house was only about ten miles away. She lived on a small ranch on the other side of Longview Ridge that she'd inherited from her grandparents, and she made a living training and boarding horses.

"Did the kidnappers make a ransom demand?" he pressed. "Or did they take anything else from your place?"

"No. They only took Cora. Who brought her here?" Ashlyn asked, her head whipping up. "Was it those cops?"

"Fake cops," Eli automatically corrected. "I didn't see who left her on my porch, but they weren't exactly quiet about it. She was probably out here no more than a minute or two before I went to the door and found her."

He paused, worked through the pieces that she'd just given him and it didn't take him long to come to a conclusion. A bad one. These fake cops hadn't hurt the child, hadn't asked for money or taken anything, but they had let Ashlyn believe they worked for him. There had to be a good reason for that. Well, "good" in their minds, anyway.

"This was some kind of sick game?" she asked.

It was looking that way. A game designed to send her after him.

"They wanted me to kill you?" Ashlyn added a moment later.

Before Eli answered that, he wanted to talk to his brother and get backup so he could take Ashlyn and the baby into Longview Ridge. First to the hospital to confirm they were okay and then to the sheriff's office so he could get an official statement from Ashlyn.

"You really had no part in this?" she pressed.

Eli huffed, not bothering to answer that. He took out his phone to make that call to Kellan, but he stopped when he saw the blur of motion on the other side of Ashlyn's car. He lifted his hand to silence her when Ashlyn started to speak, and he kept looking.

Waiting.

Then, he finally saw it. Or rather he saw them. Two men wearing uniforms, and they had guns aimed right at the house.

Don't miss
Settling an Old Score *by Delores Fossen,*
available August 2020 wherever
Harlequin Intrigue books and ebooks are sold.

Harlequin.com